FINDERS KEEPERS

SARAH MONZON

PARADISE PUBLICATIONS

Published by Radiant Publications
Moses Lake, Washington

Scripture used in this book, whether quoted or paraphrase is taken from The Holy Bible, English Standard Version® (ESV®) Copyright © 2001 by Crossway, a publishing ministry of Good News Publishers. All rights reserved. ESV Text Edition: 2011

This is a work of fiction. Characters, incidents, and dialogues are products of the author's imagination and are not to be construed as real. Any resemblance to actual events is strictly coincidental.

Front cover design by Sarah Monzon

Spine and back cover design by Perry Kirkpatrick at www.perryelisabethdesigns.com

Manuscript edited by Dori Harell

This one's for you Mom.
Thank you for always being my biggest cheerleader.

Prologue

Seville, Spain, 1689

Isabella stumbled along the rough boards of the dock, feeling exposed without her corset and many layers of petticoats. The coastal breeze tugged at the coarse wool of her stepfather's loose-fitting breeches, which rubbed the inside of her legs. A seagull cried as it soared overhead, but she refused to look up. Two miles she'd hiked that morning without giving in to the urge to glance over her shoulder, ever keeping her eyes before her—and she did not dare lose that focus now.

The first mile had been the hardest, her imagination turning every snap of a twig and falling shadow into a frightening pursuit. By the second mile she'd convinced herself that no one had even missed her yet and the plan would work. That was when the pain in her toes—from the ripped cloth she'd stuffed into Hernando's oversized boots—began to register. Despite the situation she found herself in, Isabella felt the corners of her mouth tip up. Hernando would be livid when he discovered she was missing. Her smile widened. He'd be none too happy about his absent wardrobe either, but after everything he'd taken from her, the few articles of clothing she'd filched were meager compensation.

A hand gripped Isabella's shoulder and spun her around. Her heart leapt to her throat, and she braced her feet, preparing for whatever punishment was about to befall her. If Hernando had uncovered her plans already, then *Dios* have mercy. The Atlantic's dark, churning waters beneath her feet invited her into an eternal escape.

Forcing her shoulders back, she looked at the man who had stopped her, and willed her heart to return to its normal rhythm. The tall man in front of her held no resemblance to Hernando's squat physique. Would her stepfather have sent someone to fetch her in his stead?

"What are you about, lad?" The deep voice held no malicious intent that Isabella could detect.

A small gust of wind blew over the surface of the water, causing the bright plumes on the gentleman's hat to dance. Isabella's cheeks grew warm as the breeze pulled the thin cotton fabric of her shirt across her chest. Her stepfather's tattered waistcoat added an extra layer of protection against certain feminine curves being revealed, but would it be enough? It was all she could do to resist covering herself with her arms.

The man stood with raised eyebrows, the corners of his lips turning down. She'd take impatient over the lustful stares she was accustomed to enduring.

Bueno. Her disguise was working.

"I've come..." Isabella stopped and cleared her throat. She

tucked her chin and started again an octave lower. "I've come to sign on to a ship headed to Hispaniola and the New World."

A small flock of seagulls resting on the masts took flight, squawking their protest. Isabella bit the inside of her lip. *Fuerte. Valiente.* Strong and brave—she had to encompass those characteristics now. The unknown could not be more frightening than the reality she was leaving behind.

The man regarded her, his head tilted. Isabella tried not to squirm under his scrutiny. Unable to withstand his steady gaze, she averted her eyes to the planks of the dock. Maybe a show of humility and meekness would help her acquire a position on a vessel. In her experience, it was better not to challenge a man—they being prideful creatures.

"Look at me, boy." The man's voice possessed a stern quality, but not unkindness.

Isabella slowly lifted her eyes. Black shoes with a square buckle, white stockings tucked beneath blue breeches, matching vest and overcoat. A brown leather sword belt angled across his broad chest. She forced her gaze past his waxed goatee and stopped when she met his piercing black eyes.

The man grabbed her chin between his index finger and thumb and turned her head slightly to the side. Isabella cringed. She hoped the ashes she'd rubbed on her face would hide any feminine resemblance. The lack of hair along her jaw and the smoothness of her skin could very well be attributed to a young age. As well as her slight stature. Her long, thick lengths of hair, which she had been piling high atop her head for many years, lay at the bottom of the wastebasket in Hernando's kitchen. What little hair left was now tied back in a leather thong at the base of her neck.

With a grunt, the man released her chin. "Ever been aboard a ship before, son?"

She chewed her lip. Would he hire her if she said no? The large vessel, tied to the end of the dock with thick cords of rope, bobbed with the swells of the sea. Isabella gulped. If she said yes and he later found out that she'd been lying, would she be thrown overboard like some unwanted cargo? "N-no, señor. B-but I'm a fast learner."

He sniffed and eyed the galleon. "Very well." He turned back to her. "I am Captain Montoya, and this"—he extended his left arm—"is my ship, the *Santa Rosa*."

Isabella's knees began to bend in a curtsy before she caught herself. *Estupido, Isabella. It will take more than stolen men's clothes to convince people you are not a woman. You must start acting like a man. Think like a man.* She offered a small bow.

"You will go aboard and talk to my first mate, Juan. We sail on the morrow." With that, he stalked off down the dock and toward town, leaving Isabella to stare in awe at the *Santa Rosa*, her heart soaring at her good fortune.

Fortune. Isabella's hand shot to where her ribs met to form a *V* below her breasts. Held snug in the cloth she had wrapped to bind herself lay hidden the means to her future—her grandmother's jewel-encrusted gold necklace.

The force of a workhorse shoved Isabella forward. She stumbled, her arms careening to regain her balance.

"Don't be standing there in our way, boy." Two burly men with biceps bulging carried a wooden barrel between them up the gangplank and onto Captain Montoya's ship.

Isabella took a deep breath and stepped onto the gangplank boards. It would work. She would sail across the world, and there was nothing Hernando could do to stop her.

Instead of his intimidating glares shrinking her soul, she felt dwarfed by the three center masts towering above her. Men's voices surrounded her as she stepped onto the deck. Unwashed male bodies hurried like ants on a disturbed hill.

She wanted to hide, to become small and invisible in the sea of masculinity. But that was a girl's reaction. A frightened, timid girl. She lifted her chin. Hernando's heavy hand would no longer hold her captive. This was the start of a new life, a new person.

A man approached, his cotton shirt billowing out behind him as he purposefully strode across the deck. "Excuse me, *señor*. Can you tell me where..."

The man walked past Isabella like he hadn't seen or heard her. She squared her shoulders. The times of being ignored or brushed to the side were over. She *would* be seen and she *would* be heard.

Another man came from the opposite direction. Isabella stepped in front of him. It was either he stop or plow into her, and she braced for the latter. At the last second he slowed his stride, his forehead wrinkled in a frown. "I am looking for Juan de la Cruz."

The man, or boy, really, for he looked no older than she, nodded behind him. "Captain's cabin." He scurried past her toward the front of the vessel.

Isabella stepped down into the belly of the ship. She walked along a narrow corridor, then pushed open the first door she came to. The room was larger than expected. Windows framed by dark curtains lined the far wall. Dust particles spotted the stagnant air in the shafts of light. A desk stood near the center of the room, covered with maps and charts. A man leaned over the parchments, his brow furrowed in concentration.

"Excuse me, *señor*, I am looking for Juan de la Cruz. The captain sent me, and I was told I could find him here."

The man lifted his head, and his eyes widened. "Isabella?"

Chapter 1

Off the Coast of the Bahamas, Present Day

There was no turning back. The skin on Summer Arnet's arm prickled, and she shivered. It wasn't from the sixty-degree water, either. Sharks for miles would smell the feast waiting for them just yards away. Her only protection—a few measly metal bars. No one could argue she wouldn't do anything to get her photos in *Our World* magazine.

A splash to her right, and tiny bubbles burst at the surface. The huge hunk of meat now submersed ruined the crystalline quality of the water. Bright-red blood leached out, turning a brown hue and then fading into nothing as it swirled with the ocean current.

The sound of the regulator roared in her ears as she inhaled. Bubbles floating up, distorting her vision as she exhaled. Despite her quickening pulse and the fear that threatened to strangle her, she had to keep her breathing even. If not, she'd go through her thirty minutes of oxygen in less than thirty seconds. Her hands shook, and she tightened her grip on her Sony NEX underwater camera.

She tried not to imagine the pointy head of a shark protruding between the horizontal rails. The rows of serrated teeth tearing through her wet suit, shredding her skin and crushing her bones.

Try to think of something else. Anything else.

Hadn't there been a list of statistics on her Facebook News Feed about all the things that were more deadly than sharks? For the life of her she couldn't remember any of them at that moment, except for cows. Soft-eyed, cud-chewing, fuzzy cows. Cows that only had one row of very flat teeth along their bottom jaw, none on top. That wasn't scary. And if cows killed more people than sharks, she had nothing to be afraid of, right? Somehow that didn't settle her nerves.

Off in the distance a shadow formed. The shape resembled a torpedo, long and lean. The dorsal fin jutting from the center of its back was enough to instill fear in even the stoutest of hearts. Which hers was not. With each swoosh of its massive tail, its image became more clear.

A great white.

Its white underbelly shone in stark contrast to the muted gray on top. One large black eye regarded her as the shark circled the chum in the water, swimming with its mouth slightly open.

Despite the regulator in her mouth, Summer gulped. Great white's had forty-eight exposed triangular-shaped teeth, with about five more rows in various stages of development. Not to mention they were one of the most dangerous predators in the ocean.

What I wouldn't do to be in a field full of cattle right about now.

She brought the camera to her face, focused the lens, and

began snapping pictures. She could hardly keep her hands from shaking, and hoped the photos would turn out instead of being a blurry mess. As it was, she was surprised she had the presence of mind to even push the shutter release.

As the shark opened its mouth wide, its jaws extended forward and its head receded back, making its mouth look like snarling lips. It bit down on the bait not far from Summer and shook its head violently, its gills rippling with each jerk.

It didn't take him long to devour the meat. It started to swim away, and then turned. She repressed the instinct to take a step back. The shark circled the cage, and she was able to get a few good profile shots. The lighting was perfect.

Without warning, he spun, ramming the cage with the force of a pickup truck. The cage shook, and she struggled to maintain her position in its center. She didn't dare venture too far to either side. The great white swam away and came back again, its jaws wide open. Fear clawed at the back of her throat. The shadows from the shark's gills, the pink flesh from the inside of its mouth, the creased skin between its nostrils— all details she could have lived without seeing.

I'm going to die.

Her eyes welled with tears that spilled down her cheeks and pooled in her scuba mask. This was it. She loved the ocean, and now it looked like it would be her grave.

For what seemed like forever, the shark toyed with Summer and the cage. Soon it grew bored and swam away into the ocean's depths.

At last the cage jerked upward, and she nearly lost her footing. The ascent smoothed out until stopping beside the hull of a boat dipping back and forth with the waves. Four hands reached down and gripped her extended arms, pulling her out of the cage and onto the boat.

She spit out the regulator, gulping in huge amounts of tropical sea air. Her legs trembled. The swaying of the vessel did nothing to help her gain her balance. As she lifted the scuba mask off her face, she stumbled to the left and flung out her hand, searching wildly for something to grab on to so she didn't fall overboard.

Jonathan Morris caught her hand and wrapped his arm around her waist. "Whoa there."

She yanked her hand free, curled her fist into a ball, and punched him on his bicep.

Jonathan rubbed his arm. "What was that for?"

"How could...why didn't..." Summer shook her head. The back of her eyes were starting to burn, but she refused to cry in front of the guys. "Why didn't you pull the cage up sooner?"

"What are you talking about? I bet you were able to get some great shots out there." His eyebrows drew down, creating lines on his forehead. "Besides, you agreed to the cage dive."

She pinched the bridge of her nose before walking the few feet to a cushioned seat. She ran her hand along the fiberglass of the boat in case she lost her balance again.

Her shoulders slumped as she dropped to the seat. Her nerves were raw and left her drained. "I agreed to cage dive with tiger sharks, hammerheads, lemon sharks...not great whites." She leaned her head to the side, grabbed the long, coppery strands of her hair, and twisted until most of the water had been wrung out. A puddle collected at her feet.

"You guys okay over there?" Mark asked from the rear of the boat, where he was storing the rest of the gear.

"We're fine,," Jonathan said over his shoulder, his eyes never leaving Summer's face.

She stood, her legs a little less like Jell-O. She reached up and tugged the zipper of her wet suit down. As she peeled the neoprene material off her upper body, Jonathan took a seat, resting his forearms on his knees, hands clasped between spread-eagle legs.

"You know as well as I do that great whites aren't common in these waters. You're more likely to see them off the coast of South Africa or Australia, not here."

Mark came up behind her and draped his arm around her shoulders. "Did you see the size of that thing?" His unlit cigar bobbed up and down as he spoke. "It must have been at least sixteen feet long."

Summer placed her hand against his palm-tree printed shirt and gave a small push. He was a nice man, about the age of her father, if she'd had a father, that was. But he smelled more of the salty sea and its fishy inhabitants than the sweetness of his personality.

"If only I'd have had a video camera." His arm slid from around Summer's neck, and a beefy hand landed on Jonathan's shoulder. "We could've recorded the whole thing and sent it in to *Shark Week*. They love that kind of stuff."

Was she the only one still sane here? Jonathan was brushing the whole incident off, and Mark thought it was the greatest thing since string cheese, or at least he would if he'd been able to get it on tape. Did they not get that she'd nearly been shark bait? She'd probably have nightmares for weeks.

She placed her hands on her hips, freely allowing the anger to rise and stamp out the horrendous fear that had been suffocating her. "Do you guys not realize the danger you put me in?" Okay, so maybe it wasn't fair to pin it all on them. She had agreed to the dive. But they were the ones who'd talked her into it. Or at least Jonathan was. Mark had just arranged the gear and driven the boat.

"Calm down, Summer. Everything turned out fine." Jonathan's laid-back tone did nothing to reassure her. Like fanning the flames, it only made her hotter.

"And what would you have done if he'd rammed the cage hard enough to get his nose stuck between the rails, huh? Sharks can't swim backwards. He would have thrashed around and shook his head from side to side until he was free. Who knows if the cage would've held up against something like that."

The two men stared at her like she'd grown a mermaid tail. Fine. Let them gape all they wanted. They weren't the ones who'd been trapped in a five-foot metal cage while the world's largest predatory fish eyed them like the next item on his menu.

Jonathan was the first to look away, running his hands through his curly hair. "Sorry," he mumbled.

Mark held her gaze. "Girly, I know you were scared. Shoot, I was up here on this boat, and still my blood pressure skyrocketed. But you were safe, and deep down I know a Florida girl like you knows that." He waited, brows raised.

Summer gave an imperceptible nod. She wasn't convinced she hadn't been in danger, but if she didn't concede, Mark would stand there all day. Stubborn man.

"Life is a beautiful but sometimes dangerous thing. Same as the ocean. You respect the dangers and enjoy the beauty, you hear? If you hide or shy away from something just because you might be afraid, then you're going to miss out on the best things in life."

Cold water on hot coals, Summer's temper fizzled. Who could stay mad after such words of wisdom? Would her own father have said something similar? Better not to dwell on things that never were and never would be.

Jonathan put his wrist on the top of his head, his fingers pointing straight up in a mock dorsal fin. Low and slow at first and then gaining volume and speed, he chanted, "Da-nuh...da-nuh...da-nuh, da-nuh, da-nuh."

The *Jaws* theme music. Summer rolled her eyes, but her lips tipped up.

He put his hands out in front of him, one on top of the other, like a closed mouth, then opened them and swallowed her up in his arms, play-biting her shoulder.

Mark laughed out loud, and Summer grinned as she pushed Jonathan away from her.

"Okay, okay, can we go now? I want to get back to shore and see what kind of pictures I put my life on the line for."

Mark gave a mock salute and revved up the boat's engine.

The wind whipped her hair out behind her, and she shuddered. Good pictures or not, no way was she ever diving in those waters again. She'd stick with cute little clown fish and their anemones.

Chapter 2

Two Months Later, Florida

The buttery croissant melted in Summer's mouth, her eyes closing as she savored the fluffy pastry. Oh, how she needed this small break in the middle of a hectic day. It was the first time in hours she felt like she had enough time to just breathe. The iced vanilla latte was cold and sweet on her tongue, and she held it in her mouth before swallowing. One more thing was needed to enter full relaxation mode. She plugged her earbuds into her iPhone and let Bruno Mars take her away.

A pair of clunky black biker boots appeared in her peripheral vision. A groan lodged in her throat, and she rolled her eyes. She didn't know any bikers, and none of her friends would wear shoes like that, especially when the temperature neared one hundred degrees and the humidity rivaled that of a sauna.

Not now. She started a game of Fruit Ninja on her phone. *Maybe if I ignore him, he'll lose his nerve and go away.*

Guys hitting on her wasn't anything new, but at the moment she didn't feel like putting on a fake smile and trying to let the guy down gently. All she wanted was a little time to herself to eat her pastry, drink her latte, and have Bruno Mars serenade her with "Just the Way You Are." Was that too much to ask?

Her finger hit a flying bomb, the screen exploded, and her game ended. She peeked out of the corner of her eye. Yep. Mr. Biker Boots was still there. *Until next time, Bruno.* Sighing, she took out the earbuds, forced her lips to curve into a smile, and looked up.

Whoa. All coherent thought flew from her head. Standing in front of her was the epitome of a Norse god incarnate. Blond hair grazed his shoulders, his sky-blue eyes framed by dark lashes. He had a strong square jaw and a devilish grin that lifted the corners of his mouth. His black V-neck shirt only accentuated a muscular body that would've had Michelangelo running for his chisel.

"Excuse me, but are you Summer Arnet?"

"Ah...ah..." Summer pinched the inside of her wrist to get her derailed thoughts back on track. *Get a grip.* "Yes. Yes, I am." She tilted her head to the side. No way they'd met before. She would've remembered him for sure. "And you are..."

"Trent Carrington." He eyed her, then the chair across from where she sat, and when he looked at her again, his brows were raised in question.

Lips suddenly dry, she ran her tongue along the top and motioned to the chair. "Please have a seat."

All six foot plus of him folded down into the small café chair. He leaned back, crossing one leg over the other so his ankle rested on the opposite knee. He said nothing as he regarded her. The whirl of the cappuccino machine as the barista made another beverage filled the silence at the table for two.

Seconds ticked by, and Thor's twin didn't say a word. His gaze mirrored appreciation as he looked at her, and she wasn't sure she should be flattered or offended. Mostly she was confused.

She took a sip of her latte. "Is there something I can help you with?"

"Sorry, you're different than I imaged and caught me off guard." His smile developed slowly, full of confidence. "You're the same Summer Arnet that took the photo of the great white shark featured in *Marine Life* magazine?"

Her brows pinched together. "Yes, that's me."

"Great." He leaned forward, his forearms resting on the table. "I was wondering if you could take me to where you took that shot. I'd compensate you for your time, of course."

The tattoo on his forearm caught her attention. A Celtic knot. When she glanced up, his intent gaze reeled her in, sending chills across her shoulders. She cleared her throat. "Why do you want to go there?"

His eye contact faltered and he looked over her shoulder, then shrugged. "Does it matter?" He looked at her again, one side of his mouth lifting in a flirtatious grin.

She may not know Trent Carrington, but she knew his type. He was the guy that thought all he had to do was smile and wink and he'd get whatever he wanted. Especially from women. Any appreciation that had flushed through her system at the sight of him dissolved. Looked like he needed a wakeup call. No way would she fawn over him and be as accommodating as he obviously hoped she'd be.

"Yes. It does."

His grin slipped a fraction before he tacked it back up.

Her phone vibrated on the table, and she held up a finger. Tabitha Michaels. Editor in chief at *Our World*. Summer's breath hitched. Did she finally have a shot at the gig of a lifetime?

"Sorry, but I've got to take this. It was nice meeting you."

His chair scraped against the tile floor as he stood. "Wait. What about the—"

But Summer cruised out the door, phone to her ear. She'd already let the man ruin her one moment of solitude for the day. She wasn't about to let him wreck what could be the biggest career opportunity that had ever come her way.

———

Trent slid a hand down his face. That hadn't gone at all like he'd planned. What an egotistical fool he was. If his kid sister, Amber, could see him right now, she'd laugh in his face and tell him he'd gotten what he deserved. And she'd be right. Was he really so conceited that he'd thought Miss Arnet would jump at the chance to help him just because he'd smiled at her? It was a hard pill to swallow, but it was probably the truth. Why else had he ridden his Harley over two hours when he could have just made a phone call or sent an e-mail?

Of course he hadn't been prepared for the auburn beauty, either. A quick Google search of her name had directed him to her website and studio address, but she hadn't posted a personal picture. It had been pure luck that an employee at the boutique beside her office space had been outside sweeping the sidewalk and had informed him of her whereabouts—otherwise he would've had to camp out on her front stoop. Apparently she frequented this coffee shop, because the barista had been quick to point her out—his smile had worked on the teenager in the green apron.

His mouth twitched upward. So it hadn't been as easy as he'd thought to convince the photographer to share the exact location. No big deal. He liked a good challenge. He just had to find something Summer Arnet couldn't say no to.

Trent pulled out a folded magazine from his back pocket and opened it to page 14. Summer's photo. While she'd captured harrowing detail of a dangerous creature, he could really care less about the shark. What had snagged his attention from the first time laying eyes on the photo were the shadows in the bottom right-hand corner. Maybe it was wishful thinking or his imagination playing tricks on him, but he swore he could make out the bowsprit, forecastle, and foremast of a seventeenth-century Spanish vessel. A galleon used in the country's treasure fleet.

Ever since Christopher Columbus accidentally landed in the New World in 1492, ships had been bringing back the exploitations of the land—with silver and gold mined from Peru and Colombia among the exports. Pedro Menendez de Aviles, a personal advisor to King Phillip II and an experienced admiral, designed both the treasure fleet system and the galleons used to protect the trade. The fleet stuck to two main routes, so Trent could narrow down the possibilities as to where Summer had taken the photo, but even then it would take longer than his lifespan to search the entire route, and that wasn't taking into consideration the fact that a strong storm could've blown the ship off course and been the means for it sinking in the first place.

He could just imagine the history and wealth locked within the hold of the galleon, preserved in the depth of the earth's seas.

An image of his mother, concern in her eyes, overshadowed the excitement building inside him. He pushed it to the side. Her concerns were unfounded. Searching for the ship was neither dangerous nor illegal. And just because he liked to look for lost things and have a good time didn't mean he was trying to fill a void in his life—that was her favorite lecture to date. Besides, even if there was a void in his life—and he wasn't admitting there was—it was his parents' God who had created it in the first place. Trent shook his head. His mother pictured him a lost little boy searching for his way home, when in reality he was more like Ponce de Leon and Hernando de Soto, an adventurous man on the cusp of a great discovery. If he happened to have a few conquests along the way...well...what was the harm in that?

"Hey, do you mind if I borrow this chair?" Trent looked up at a middle-aged gentleman in a business suit. At a table behind him sat two men and two women, all similarly attired. One had a laptop open in front of him.

"No, go ahead. I was just leaving." Trent stood and walked out the door. The afternoon sun blinded him, and the warm humid air hung heavy in his lungs. He pushed a pair of sunglasses up the bridge of his nose before unhooking his helmet from the handlebars of his Harley. After tucking his hair behind his ears, he slid the helmet on and revved the V-twin engine.

As he pulled out into the palm tree–lined street, the coastal breeze swaying the fingerlike fronds, his thoughts traveled back to Miss Arnet. What had made her say no without even hearing him out first? More importantly, what would make her say yes? Most people could be motivated by either love or money.

He grinned. He wouldn't mind offering a little of both.

Chapter 3

Summer walked up the two steps to the front door of her home, her movements automatic. It was a good thing unlocking the door and stepping over the threshold required no brain power. The conversation with Tabitha Michaels had tased her mind, leaving it incapacitated to form any coherent thoughts.

Shooting for *Our World* was a farfetched dream, but didn't fantastic and implausible things happen every day? Apparently they happened every day for other people. Not for her. She fought back the sting of rejection as her mind played over Tabitha's words. *Your pictures are beautiful, Summer.* That was when she'd paused, and Summer had let her heart soar with hope, with possibility. Too bad it'd crashed and burned with the next breath. *But they aren't unique. We've seen pictures like yours from hundreds of other photographers. If you want your photos to be published with Our World, then I need to see something truly original. Something new, edgy. Something that will wow our readers, create dialogue, and entice new subscriptions.*

Rejection wrapped in a pretty package. Thank you, but no

thank you. *Your work isn't a good fit for our company at this time. Good luck on your future endeavors.* Tiny darts puncturing holes in life's dreams.

She flopped onto the swivel chair behind an oak desk she'd splurged on, and buried her face in her hands. What was edgier than cage diving and photographing a great white shark?

The strip of rubber dangling from the underside of the front door swept across the stained concrete floor. Summer peeked between her fingers. If she'd had the presence of mind, she'd have locked the door. Who cared if it was still business hours? Right now she considered the space more her home and less her studio.

The self-absorbed Norse god from the coffee shop entered and closed the door behind him. What was he doing here?

"Are you following me?" Summer's voice held both accusation and apprehension as she eyed the man. He was turned away from her, studying some of her favorite photos displayed on the opposite wall.

"Actually, yes," he said without bothering to look at her.

She stared at his profile and silently pulled her phone out of her pocket in case she needed to call the police. Too many late nights watching crime shows had her imagination running wild.

He turned. "I came to make a proposition."

"A proposition?" Wariness coated her voice, and her eyes darted around the room. Was there anything handy she could grab to wield as a weapon if the need arose?

Trent came and sat on one of two metal folding chairs she had in front of her desk. "Yes, a proposition. I need you to take me to where you took the picture of the great white."

That again? Curiosity warred with her unease. What was so special about that location?

"Why?"

He eyed her and looked to be weighing his options before shifting in his seat. She squeezed her phone. Reaching behind him, he withdrew a folded magazine from his back pocket. He flipped pages and creased the center. Turning it around, he placed it on the desk and pushed it toward her.

Summer leaned forward. What was she supposed to be looking at that was so mysterious? All she saw was evidence of a harrowing experience. She huffed as she sat back. "It's my photo. So what?"

Trent scooted forward until he was on the edge of his chair. A strand of hair came loose from behind his ear and fondled his cheek as he pointed to the bottom corner of the page. Dangerously beautiful. Like fire coral. *Mesmerizing to look at, but don't get too close, or you're liable to get hurt.*

Her eyes slid to the spot where he indicated. Nothing. There was absolutely nothing there besides the vastness of the open ocean. She lifted her gaze and met his look of expectation. Was she missing something? Her feet pushed off the ground, and her chair rolled closer to the window. The natural light shone on the glossy pages. She squinted and inspected every inch of the corner before shaking her head. Too bad Thor's twin was crazy. She eyed him again. Hopefully not crazy and dangerous.

"You don't see it?" He sounded disappointed.

"Why don't you just tell me what it is I'm supposed to be looking at?"

Trent stood and walked to the other side of the desk. Summer rolled her chair away from him. No use letting him get too close, in case he did have some nefarious intentions.

"Right here." He pressed his index finger to the page. "I'm convinced these shadows are from a seventeenth-century galleon that was a part of the Spanish treasure fleet."

She stared at him before returning her gaze to the picture. All she saw were highlights and low lights—shadows created in the ocean's depth. "I don't see anything."

He took the magazine, folded it, and put it in his back pocket. "Look, I'll make it a win-win situation for you. Take me to where you took this picture. If there isn't a sunken ship, I'll still pay you for your time, but if there is a Spanish galleon down there, well, I'll share a portion of the treasure with you."

Sunken ships? Treasure? Was he going to produce a map with a giant *X* that marked the spot next? The notion was ridiculous.

Wait. That was it. This whole thing was some practical joke. Of course. It all made sense now. Summer grinned. They'd almost had her. "So who put you up to this? Mark? No, I bet it was Jonathan, wasn't it?"

She stood and searched the room for a hidden camera. If her place wasn't so small, she would've expected Jonathan to jump out from behind a piece of furniture with his crooked grin in place. The practical jokester.

No hidden cameras she could see on her desk. The top of the fish tank maybe? Three long strides and she was there. The sound of the water overflow as she scanned the top of the tank was interrupted as Trent spoke from behind her.

"What are you doing?"

She glanced over her shoulder. "Looking for the camera. Jonathan's going to be disappointed I didn't fall for his little trick this time." Not on the fish tank. Where could it be? There couldn't be too many places in the six-hundred-square-foot room to hide a camera. The kitchenette counter?

"Who's Jonathan?"

Summer stopped scrutinizing the counter around the coffeemaker and turned. "What do you mean, 'Who's Jonathan?' Jonathan is the guy who put you up to this whole prank." She raised her hand about four inches over her head. "He's about this tall, curly brown hair, glasses. Ring a bell?"

Trent still sat in the metal folding chair. He'd lost his air of excitement and was once again carefree personified as he leaned back and placed his interwoven fingers behind his head. The dark ink of his woven triangle Celtic knot tattoo on his forearm contrasted with his fair complexion. "Sorry to disappoint you, babe, but I don't know anyone named Jonathan."

Babe? She raised her chin and tried not to grind her teeth. A dentist appointment wasn't in her budget. "First of all, never ever call me babe, capisce? I'm a grown woman and not some infant that needs a daddy to take care of her, you got it? And second, if Jonathan isn't behind"—she waved her hand —"this, then why are you here?" Without taking her eyes off him, she slid her hand back across the counter until her fingers rested at the base of the knife block. "How did you find me?"

He shrugged. "Your website lists your physical address. I live in Cape Coral, so it only took a couple of hours to get here, no big deal. As for what I want...well...I just want you to take me to where you took that photo." His gaze shifted to her hand near the knives. "No need to stab a guy over something as simple as that, is there?"

"You're serious?" She leaned heavily on the counter.

He nodded, but his lips trembled. Was he trying to stifle a grin?

Her arms crossed over her chest. "Treasure hunting, *pirating*"—she spat the word. Just saying it left a bad taste in her mouth—"is illegal and destroys submerged cultural heritage all for the sake of man's greed."

Trent's jaw began to tick, but that was the only clue to his frustration. The rest of his body remained the epitome of relaxation. "If you want to get off your high horse and look up the laws, go right ahead. Permits are required, and the state takes twenty percent of the articles found for museum exhibits, but it isn't illegal."

"My high—" Summer repeated and then clamped her lips shut. This would be a good time to count to ten before speaking. "My answer is no. I didn't see a ship anywhere in sight when I dove there, and even if there was one, I wouldn't take you there so you can rob a historical landmark."

Trent stood and held her gaze. Her chin jutted forward. No backing down. No matter how much his blue eyes were melting the heat in her veins. His mouth opened, then shut with a small shake of his head. After a second of skimming her desk, he reached for a pen and Post-it Note and then bent to jot something down. The pen landed with a soft thud on her desk.

He paused, the door open a crack, and turned back to look at her. "If you change your mind, here's my number...babe." He smacked the paper onto the inside of the paneled door and ran his finger over the top to make it stick before stomping out into the blinding Florida sunshine.

———

Infernal, insufferable woman. All she had to do was take him to a specific spot so he could look around, and she'd called him a pirate. Might as well have tacked on looter and thief. Trent shoved the helmet onto his head and straddled his bike. He gripped the throttle, and he pictured his hands around her shoulders. Maybe a good shake would knock some sense into her. With a rev of the engine, he peeled out of her street faster than a streak of heat lighting. Burned rubber singed his nostrils, and a glance over his shoulder showed skid marks where his bike had been parked.

He wanted to hit his head against a wall. Without Summer's help he'd never get to search the galleon. Why did she have to make it so difficult? He shook his head. His departing "babe" remark was sure to be the preverbal nail in the coffin of his dreams. What was with her reaction to that word anyway? A bit touchy.

Trent merged into northbound traffic on I-75. He'd planned on sticking around Fort Lauderdale for a few days while he and the photographer hashed out and finalized the itinerary for the diving trip, but with her refusal to participate and decision to be tight lipped about the location, he had no reason to stay in town. He wasn't the type to wait around for a woman's call. Especially if the likelihood of that even happening was nonexistent.

A large, anvil-shaped thundercloud loomed in the distance. The dark underbelly cast a gloomy shadow while the sun illuminated the puffy whiteness of the rest of the cloud towering above. It would be just his luck to be caught in an afternoon rain shower.

A cherry-red Corvette sped past and wove through traffic, nearly clipping him. Trent swerved and swore. What was with people today? Did everyone wake up without a brain in their head? He'd already received a verbal lashing. He didn't want to add road rash to the list of wounds he'd need to lick.

The power of his Harley and the wind of the open road helped him regain some of the control he'd lost. So things hadn't gone according to plan. That was no reason to give up. Especially since he was so close. Plan B started to formulate in his mind. Maybe he didn't need Summer Arnet after all.

Chapter 4

Seville, Spain, 1689

"*Tío* Pepe?" Isabella stood agape at the man in Captain Montoya's cabin. Her mother's brother had reportedly been lost at sea, but there he was in the flesh, and very much alive. "What are you...but I thought...how did..." She shook her head, unable to sort out the evidence in front of her.

Juan de la Cruz, Pepe to Isabella, rushed forward and enveloped her in his arms. He squeezed her close, then released her, cradling her head in his large hands and smoothing away chopped strands of hair from her brow. "It looks like we both have a lot of explaining to do." His voice held only tenderness, and Isabella was relieved to note no censure or condemnation, in his words or gestures, for her appearance.

Juan walked to the still-open door of the cabin and closed it. "Now then." He returned to Isabella and took both her hands in his. "Tell me why you are standing before me dressed as a lad and not the beautiful girl I last saw four years ago, hmm?"

Isabella worried her lip. How much should she tell him? She'd like nothing better than for Hernando to get what he deserved, and she had no doubt her uncle would give it to him. But that would leave Pepe rotting in a prison cell and her alone again with no family.

She looked into his concerned face, then down at her clothes, pinching the seams of her stepfather's breeches and pulling them slightly out at the sides. "If I'd known how freeing men's clothes were, I might have started wearing them sooner."

Her uncle quirked a brow and folded his arms over his chest.

"I'm off on a grand adventure, Uncle. It's time to start a new life in a new world. There is nothing left for me here in Spain now that Mother is gone." The thought of her once graceful mother strangled her. It had only taken Hernando two years of marriage to rob her mother first of her spirit and then her very breath of life.

"I was sorry to hear of her passing. If circumstances had been different...if there had been a way to return to Spain sooner..." Juan spoke barely above a whisper, emotion choking him. He cleared his throat. "But what of the prospect of marriage? If your stepfather no longer wanted the responsibility of your care, surely he could have arranged a suitable husband for you."

It took all of her control not to bark out a sarcastic retort. As if Hernando were ever interested in her care. He was only interested in control, and if the way he'd kept looking at her, touching her, was any indication, the only prospective husband for her he would have sought was himself. She would rather die than become his wife.

"There is no husband in my future, Uncle."

He rubbed his chin with the back of his fingers. "I see. So you are to be a sailor then?"

"*Sí*." She stood a little straighter. The king's soldiers stood at attention when receiving orders from their commanding officers; maybe sailors did the same aboard merchant ships. "That is why I am here. Captain Montoya has just hired me on to his crew and sent me to find his first mate, that is, you. I was to report for duty." She relaxed her stance and eyed her uncle. Had *Dios* answered her unspoken prayer? She'd thought he'd stopped listening to her cries long ago when her mother had perished and Hernando had not. But what else but the hand of God would bring a dead uncle back to life to be the first mate on the vessel to her freedom?

Juan began pacing the large cabin, his index finger hooked to his chin and his lips pursed. Isabella followed him with her eyes, waiting with hitched breath. Finally he stopped and turned toward her, his eyes clouded.

"There is more to this story I think than what you have told me, but I will not press. I know I should force you off this ship to ensure your safety, but my selfish heart wants you close. I have not seen family in four years, and I find I cannot let you go so readily."

Isabella rushed forward. "Oh, thank you, Uncle. You have no idea—"

A hand in the air stopped her midstride and midsentence.

"This will not be easy, my dear. The sailor's life is no *fiesta*, and the high seas a temperamental mistress."

"Yes, but—"

"Let me finish." She hung her head, and he tipped her chin

up with a finger. "I will try to protect you as best I can, but I have my own duties to perform, and I fear if I give you special treatment, the other men will notice and begin to question." His eyes roamed her face. "Your disguise is good, but nothing could hide the beauty of your eyes and the delicate features you inherited from your *madre*."

She patted his cheek, the stubble rough on her palm. "I'll be careful. I promise."

"*Señor* de la Cruz." The door burst open, and Isabella dropped her hand. The lanky man in ill-fitting, sweat-stained clothes halted just inside the cabin. His scraggly hair was pulled back in a queue, but a strand hung in front of his eyes as they darted from Juan to Isabella and back again. She shifted her weight away from her uncle. No doubt it appeared strange to see two *men* standing so close together. She must be more careful in the future. One slip of the tongue, one wrong move, and she could be found out. No telling what her fate would be then.

"What is it, Luis?"

"A fight has broken out on the main deck between two of the men."

Juan swore under his breath and trotted out the door, Isabella close on his heels. Her eyes took a moment to adjust from the dark interior of the cabin to the bright sunlight. Men's voices shouted and cheered, but she couldn't see past the wall of muscular backs.

"Psst...up here."

Isabella turned and found a young boy of about ten years hanging from the rigging that led from the side of the ship all the way to a contraption that resembled a bucket at the top of the center mast. She remembered looking at one of her uncle's books as a small girl, and if she remembered correctly, the large bucket at the top of the mast was called some kind of bird's nest.

The boy motioned her over with his hand. "You can see better from up here."

Tentatively she gripped the coarse rope above her head and set her booted foot on a low rung. The rope ladder groaned and swayed under her weight. White-fisted knuckles clung to the rope. Her stomach jumped to her throat.

"Hurry up or you'll miss it. *Señor* de la Cruz is already starting to break up the fight." The boy's voice beckoned from above.

She managed to balance her weight on the unstable cords and hoist herself up beside the boy. The ocean breeze pulled at her linen shirt and dried the perspiration beading on her forehead.

"My name is Luis."

Another Luis? Isabella's brows puckered.

"I am named after my father." Luis indicated with his head toward a man on the outskirts of the crowd. The same unkempt man who'd retrieved her uncle.

The circle of bodies began to disperse, the presence of the first mate and threat of punishment having cooled the men's passion for a fight.

"What is your name?"

She turned back to the boy. He was small for his age, and skinny. The odor emanating from his body made her want to pinch her nose. As it was, she had to wrestle the reflex to gag. A few of his teeth were black with rot as he smiled at her.

A name. She couldn't very well tell him her name was Isabella. "Benito."

"First time aboard a ship?"

She grinned. "Is it that obvious?"

He wiped his nose with the back of his hand. "Don't worry. Stick with me, and I'll show you everything there is to know about living on the high seas."

"Thank you, Luis. I shall forever be in your debt for your kindness."

Luis laughed and started to climb down the rigging. "You talk funny." He jumped and landed on the wooden deck with a *thud*. He waved and scurried away down some steps and into the belly of the ship.

Isabella winced. She'd been on board Captain Montoya's galleon less than an hour, and already she'd raised suspicion. She had to do better. Be better. No one could suspect who she really was. If anyone ever found out… She shook her head. Best not to entertain that as even a possibility.

Juan's gaze caught hers, and a jerk of his head had her descending her precarious position. Relief washed over Isabella as her feet touched the solid boards of the main deck. She hoped she'd never have to climb the unstable rigging again.

She caught up with her uncle at the top of the same stairs Luis had descended moments earlier. As they took step after step, leaving the bright sunlight for the dim quarters of paneled wood, Juan spoke over his shoulder, his words drifting back to the wide-eyed Isabella.

"This galleon has five levels—the half deck, upper and lower gun deck, the orlop deck, and the hold."

They stopped at the bottom of one flight of stairs, sunlight streaking in from small windows and dancing off dust particles drifting in the stagnant air. Large, heavy cannons aimed out of the square holes spaced along the outer wall. Isabella wasn't sure if she should feel safe with their presence or nervous at the possibility of a danger so great that their use was warranted.

The fast-paced tour ended in the hold of the ship. Isabella's head spun. How would she keep it all straight?

Juan's lamp illuminated countless barrels. "These contain our survival for the next months—fresh water, wine, dried fruit, salted beef." He turned and looked her in the eye. "This will be a completely different life than you are used to. Most of the food we eat is not fresh, nor is it hot. Fires are a dangerous thing on a vessel built of wood. We limit the use of a cooking fire to once a day."

She smiled. "Do not worry about me, Uncle. I will be fine."

"There is only a small supply of fresh water. After so many weeks in the heat, it begins to grow algae and is unsuitable, so we mainly drink wine. There is no luxury of a bath either."

Isabella patted his arm. "The more unpleasant I smell, the less likely the other men will suspect I am something other than what I appear."

Juan huffed and turned to scale the steps from the ship's depths. Isabella's lips curved. She could see right through Pepe. He was trying to change her mind. Sweet man, but he did not understand that stale food, dirty skin, and hard work sounded like heaven to her.

They ascended to the half deck through an opening Juan had called the great skylight. Now near the stern of the vessel, the mizzenmast towered above them. Isabella had no idea how she was going to remember all the information and terms of things that Pepe had told her. Why couldn't sailors use the same vocabulary as everyone else? What was wrong with using front, back, left, and right to refer to the parts of the ship?

"Are you listening to me?" Her uncle's voice snapped her

out of her musings. She caught the smirk of one of the other sailor's behind Juan's back, and her cheeks flushed hot. She gave a small shake of her head and mumbled an apology.

"As I was saying, you are new to the ways of the sea and you are young. I am going to assign you a number of duties so that you can acquaint yourself with the ship and survival upon it." He clasped his hands behind his back and rocked on the balls of his feet. "You will help young Luis with his duties as cabin boy when the captain has need. On top of that you will swab the deck and keep her surfaces clean. In the case of an attack, you will work as a powder monkey and transport gunpowder from the orlop deck to the cannons on the upper and lower gun decks."

"Juan! In my cabin now!"

Isabella turned and watched as the captain stalked across the deck, his boots thunking on wooden boards. A scowl etched deep lines in his striking features.

Juan tilted the handle of a swab in her direction, and she reached out to take it. As he passed her, he tipped his head and whispered in her ear, "Keep your head down and try to stay out of trouble."

Chapter 5

Florida, Present Day

The room nearly vibrated with each rapid rotation of the three commercial-grade dryers in the laundry room at the upscale hotel where Summer's mother worked. The moisture from the steamers and the heat from the dryers weighed down the air and caused perspiration to drip down Summer's spine. She took a swig from her water bottle and fanned herself with her hand. How anyone could work in the windowless room, with the constant noise and energy-sapping humidity, was beyond her.

Mom brought two corners of a pillowcase together and with the flick of her wrists, snapped the soft cotton fabric. She laid it on a long work countertop and smoothed out the wrinkles before folding it over again into a perfect square.

How long had her mother worked as a maid in this hotel? As far back as she could remember, her mother had donned the drab gray work dress with freshly pressed white collar and cuffs and tied a matching pristine apron around her waist. Her name tag pinned to her breast and her curly silver hair twisted into a bun, completed the uniform that bespoke a station in life in a country that professed to no longer have a caste system.

"If you're going to sit there and sulk, you might as well help me." Her mother held a bundle of sheets in her arms.

Summer slid off her stool and grabbed one end of the bedding, stepped back, and shook the fabric. It was light and smelled like lavender and honeysuckle.

Mom eyed her. "What's with the sour face? You look like you've been sucking on lemons all morning."

Summer brought her end of the sheet to her mom and kissed the older woman's cheek. "I just needed a bit of your sugar to make lemonade, Mom." She slid her hands down the cotton weave and stepped back to pull taught the fabric and fold it over once more.

The lines around her mom's eyes and mouth softened. "So tell me, what has my sweet girl down in the dumps?"

Summer took a deep breath and let it out slowly, lungs deflating—just like her dreams of ever making a career out of her photography. "You know the magazine *Our World*? The editor called me today."

"You've wanted to get a photograph published in that magazine since you were twelve."

"Yeah, and I thought I'd finally have a shot at it, but—" The buzzer on one of the dryers rang out loud and long. "But the editor said my photos aren't edgy or unique enough."

Mom wheeled over a metal cart to the large machine and started transferring warm bedding into it. She paused and looked up. "And?"

"Isn't that enough?"

"It is, but something tells me there's more." She pushed the cart to the counter, then slid a large black leather purse toward her, rifled around in it, and brought out a few coins. "Want a Coke?"

Summer shook her head and held up her water bottle.

"I'll be right back." Mom walked out the door toward the long hotel hallway. Around the corner was a vending machine.

Summer puffed out a breath and massaged her temples. She should have brought along her bathing suit and soaked in the hotel hot tub. That would have released the tension constricting the muscles in her shoulders. It wouldn't have been the first time her mom had snuck her in either. Not that she really needed to do any sneaking. The hotel was Summer's second home growing up. She'd spent hours back here in the laundry room, pouring over her homework, eating snacks from the vending machine, and swimming in the indoor pool.

The door opened and Mom walked through, a Diet Coke in her hand. She pulled up a stool from under the counter and took a seat. The bottle hissed as she twisted the lid. "Okay, spill the rest. The phone call was bad, but I sense there's more."

"You're right." Summer fiddled with her bottle. "I thought it was a practical joke at first, but it turns out he was serious."

"Wait. Wait. wait." Mom waved at her. "Back up. You're not making any sense. What did you think was a joke, and who was serious?"

"Get this. So earlier today I was at the coffee shop trying to get a moment to myself just to breathe, and this guy I've never met asks me if I'm Summer Arnet."

Mom's eyebrows rose.

"I know, right? He wanted me to take him to the dive site

where I photographed the great white. That's when the editor at *Our World* called and I left the coffeehouse. Well, I hadn't even been home five minutes before the guy comes busting through my front door."

"He followed you?" Mom's hand flew to her heart. "Should we call the police?"

"Calm down, Mom. Everything's fine. I was a little scared at first, but he's harmless. He got my address off my website."

Mom jumped from her stool. "You have your address on your website!"

"Anyway…" Summer said it slowly, exaggerating every syllable. "He finally told me why he wanted to go to that particular site. He thinks there's a sunken treasure ship down there." She snorted. "Said he'd spilt the treasure with me if I took him."

Mom settled back on her stool, but her lips were pressed in a thin line. "So it wasn't a practical joke?"

"Nope. He was dead serious."

A moment of silence followed. "So when are you taking him?"

Summer's eyebrows knitted together. "What? I'm not taking him anywhere."

"Why not?" Mom stood and walked to Summer, taking her hands in her own. "Listen, honey, this may be the big break you've been looking for."

"What do you mean?"

"That editor said she wanted something new, right? The ship may not be new—I'm sure it's quite old. But the discovery will be…new, that is." She brushed a strand of hair off Summer's forehead and tucked it behind her ear. "And exciting."

"You're not making any sense." The plastic bottle in Summer's hands crinkled as she twirled it in her fingers.

"The ship." Mom smacked her thigh. "You take that man and do the dive and take some fabulous pictures, and voila, you'll have that editor eating out of your hands. Not to mention be half a treasure richer."

"Mom! Looting that ship would be the same as stealing from a culture, from history. I might as well get a parrot, put a patch over my eye, and start making people walk the plank."

"Arg!" One side of Mom's mouth lifted, and the opposite eye squinted as she tried her best pirate impersonation.

Summer crossed her arms, but her lips twitched. "It's not funny."

"Then why are you trying so hard not to laugh?" Mom's eyes twinkled.

"Okay, fine, it's a little funny."

Mom pulled her stool up close and laid her hand on Summer's knee. "Sweetheart, I admire your moral stand, but this is the real world. Do you think if I had a chance at half a treasure I'd still be living in the single-wide at the trailer park or cleaning up after people here at the hotel? Besides, what's a bunch of Spanish doubloons, or whatever's on that ship, doing for their culture or history? Nothing. No one can appreciate or benefit from it buried under gallons of water."

Mom cupped Summer's cheek and brought her face around to look her in the eye. "But you, you could make your dreams come true." She stood and kissed Summer's forehead before picking up a fitted sheet to fold from her pile in the cart. "Think about it."

The door that led to the front desk opened, and a head peeked around the edge.

"Oh, hi, Summer," the middle-aged woman said when she spotted Summer on the stool. "Your mom here?"

Summer pointed as her mom answered. "What do you need, Liz?"

"Suite 315 called and said they'd be checking in early, and Tanisha isn't finished cleaning in there yet. I'd put them in another room, but they're regulars and will only stay in that suite. Crazy rich people. A bed is a bed, am I right?"

"Don't worry about it. I'll head up and help Tanisha finish." Mom grabbed supplies from the closet.

"You're a lifesaver, Patti." Liz blew the woman a kiss before ducking back out the door.

Arms loaded with a few extra rags and cleaning chemicals, Mom turned back to Summer. "Call him. Today. Don't be the one standing in the way of your dreams. All it will get you is calloused hands and neighbors five yards away."

"I'll think about it." She replied to her mom's retreating back.

Should she call? The discovery of a sunken ship possibly hundreds of years old did sound exciting. And it wasn't the discovery of it she was morally against—it was the robbery of items that belonged to a culture of people. They didn't belong to a single person for personal gain. He had said he'd share half the treasure with her. What if she donated her half to a museum? If the treasure stayed on the ocean floor, then no one could appreciate or benefit from it, right? And if she did take him down there, she was only doing it for the pictures she could take, anyway. They would be sure to impress Tabitha Michaels. Maybe even get Summer a regular spot in *Our World*.

She stood and reached into the front pocket of her khaki

shorts. She pulled out a small slip of paper and unfolded it, staring at the numbers written in black ink. Call or not call? She held her bottom lip prisoner between her teeth as she vacillated. Her eyes closed. Boy, was her pride going to sting when she told him she'd changed her mind.

She grabbed a memo pad with the hotel logo at the top and scrawled a quick message for her mom. *Calling him. Xoxo, Summer.*

With a wave to Liz at the front desk, she exited the automatic doors. Maybe this would be fun. What was the word her mom had used? Exciting. A definite adventure. An image of rows of razor-sharp teeth tearing her from limb to limb flashed through her mind, and she shuddered. Maybe she'd say a prayer beforehand that all sharks, at least the more aggressive ones, were no longer roaming the vicinity. She glanced to the cloud-dotted sky. If God was up there, it wouldn't hurt to cover her bases.

Fishing the square fob out of her small clutch, she unlocked her silver PT Cruiser and opened the door. A wave of heat surged from the inside of the vehicle. Summer crouched under the car's soft top, reached out, and pulled the D ring at the center where the roof and windshield met. A press of a button and the top folded down. She unplugged her phone from the car charger. Eyes darting between her phone and the paper with Trent's number scrawled on it, she punched in the numbers.

The phone rang, and she toed a pebble in the road. An elderly man with a *Gone Fishin'* cap rode by on a motorized scooter. The Chihuahua he had tucked under his arm barked at her as they passed. The ringing stopped, and a default greeting on the answering service responded with a short message and a long beep. "Mr. Carrington, this is Summer Arnet. I've changed my mind. If you still want me to take you to the dive site, then call me back, and we can work out the details." She punched End and dropped the phone into her clutch.

Chapter 6

Morning sunlight squeezed through narrow slats in the window blinds. Trent stretched, his arm brushing the empty, cold space beside him on the bed. Turning his head, he squinted, seeing through sleep-filled eyes. Alone. He felt a familiar stab in his chest. Guilt? He pressed a fist to his sternum, pushing against the pressure, weeding out the roots of remorse. He had nothing for which to be ashamed. It was only his Christian upbringing, the indoctrination of his parents' faith that nicked his conscience. He propped himself up on his elbow and reached for a small piece of paper lying on the pillow next to his.

There's coffee in the pot and a cup on the counter. Had fun last night. Maybe we can do it again sometime. Red lipstick colored the corner of the paper where she'd pressed a kiss.

A grin pulled at the corners of his mouth. Last night *had* been fun. His smile faltered. But why did he feel so empty this morning?

He pushed back a purple paisley-printed comforter and then padded across plush carpet on bare feet. The shower turned on with a squeak, and he ran his fingers through his hair as he waited for the water to heat. Steam rose from behind the curtain, and he stepped in, warm water washing away vestiges of drowsiness.

His forehead rested on cold tile as warm water ran down his back. The hollow ache returned and caved in his chest. He was still waiting for it—the assurance of happiness, of the fulfillment society promised. Was this all there was? Brief moments of pleasure and then back to a half existence? He lifted his head and let the water pound his scalp.

Jesus wants to make you whole. To give you an abundant life.

Trent snorted at the remembered words of his mother. His parents seemed to forget that God not only gave, but also took away. If God was all-powerful like his parents proclaimed, then it was He who'd torn Trent in two in the first place. He didn't want anything to do with a God like that.

He turned off the water and stepped out of the shower. After drying himself off, he used the towel to wipe away the fog from the mirror. Empty eyes stared back at him. No. God simply could not be trusted. It was up to him alone to make the most out of life. He'd steal his moments of pleasure. Buy his happiness, if need be. One side of his mouth lifted in a smirk. With the amount of antiquities he was hoping to salvage from the sunken galleon, that could be a lot of happiness indeed.

Who would've thought the photographer would change her mind? He picked up discarded jeans from the bedroom floor and shimmied into them. Where would she take him? Off the coast of South Carolina? Mexico? In the Gulf around Louisiana? He doubted Cuba. Too many politics involved. Maybe more local. Could the ship be in the waters around

Florida? For some reason the magazine hadn't noted where the photo had been taken, which was unusual.

Trent retrieved the mug from the counter and poured a cup of coffee. Four clear cylinders lined the back of the counter. He licked his finger before pressing the tip into the contents of the second-smallest container. He popped the digit back into his mouth. Sugar. He had to open three drawers before he found a spoon. Two scoops, stir, and his coffee was perfect.

How would Summer Arnet react when he arrived at her studio again today? He imagined her green eyes widening with surprise, her pert little mouth opening in a small O. A few fun ideas of how to occupy that cute mouth flashed through his mind, and a mischievous grin split his face. Who said you couldn't mix business with pleasure? Maybe he should prove them wrong.

He drained his mug and rinsed it in the sink.

———

Trent dismounted his Harley and clipped his helmet around the handlebars. He took a deep breath in and let it out slowly, hands on his hips. Man, it was going to be a good day. He could feel it. All the pieces in the puzzle were finally coming together, with no need for plan B.

Summer's studio was in a fun, artsy part of town. Small bungalow-style buildings with vertical siding lined the street, each painted a different tropical color—coral, lime, sunshine yellow, and lastly a sky blue. The blue one was Summer's.

He jogged up the few steps to Summer's studio and opened the door, a dashing smile in place. Three pairs of eyes lifted at his entrance. Summer sat behind her desk, flanked by two men. They straightened from their hunched positions behind the computer screen.

Summer stood, hands on the desk. "What are you doing here?"

"Nice to see you again too." Trent winked. He was tempted to tack on "babe" just to get a rise out of her, but the older gentleman was watching him, a warning in his look. Her father maybe?

"Sorry," she mumbled as she sat and started rearranging pencils on her desk. "I figured you'd call, not show up unannounced. Again."

The younger man's eyes darted between Trent and her. "You know this guy, Summer?"

She exhaled. "Yeah. I'm taking him diving."

"Oh, come on now. Don't say it like that." Trent sat in the same chair he'd occupied the day before, and stretched out his legs, crossed his ankles. "Try saying it without looking like you just found a worm in your boiled peanuts."

Summer's eyes narrowed. "When do you want to go?"

The younger man shook his head. "Wait. You're not taking him by yourself, are you?"

Who was this guy? He didn't share any resemblance with the photographer, so he couldn't be her brother. Boyfriend? Well, that would be a serious damper on Trent's fun.

Trent folded his arms, mirroring the two men on both sides of her. "Does she need a chaperone, Sparky?"

Folding her own arms, Summer leaned back in her chair. She smirked. "You know, Jonathan, that's a great idea. You and Mark should come with us."

Trent leaned forward. "Hey, now, wait a minute. That's not what we agreed to."

"We haven't agreed to anything, Mr. Carrington."

"Trent. And I'm not splitting…I'm not paying more than I already offered."

"No problem."

"Great."

"Terrific."

Summer glared at him, a challenge in her eye. As for Trent, he schooled his features, swallowing a genuine smile. Who was this woman? Not only was she unaffected by his charms, something he rarely encountered, she also had grit…and sass. A beguiling combination.

The middle-aged man on the right hid a chuckle behind a cough, and the photographer speared him a look out of the corner of her eye.

"Can someone please fill me in here?" The man she'd called Jonathan was beginning to grate on Trent's nerves.

Summer flung her arm out in his direction. "This man—"

Trent stood and extended his hand first to one man and then the other. "Trent Carrington. Nice to meet you."

"Like I was saying—"

"Summer's not a dive instructor or excursion guide." Jonathan gripped Trent's hand—hard.

Make that his last nerve. "I don't think she needs someone to fight her battles for her either, Sir Galahad. But to put your mind at ease, I don't need an instructor. I'm scuba certified."

"How about some iced tea, Summer? Before these two go outside to see who can spit the farthest."

"Right, Mark." She stood. "Four sweet teas coming up."

Minutes later, she returned holding a tray with four tall glasses filled with russet-colored liquid.

"Let's start over." She handed a glass to Trent. "Trent Carrington, this is Jonathan Morris and Mark Sutton. They were both with me on the great white dive."

Jonathan's eyebrows shot up. "He wants you to take him *there*? But you said you'd never dive there again."

Interesting. Summer cast a quick glance in Trent's direction before looking back at her friend. "Sometimes you have to do things you don't want to. It's called life."

"Yeah, but—"

Trent set his glass down and clasped his hands together, resting them on the desk. "So, are we all in?" Summer looked at him, gratitude in her eyes. He liked the spit and fire—it was fun. But this...this he could get lost in. He cleared his throat. "I was hoping we could head out in two weeks. That would give us enough time to make any arrangements for equipment and boat rentals and buy plane tickets, if need be."

"I don't have any major photography plans scheduled since hurricane season is coming up, so that works for me." Summer turned to her friends. "What about you guys?"

Mark shook his head. "Sorry. I promised your mother I'd help patch up her roof."

All eyes turned to Jonathan. "I wouldn't miss it for the world."

Trent resisted the urge to groan. It wasn't like he minded the extra person along for the trip. He just minded *this* person. Less than ten minutes and the guy had gotten under his skin like a festering splinter.

Why was that, anyway? Maybe it was the way he hovered over Summer. He might as well have hiked a leg and marked his territory. But why should that bother Trent? If he needed company on the trip, there were bound to be women who'd be willing companions. In fact, he should be happy. With Secret Service Skippy acting as bodyguard, there'd be no distractions. He could keep his eye on the prize...literally.

Then why did he feel like there had been something great

right in front of him, and when he'd reached out, it had dissipated like a mirage, his hands empty, as always?

"I'm going to need a credit card."

Trent blinked, his mind racing to get back on track from its pit stop.

Summer's hand was held out, palm up. "To reserve equipment and book hotel rooms and airfare."

Airfare. So, not in Florida. And no way was he handing over his credit card to someone he'd just met the day before. "So where is it we're going, anyway?"

"Bahamas." With eyebrows raised, she gave her open palm a pointed look.

Mark set his glass down. "I'm going to head out, Summer. You guys sound like you have plans to make, and I have a few errands to run." He turned to Trent. "It was nice to meet you."

"You too, sir."

"Guess that means I'm out of here too." Jonathan blew out a breath. "I hitched a ride over with Mark."

"I'll see you guys later."

The door closed, and Summer looked at him expectantly.

"I'm not giving you my credit card."

She huffed and grabbed a pen and a notepad. "Fine." She scrolled through her smartphone, bent, and then copied something onto the paper. Straightening, she handed him the paper. "That's the name and number of the company we rented the boat and equipment from last time."

"Thanks." He paused. "I really appreciate this, you know. I don't know why you changed your mind, but I'm glad you did."

She studied him as he stood.

"I'll call you with the details."

His hand was on the doorknob when she spoke.

"It's about more than the money for you, isn't it?"

First his mom and now her? Why couldn't it just be about the thrill of the chase? The intrigue of a mystery? Uncovering something that had been hidden for centuries? And of course, amassing a fortune. Why did they think something deeper was driving him?

The hollowness that had caved in his chest earlier that morning returned, leaving him empty. He swallowed and sidestepped it as he would a small sinkhole in the soft Florida sand. "I don't know what you're talking about."

She regarded him a moment before her slight shoulders rose and fell in a small shrug. "Your business is your business."

"Uh, right. Well, I'll be in touch." He exited without a backward glance. Without a chance for her probing looks and curiosity to unearth something...that wasn't there? He beat the heel of his palm against his skull a few times. These women needed to get out of his head. There was nothing wrong with him. He wasn't on some quest to fill a void in his life. He was simply a man about to undertake an underwater exploration with the hope of making the greatest discovery of the decade.

Breath puffed out his nose in a snort as his thoughts turned sarcastic. *I wonder if the women in Lewis and Clark's lives pestered them about* filling a void *when they set out to find a Northwest Passage.*

He was face value. The sooner everyone accepted that, the better.

Chapter 7

I'm going to go cross-eyed if I stare at this screen any longer. Summer scrubbed at her eyes, then blinked hard a few times. Over a hundred photographs to edit and she was only halfway through. At this rate her backside would be glued in this seat for the rest of the day. She twisted in her chair, the top half of her going one way and the bottom half going the other. A satisfying crack sounded from her lower spine. A chiropractor would scold, but it alleviated the pressure. Now back to photo number fifty-three. She covered the computer's mouse with her hand and made a few clicks.

Her cell vibrated on the desk next to her outstretched hand. The ID registered a number she didn't recognize. She tapped the green Accept button.

"Hello?"

"Hey, beautiful, you want to grab some coffee?"

Furrows formed between her eyes. Who in the world? "I'm sorry. You must have the wrong number."

She pulled the phone away from her ear but stopped short

of disconnecting when she heard the voice on the other end say her name.

Her lips turned down. "Who is this?"

"Who do you think it is, babe? I told you I'd call." Summer hadn't known it was possible to hear a smile until then. The flirtatious, mischievous smile she'd seen on Trent Carrington's face before resounded over the phone lines. And babe? Really? She set her teeth. The guy knew it irked her to be called that, but it seemed he got perverse pleasure in pushing her buttons.

Ignore it. If he can't get a rise out of you, he'll eventually stop. At least that was how it had worked when the boys had teased her in elementary school.

Summer stared at her computer screen. She really needed to get these photos edited by the end of the day. "I'm in the middle of something right now, Trent. If this is about the trip, you can e-mail me the itinerary."

The door to her studio pushed open, and there stood Trent. All six foot plus of him. The sun shone through the open door, causing his blond hair to glow like gold. One side of his mouth whirled up in a lopsided grin. Her breath whooshed out of her. From irritation. Obviously. The reaction couldn't have been for any other reason.

"I'm not taking no for an answer." Summer heard his voice from across the room as well as from her cell. She hung up and sent him a glare.

"As you can see, I'm working." She indicated the screen in front of her.

He walked across the room and sat in one of the chairs opposite her desk, leaning back in it like he had all the time in the world.

"Coffee will only take fifteen minutes." He bestowed one of his flashing smiles upon her.

Summer looked at him. She took in his laid-back manner, the way he was quick to smile, and the ease in which he charmed. For goodness' sake, the man thought all he had to do was smile and he'd get his way. She pursed her lips. Already she'd given in to him, but that was because she needed some edgy photos for *Our World*, not because he'd smiled at her, said *pretty please*, and made her go all gooey inside.

Someone needed to start telling this man no.

"Thank you for the offer, but I really don't have time right now."

He continued to lounge in her chair, his gaze never leaving her face, the lopsided grin never faltering. "All right. No problem."

Really? He wasn't going to put up more of a fight? No cajoling? No begging? No persuasion of any kind? Summer was surprised at the twinge of disappointment in her midsection. Guess he didn't think her worthy of any added effort.

Trent stood, and Summer's eyes followed the motion. His gaze continued to lock on her, and she swallowed hard.

"I'll just go and bring some coffee back. Better that way anyhow. Now I won't have to worry about getting you back at a specific time. And since I don't have anything else going on right now, I can stay and keep you company while you work. I could stay all day if I wanted to."

All day? Her nerves already stood on end with his constant stare. No way she'd be able to get any work done. And how so like him to manipulate a situation so he got exactly what he wanted. Any twinge of disappointment was replaced with annoyance.

She met his gaze and took in the cocky slant of his eyes.

He thought he was so irresistible. One look, one smile, and she'd fall all over him. Not going to happen.

"Do you always get what you want so easily?"

His head tilted as if thinking it through, then his eyes bored into hers once more. "No. Not everything is worth pursuit. But when I find something special, I'll do everything within my power to claim it as mine."

Her breath came in a short gasp. Words. That was all they were. Words he'd probably used a thousand times before on a thousand different women. That was what her head told her heart. But the way her heart hammered against her chest, it didn't feel like it was listening.

Summer licked her lips and tore her gaze away from his. It was like pulling apart strong magnets. In fact, his gaze already drew her back in. She fiddled with her mouse, attempting to ignore the compelling figure standing now in her peripheral vision.

Oh, what was the use! She'd never get any work done with him standing there, and if she didn't say or do anything soon, he was bound to leave only to come back for an indefinite period of time. If she wanted to get any work in the next five hours, the only recourse was to take a break and appease the man by having coffee with him. Fifteen minutes away was better than a whole day wasted.

She sighed heavily to let him know she wasn't happy with the interruption or his manipulation. "Let me grab my purse."

His grin widened.

She had to concentrate to keep her brow furrowed. Her rebellious lips wanted to turn up to answer his bright smile, and she didn't want him to get the wrong impression. She wasn't falling for his charms. She was doing what she had to do in order to get back to work without any distractions.

Trent held the door open, and she felt the pull of him as she passed. He closed the door, and she turned to lock the dead bolt. She started down the steps ahead of him and turned right. Her car was parked on the side of the road a few yards away.

"Where are you going?"

She stopped and turned around. "My car is right up here."

"Yes, but my bike"—he pulled a helmet from the handlebars—"is right here."

She propped a hand on her hip. "I'm not riding that thing. I'll meet you at the coffee shop."

One eyebrow rose. "Scared?"

Not of riding the Harley. It was more the thought of where she'd need to put her hands to stay on that frightened her. If a girl didn't want to get burned, then she'd better not put her hands to the fire.

"How about I make you a deal?" His words stopped her from turning back around and marching to her car. "We'll take my bike, but you can drive."

"Me drive your Harley?"

"Mmm-hmm."

Tempting. She'd always wanted to drive a motorcycle. Dirt bikes had been fun in her teen years, but she'd never gotten a chance to ride a real hog. "Don't you have to have a special license to drive?"

Trent shrugged. "It's only a few miles to the coffee shop. Besides, what's a little adventure without a little rule bending?"

Summer tucked her bottom lip between her teeth. The coffee shop was only a few minutes down the road, and when would she get another chance to drive such a powerful machine? Her hands itched to encircle the throttle. She released her bottom lip and let it curve in a small smile.

"Deal." She eyed the helmet in his hands. "You have a second one of those?"

He retrieved another helmet from the leather saddlebag in back. "I always carry a spare."

How many women had wrapped their arms around him and pressed their cheek to his back as he took them for a ride on his Harley? Her grin broadened. The real question was, how many women had he let drive? She guessed not many.

She pulled on the elastic band holding up her high ponytail and shook out her hair. With an outstretched hand, she wordlessly asked for the helmet in his hands. Their fingers brushed, and an electric current zinged up her arm. Must be the adrenaline in anticipation of finally getting to drive a motorcycle. The only possible explanation.

The helmet slid over the top of her head, and she secured the strap under her chin. She slung her leg over the seat and settled into the leather under her backside. The sun reflected off the polished chrome, nearly blinding her. She gripped the handlebars, appreciating the Harley's power. A machine like this deserved respect.

A warm hand cupped her upper arm before Trent descended onto the seat behind her. Florida was hot enough, but the heat emanating from his body made her only too aware of his proximity. He leaned down even closer to her, his chest brushing her back. Adrenaline surged again. His arms came up alongside hers, and his hands covered hers on the handlebars. She licked her lips and willed her heart to stop pounding so quickly.

His right hand squeezed hers. "This is the throttle. A little goes a long ways, so don't give it too much, or we're going to be popping wheelies down the road." Two of his fingers lifted from the back of her hand. "This is the front brake." He shifted so he was now speaking into her left ear. "On this side you have the clutch. Disengage the clutch with your left hand, shift with your left foot, and then engage the clutch again. Got it?"

She nodded, but she felt the confidence draining out of her. Hopefully, she wasn't about to kill them both.

"You'll be great." Trent squeezed her shoulder and then settled his hands on her hips.

Summer sucked in a breath, her body going still. How had she thought driving would be a safer option? Obviously she hadn't thought it through. Hadn't thought about the way his hands would circle her waist. And now that they were, she couldn't think at all. What had he said to do to make the thing go?

Right. Throttle. She twisted the throttle toward her. Miraculously, they moved forward down the street. A Harley had probably never been ridden so slowly, but her concentration was split between remembering Trent's instructions and the feel of his strong hands resting on her hip bones.

The ride was anything but smooth, but at least they made it to the coffee shop in one piece. She parked the bike along the side of the road and heaved a large sigh. Not exactly the thrill she'd hyped it up to be.

Trent hopped off the motorcycle behind her, and she felt her body relax with the added space between them. She hadn't realized how tight she'd been holding herself while he'd been so close.

She swung her leg over the seat and unclasped the helmet from under her chin. After handing the helmet to Trent, she ran her fingers through her hair a few times and then gathered the mass at the back of her head and secured it with an elastic band. A messy ponytail was the best defense against helmet hair.

A small bell jingled as they stepped into the coffee shop. Summer inhaled deeply, her body relaxing the rest of the way. She'd earned a vanilla latte.

They stood behind a small line and waited to order. When it was their turn, they stepped up to the counter.

"A black coffee for me, please, and she'll have a..." Trent turned toward her, his question dangling in the air.

She shook her head. "I'll get my own."

Lips that had been smiling all afternoon turned down. "Don't be ridiculous. I dragged you out here. I'm going to pay, so order."

Irritation flushed her skin hot. "I can pay for my own."

He pinned her with a look. "I know you can, but you aren't. Now order. You're holding up the line."

"Fine." She glared at him before turning to the barista. The girl's eyes widened, and Summer suddenly felt embarrassed at having caused a scene. Why should she care so much that the guy always got what he wanted? At least this time she was getting a free coffee out of it. "Vanilla latte, please."

A few minutes later they collected their drinks and sat at a small table in the corner of the café.

Summer sipped her latte. "So what are you doing here anyway? I thought you lived on the Gulf Coast."

Trent's forearms rested on the table as he cradled his paper cup. Summer was mesmerized by the tattoo on his right arm, which stretched from his wrist to near his elbow. It was the first time she'd been able to see it up close. The intricate detail held a quality of artistry that intrigued her. What did the symbol mean? She wasn't familiar with Celtic knots. Didn't different ones hold significant meaning?

"I'm doing research at the university library."

His voice drew her gaze back up to his face. Research? Really? "What kind of research?"

"I've been looking at blueprints of ships built in different eras and from different regions. My gut tells me we're going to find a seventeenth-century Spanish galleon when we dive, but it seems like a good idea to be prepared in case my gut turns out to be wrong." He took a sip of his coffee before continuing. "I don't want to be who knows how many feet below the surface and not know what I'm looking at."

Smart. And surprising. She hadn't pegged him as the planning type. Maybe he'd learned from experience? "How many of these treasure hunts have you been on?"

"I have connections in the archeology department at the university, so I've tagged along on a few dives and a couple of digs."

Interesting. "Have you thought of actually going to school and majoring in archeology?"

His lopsided grin returned. "I have a bachelor's degree already, although not in archeology."

She felt her jaw unhinge. Maybe there was more to Trent Carrington than he let people see. "What did you major in?"

"History. I have my teaching credentials as well."

There was nothing he could say now to surprise her. "You're a teacher?"

He chuckled and shook his head. "Not yet. I want to experience history first. Maybe even contribute to it. I promised myself one year of exploration and adventure before I settled down like a responsible adult with a regular day job."

"High school history?"

He inclined his head. "That's the plan. Although if I strike it rich with a certain Spanish treasure fleet vessel, maybe the plan will change."

She stared across the table. No way would she have learned anything in high school history class if he had been her teacher. What teenage girl could concentrate on boring dates when the teacher made her hormones go haywire? Here she was, a grown woman, and already her imagination was decking Trent out in knee-high boots, a shiny metal breastplate that nipped at the waist, and a thin rapier dangling at his side. *Talk about making history come to life!*

She took another sip of her latte. For some reason, her mouth had suddenly gone dry.

He looked at her in his unnerving way. "What about you? What are your plans? Why did you change your mind and decide to take me on the dive? Somehow I doubt the idea of a vast fortune swayed your moral compass."

A small chuckle carried on her breath. "No. Greed was not the deciding factor. In fact, I'm going to donate my portion of whatever we end up finding."

"So, if not for the money, then what?" His eyes roamed her face and upper body visible above the table, his eyes crinkling at the corners. "It wasn't because of the adventure."

Her brow furrowed. *What was that supposed to mean?* She glanced down at what she was wearing. Fitted shirt with a Peter Pan collar, dark skinny jeans, and ballet flats. Did her outfit scream cautious and collected? What about Trent? His white V-neck shirt hugged corded biceps. Jeans ripped at the knees, and the black leather jacket hung haphazardly across the back of his chair definitely lent to his adventurous spirit and bad-boy persona.

She lifted her chin. "I'm just as adventurous as the next person."

He smirked in response.

It was on the tip of her tongue to argue with him, to prove that she knew how to have adventures, but then she clamped her jaw shut. What was the use? She'd already verbally disagreed with him on a number of things that day, and she'd lost every argument. She'd said no to getting coffee and no to him paying for said coffee, but where was she? Sitting in the corner of her favorite coffee shop, cradling a free vanilla latte in her hands. It wasn't worth the energy to disagree with him again. Especially since she was sure he'd somehow end up getting his way once more.

Lifting his hand, he ticked off two fingers. "Not for the money and not for the adventure. Are you going to reveal your motivation, or am I going to keep guessing all of the reasons it wasn't?"

The stubborn man wouldn't let up. "Fame." Okay, not the real reason, but something he'd understand. Maybe that would appease him.

His brows flattened, and he crossed his arms over his chest. The motion tugged his shirt down a tad, and she had to look away from the blond tuft of hair peeking out from the V of his shirt. Good grief. She'd grown up in Florida and spent half her life on the beach. She'd seen plenty of men completely shirtless. So why did the display of a small patch of skin have her mouth going dry?

"I don't believe you. Fame isn't in the direction of your moral compass either."

Okay, moment of attraction over. This guy was far too perceptive for his own good. It was downright irritating. In fact, everything about him irritated her. The way his blue eyes danced like the waves, reaching out to her and pulling her in. The way his half grin made her stomach feel funny, not unlike being out to sea in a small raft after a big storm. The way he seemed to look at her and see her. Not a Photoshopped version of who she was, but the real, unfiltered Summer Arnet. The man was totally and completely irritating.

He smiled at her again, and she almost rummaged through her purse for some Dramamine. "You might as well spill it. You know how stubborn I can be. If you want to get back to your studio and finish whatever it was you were working on, just tell me why you changed your mind."

Hmmm...she'd forgotten about those photos that still needed editing. "Fine. It's always been my dream to have a photo selected for *Our World* magazine. I thought the great white photos would be well received with the editors, but they were rejected with instructions to find a more edgy approach for their subscribers."

"Edgier than a great white?" His incredulous look made her laugh.

"Pretty much my reaction."

"So you're hoping photos of a four-hundred-year-old sunken ship will be edgy enough for them."

Summer nodded. "That's the plan."

A plan she'd better imprint in the soft tissues of her brain. No deviations. No detours. No entanglements.

Especially not with Trent Carrington.

Chapter 8

"Flight 5250 to Detroit will now depart from gate A24."

The conversations held in the terminal resumed as the announcement ended and the light music started once again over the speakers.

Summer checked her watch. They'd be boarding in less than half an hour, and Mr. Hotshot still hadn't shown up. She peered out the large window covering the majority of the exterior wall. The plane was parked at the gate, the accordion attachment bridging the aircraft's door to the Jetway.

"Worried he won't make it?"

Jonathan leaned closer from his seat beside her and bent his head toward her ear. He smelled fresh. Like Irish Spring soap. Nothing overpowering. Was it weird that she could tell the difference? Probably not, unless the fact every time she went shopping—mostly as a teenager, but occasionally now too—she'd detour to the soap aisle and sniff the contents, conjuring up an image of a father she'd never met.

Jonathan waved a hand in front of her face. "Yoo-hoo, earth to Summer."

Heat infused her cheeks as she blinked. "What? Sorry."

One eyebrow rose, but he let it go.

Bless him. No one needed to know how pathetic she was.

He nudged her with his elbow. "So, if he doesn't show, you want to have the pilot marry us and make this our romantic Bahaman honeymoon?"

Always a kidder. Well, she could play along.

"Absolutely. Your mom would forgive you for eloping in about ten years."

Jonathan shrugged a shoulder. "Nah. You've always been like a daughter to Mom. She'd kiss me for making you an official part of the family."

Summer wrinkled her nose. "If I'm like a daughter to her, then that makes you my brother, and incest is illegal, last time I checked."

"What's illegal?" A deep voice resonated from behind, and Jonathan and Summer swiveled in their chairs.

Trent looked more ready for bike week in Daytona than plane travel, with his clunky black boots, ripped jeans, oversized belt buckle, and red-and-black plaid button-up under a black leather jacket. Summer preferred her men more GQ—what girl wouldn't swoon over a tailored suit?—and a little less Hell's Angels. But if that were the case, why had her mouth suddenly gone dry?

"Glad you finally made it." Jonathan's voice held an edge of steel.

She considered Jonathan out the corner of her eye. The muscle in his jaw ticked. Maybe it hadn't been such a good idea to have invited him along after all. Playing referee was going to get old fast. But what was his deal? Why the animosity?

"Miss me?" One corner of Trent's mouth tilted up.

Trouble. With a capitol *T*. The song from *The Music Man* crescendoed in her mind. She'd need to do a better job of steering clear of this smooth talker than Marian did of Harold Hill.

Summer stood, her long maxi skirt tickling her ankles. "Like a dog misses fleas." She tugged the bottom of her teal tank top. "I'm going to find a real bathroom before it's too late. Excuse me, boys."

———

Trent watched Summer walk away. People came to Florida all the time for the view, and right now he couldn't blame them.

"You're not her type, you know."

Of course, the state did boast annoying insects as well. This one of the human variety.

The leather of Trent's jacket crinkled as he crossed his arms. "Oh yeah? And what type is that?"

Behind his square hipster glasses, Jonathan's eyes never blinked. "The type that think they're God's gift to women. That the rules don't apply to them." He paused as a mother and young child squeezed their way past them to the other end of the row of seats. "I bet you've been with a dozen women at least but haven't had a single lasting, meaningful relationship." He pointed a finger at Trent's chest. "You can't use Summer like that. I won't let you."

Trent splayed his hands in front of him. "Dude, you need to chill. Seriously. I haven't ever forced a lady to do something she didn't want to do, and I'm not about to start now."

"Good. Because if you—"

"Hey, guys, you coming?" Summer called and motioned them into line.

When had they started boarding?

Trent stood and pulled out his boarding pass from the front pocket of his laptop case before stepping into line beside Summer.

She angled her head his way. "What seat are you in?"

He held out his pass so she could see while he zipped his bag closed. "6B."

"I'm 6A, so I guess that makes you 6C, Jonathan?"

Trent didn't need to turn around to see Jonathan's face, because he could feel the heat of the other man's glare through the back of his head. Trent's lips threatened to curl into a smirk. Feigning a cough, he covered his mouth with his hand. The seating arrangements had been a perk of making the reservations. It might not be within his means to stop the third wheel from coming on the exploration, but he jolly well didn't have to sit beside him on the hour flight across the Atlantic.

"No. Apparently I'm all the way in the back of the plane—28B."

Perfectly sculpted eyebrows rose high up Summer's forehead. "Really?"

She turned her gaze to Trent, expectant.

He cleared his throat. "Yes, well. It's a packed flight. There weren't three seats available together when I booked it." Little white lie, but *I couldn't bear the thought of spending more time in your friend's company than absolutely necessary* wasn't going to win him any brownie points.

Full lips pressed into a thin line. "No problem." The little minx turned and held her boarding pass out to Jonathan. "You can take my seat, and I'll sit in the back."

Trent snatched the pass out of her hand and gave it to the

airline worker scanning them into the computer. "No can do. We need to discuss the dive."

Nostrils flared on her button nose. "Fine."

It was amazing she got the word out past her clenched teeth.

The trio walked down the Jetway and stopped as the line clogged just before entering the aircraft. Summer reached out and touched Jonathan's arm. "Maybe the person in the seat beside us will be willing to switch with you so we all can sit together."

Jonathan gave Trent a hard scowl before his eyes softened and he looked to Summer. "I doubt anyone will want to give up their seat close to the front to sit near the back, but thanks."

The line resumed, and Trent smiled and nodded at the flight attendant welcoming the passengers. The woman's gaze raked over him, a spark of interest in her eyes.

Funny. There was no answering fire in his belly raising his body temperature. No desire...for her. He took a second look, and her lips parted. Bad idea. Now she'd think there was an interest when there wasn't. But why wasn't there? The airline's uniform shorts exposed long, well-shaped legs, and the tailored top tucked in to a trim waist. Thick, wavy brown hair framed an oval face, and intelligent hazel eyes followed him as he entered the aisle. She looked like she wouldn't mind getting to know him better—his usual prerequisite to pursuit —so why did that thought hold no appeal for him?

His hip bounced off a seat to his left. He felt like a human pinball machine as he shuffled down the aisle. Ahead of him, Summer's long red hair fell from over one shoulder and tumbled down her back as she turned her head and looked up at the seat numbers posted under the overhead compartments. Milky white skin dotted with adorable freckles peeked behind the thin strip of her tank top strap along her shoulder. His breath hitched, and his fingertips tingled with the urge to trace the line along the curve of her neck.

Could she be the reason the flight attendant hadn't stirred any cravings inside him?

Summer sank into the gray cushioned seat, head back and eyes closed. Trying to ignore him? He took his place beside her and pushed his canvas laptop case under the seat in front of him.

People continued to shuffle along the aisle, carry-on cases getting shoved into overhead compartments. A baby started to cry somewhere near the rear. Trent pulled a hand across the back of his neck. This could be a long hour.

An overweight gentleman squeezed past rows of seats by walking sideways. He paused beside Trent and looked up.

Oh, please, no.

The man fell into the seat beside Trent with a puff of breath. A puff of rancid onion breath.

So this was to be his punishment for banishing Jonathan to the back of the plane.

Seat 6C shoved in a pair of earbuds and opened a creased paperback. At least Trent wouldn't have to endure holding his breath over small talk.

Glancing back over to Summer, he leaned his elbow on the armrest between them. The woman scooted away even farther. Another inch and she'd be taking this flight sitting on the wing of the plane.

She couldn't avoid him forever.

His eyes snagged on the small rectangular window. The plastic shade had been pulled down. He grinned. Come to think of it, the cabin was a little dark. With deliberate movements, he leaned over Summer, his arm skimming hers, and tugged the covering up. He paused as he leaned back to his side. Summer's green eyes narrowed to thin slits. Trent winked, and her eyes widened, her cheeks infusing with color.

So, she wasn't immune to his charms after all.

The revelation brought an unexpected lightness to his chest. It was as if he had been holding his breath since meeting her and now his lungs were able to work to their full capacity again. Interesting. What was it about this woman that affected him so?

Summer pulled out an in-flight magazine and flipped through the pages.

A flight attendant stood at the front of the aisle and began going through the safety information. He'd heard it a thousand times. Life vests under the seats, put your own oxygen mask on before helping a child, yada yada yada.

"Cabin crew, please prepare for takeoff."

The engines roared to life, and the plane gained speed on the runway. Soon the force pushed him back against the seat, and the plane was in the air.

Summer's nose was still buried in that stupid magazine. There couldn't possibly be anything in all that junk advertised that she actually would consider buying. He had to hand it to her. She was pretty good at the silent treatment.

"Can I get y'all something to drink?"

Trent looked over to find the pretty flight attendant in the aisle. 6C ordered his drink, and then the attendant turned her eyes on Trent.

"And how about you, sugar? What can I get for you?" Her words were innocent enough. Probably the same two questions she asked all the passengers. But the *way* she said it. The look in her eyes and the tilt of her head. Oh yeah. She was asking for much more than what he wanted to drink.

Twin holes burned into the back of his head, and he knew Summer was glaring. He gave himself a little mental high five. Someone completely indifferent wouldn't care a twit that another women was flirting with him. But it obviously bothered Summer. Which meant he had a chance.

"I'll take a water, thank you."

The flight attendant turned to Summer after a few more beats of solid eye contact. "And for you?"

"Water."

Summer jammed the magazine back into the seat pouch in front of her. She crossed her arms and stared out the window.

Man, but she was cute. Time for a little peace offering though. An hour on a plane with nothing to do and no one to talk to would seem like a lifetime. Trent reached into a pocket in his jacket and pulled out a pack of gum. He held it out to her, letting his arm brush against hers.

"Want a piece?"

She turned slightly. Looked at the gum and then at him.

"For your ears."

She took a piece, and the lines around her mouth softened. Finally.

The gum wrapper crinkled as she unwrapped it. "So what are you hoping to find in this ship of yours?"

Good question. "That depends. If the galleon was traveling from Spain to the New World, then it would be loaded down with tools, books, clothing, and other European-made luxuries. On the other hand, if the ship was headed to Spain, the possibilities are a little more monetary. A galleon in the treasure fleet could theoretically hold two million pieces of eight." He paused. "You do know what pieces of eight are, right?"

Slender arms folded over her chest, and her lips pursed.

Man, it was fun to rile her.

"Like anyone born and raised in Florida, I know my share of Spanish history, Trent. Pieces of eight are silver coins, also known as Spanish dollars." Her arms unfolded. "You know the galleons in the Spanish treasure fleet carried other cargo besides gold and silver though. Many carried tobacco, sugar, silk, even lumber. None of which would be valuable now, and all of which would be ruined. What if we go through all this trouble and you're left with an empty ship?" She glanced away and muttered under her breath, "If there's even one there."

Doubter. Well, she didn't have to believe a piece of history lay in that specific spot in the ocean, but he did. He could feel it in his gut.

The plane suddenly dipped, and Trent's stomach shot to his throat. Reflexes had him white-knuckling his armrests. Summer screamed beside him and gripped his arm. Her fingernails dug into the skin surrounding his bicep. Too bad the situation was too dangerous to relish her closeness.

The plane shook and bounced more than the wooden roller coasters he used to ride as a kid. A thousand times scarier though. His palms grew sweaty, and he couldn't rein in the speed of his pulse. Prayers could be heard throughout the cabin as well as chants of "We're gonna die. We're gonna die." Up and down they bounced before the plane plunged again and the air masks dropped in front of their faces.

The chanters had been right. They were all going to die.

Chapter 9

In the Middle of the Atlantic, 1689

Metal clashing pulsated the air surrounding the ship. Isabella whipped her head around, her hands wrapping tighter around the handle of a swab.

Ting. Ting. Grunt. *Zing.*

What was going on? Curiosity propelled her forward. Two men stood on the main deck, feet braced and swords flying. The captain looked poised as his arm arched behind him, sunlight reflecting off the brass buttons on his doublet. His dark hair bounced around his shoulders as he thrust his rapier at his opponent.

The challenger swung his own sword downward, successfully deflecting the offensive strike. He moved back, but the captain did not follow.

Isabella's breath hitched as she watched the standoff. Who would attack next? Sweat beaded off the sailor's forehead, his lightweight shirt clinging to his back. His chest heaved from exertion, while Captain Montoya didn't even appear winded. The man juggled the hilt of his sword in his hand, and with a primitive roar, lunged toward the captain, the tip of his rapier aimed at the heart. Isabella covered her mouth and the gasp trying to escape. Was this mutiny? Should she try to find help?

Like a flash of lightning, Captain Montoya's sword struck —down, up. Small, short strides propelled him forward while the other man stumbled back, his parries slower and the determination seeping from his eyes. Isabella wasn't sure how the captain did it, which expert maneuver had unarmed his opponent, but the other man's sword clanged on the wooden deck and rolled toward her feet. She picked it up, the weight unfamiliar in her hands.

"You need more practice, Mario. His majesty expects the shipment we are to bring back to reach Spanish soil and not to fall into the hands of thieving pirates. Understood?"

Captain Montoya didn't wait for a response, but turned, eyes scanning. His penetrating look stopped on her and the weapon she held in her hand.

Heat flooded Isabella's cheeks, and she averted her eyes.

In three long strides he stood before her. "Come. You will be my next opponent."

Her head snapped up. "Me?"

He turned and walked back to the middle of the deck. She shuffled forward, the hilt of the rapier held tight in both fists. The captain stopped and took a stance Isabella could only assume was the starting position for a spar. She raised the sword in front of her, her arms already shaking and wrists aching from the weight.

The captain lowered his sword and regarded her. "Have you never sparred before, boy?"

"N-no, sir."

He shook his head and muttered something under his breath. With a look of annoyance, he approached her. Large hands cupped the top of her shoulders and pressed. "Shoulders down."

The rapier wobbled, and she tried to keep her hand steady. He tapped her right arm. "This hand holds the sword. Up a little more. Good. Now your other arm is going to work as a counter balance, and you hold it out behind you just so."

He demonstrated the stance, and she attempted to imitate it.

"Now, when I attack, try to block my strikes." Slowly he brought the sword toward her. Right, left, center. Each strike she blocked reverberated down her arm and echoed up her spine. She gritted her teeth and adjusted her grip.

Displaced air zinged in her ear, and too late she brought her arm up to block. The side of his rapier smacked her upper arm. Her eyes went wide at the sting. A flash of metal caught in her peripheral vision before her thigh exploded with pain. The point of her sword dropped, and he caught her again on the shoulder.

Her body screamed. Muscles already fatigued from work aboard ship protested at the unusual abuse. Chapped skin that had once been as soft as rose petals shrieked with each hit of the captain's sword. Images, unbidden, came from the recesses of her mind—the hiding places where she thought they were locked away. Hernando looming over her mother's hunched form. A fist raised, a black eye, and a lie on her lips for its cause. Bruises in the shape of fingers.

Resolve hardened Isabella's spine. No more would she allow men to have the power over her to cause harm. It was time to fight back.

She bore down and braced for the strike she knew was

going to fall. Willing to take the hit in order to make an attack of her own. As Captain Montoya's sword ripped through the air and landed on her shoulder, she struck.

Using her smaller stature to her advantage, she swung her sword upward, muscles in her arms, legs, and back jumping to attention and straining in their frontal assault. She caught the captain under his arm, her movement mired as the sword came in contact with his body. Surprise registered in his eyes, and a thrill of triumph surged through Isabella's body.

She had no idea what she was doing. No training or strategy on which to rely. An innate need to no longer be on the defensive, to no longer be the victim, powered her attack. Fear had made her a prisoner in her own body, but now she was breaking free.

Her sword never touched the captain again. He parried her every move, and exertion overtook the wildness of her movements. Soon she doubled over with her hands on her knees, gulping in deep breaths. Her side ached, her skin stung, and her hands and arms tingled from the reverberation of clanging swords. But most of all, her spirit flew.

Captain Montoya stood beside her. "Again. Tomorrow at dawn." He strode away without a backward glance.

Pepe rushed toward Isabella, his hands reaching out, then retracting back to his sides. "What were you thinking?" he hissed.

She turned her head and looked up at him, a grin in place.

Juan clucked his tongue. "It is lucky for you the captain is a fair man. Another not so noble would have taken it upon himself to teach you a lesson."

Isabella kept silent as she straightened. She had not asked to spar, nor did she have a choice when he'd commanded her to. She'd not apologize or explain herself.

"You are fortunate they were only practice swords." He ran a hand down his face. "I cannot imagine how you'd look otherwise." He shook a finger at her. "No more sparring. If you see the captain or any of the officers practicing, then make yourself busy on one of the other decks."

"I am to meet Captain Montoya again at dawn for another bout."

Isabella flinched at the fire in her uncle's eyes. It slowly died, and he began to pace in front of her. "The captain is a good man. I will tell him your situation, and he will work everything out." His arms moved in wide gestures. Was he talking to her or himself? "I may lose my position, but what is that compared to your safety?"

Isabella reached out her hand and touched his arm, stopping him midstride. "You cannot tell. I will not allow it. You said yourself the captain is fair. He would not harm me. And if I learn to defend myself with the sword, then I will be even safer than I am now. I would have a way to protect myself." Her eyes pleaded with him. "Please. This is something I must do."

He sighed and looked out at the horizon. When he met her gaze, she knew she had won. "Your *madre* would kill me if she knew what I was allowing to happen. I only pray to *Dios* you know what you are doing."

———

Isabella awoke and groaned. She hurt everywhere. Muscles she didn't even know she had protested as she slowly stood. Her hands curled into themselves and then extended back out. How was she going to be able to hold a sword, let alone lift or swing it?

The ship tilted and she stumbled, arms outstretched to try and catch herself. Her fingers scraped along a wooden beam, and a splinter pierced her skin and lodged itself there. Ah! Sticking the offended digit into her mouth, she sucked hard. As she took the finger out of her mouth, she shook her hand vigorously, trying to shake out some of the sting.

How long had she been aboard this ship now? With no calendar, she hadn't kept track. Hard work and the necessity to remain unseen marked each day. That had been accomplished. Until yesterday. A snort escaped as she thought about all the times she'd been in the captain's cabin performing her duties without any notice. She should have left the sword where it had lain.

I may be trading my prison of fear for an actual prison if I am found out.

A candle and tinder pistol lay in the bottom of a small box by her bed. She retrieved both and lit the candle. The stench of burning tallow wrinkled her nose.

With caution, she descended to the hold. She'd discovered a small alcove among the barrels when she'd been searching for some dried apples near the beginning of the voyage. Her grandmother's necklace bit into her side, and she needed the privacy the alcove afforded to rewrap the jewelry into her bindings. Her fingers wrestled with the tightened knots on the strips of cloth encircling her chest. The ends were frayed, and the fabric showed spots of tearing. What would she do if the fabric didn't hold up for the entire voyage? She folded the linen, creating a pouch for the necklace, and began rewrapping it.

Footsteps sounded on the stairs, and Isabella froze. She tucked her body more fully behind a large crate and blew out her candle. The hold plunged into total darkness, but Isabella crouched wide eyed. She prayed the strong smell of moldy cheese and wine would overpower the lingering fumes from the flame.

Light flickered and expanded as two men descended into the hold.

"Have you thought more about what we discussed?"

"Are you sure the plan will work? If we are found out beforehand or your men have second thoughts and we are outnumbered, then the penalty is death."

Isabella's heart drummed in her ears. She covered her mouth with both hands, afraid to make a sound.

"Of course I am sure. It would be easier if Captain Montoya was not so loyal...or at least more loyal to himself than the crown. But it is of no consequence. More of the men have sailed with me than the captain, and those not already on our side...well...let's just say they can be persuaded."

"I do not know..."

"Think about the gold. Ingots the size of your head. Hundreds of them. Why should King Charles benefit from all of our hard work? I say we take what is rightfully ours."

"Shhhh. Keep your voice down. Do you want someone to hear you?"

"Like who? The rats? Are you in or not?"

The silence stretched, and Isabella was afraid to breathe. If the consequence of their plans was death, she did not want to think of what they would do to her if they found out she had overheard.

"I am in. You will have to fill me in on the details later. I am late as it is to report to *Señor* de la Cruz."

Boots thudded against plank stairs, and Isabella exhaled. Now what? Should she run to her uncle and inform him about what she'd heard? No, she couldn't do that. At least not yet. One of the men said he had to report to the first mate. And she was supposed to meet the captain. In fact, she was probably already late. Should she tell him? If she told him, she would have to explain what she had been doing down in the hold in the first place, and she couldn't do that without exposing her secret. Besides, she had been so scared that the men would see her that she hadn't peeked from her hiding spot to get a look at them. She would never be able to identify the sailors behind the heinous plot. Nor did she know what the plot was.

Something scurried along the floor and over her booted foot. She sucked in her breath and swallowed a scream. Time to head to the surface and the light. Stretching her hands out in front of her, she felt along the barrels and crates until she reached the small circle of light that spilled through the opening to the orlop deck. The boards creaked as they bore her weight, and she hoped the men hadn't lingered on their ascent.

As she rounded the corner to take the last flight of stairs to the surface, Luis's small frame almost collided with hers. She reached out a hand to steady him. "Slow down, *hijo*."

Large, round eyes brimming with fear stared up at her. He tried to sidestep her, but she kept a grasp on his shoulder.

"Let me go. I have to go."

She knelt down in front of him, and he wiggled under her hold. She pinned him with a look, and He quieted, scrubbing balled fists over bloodshot eyes.

"*Mi papá…*" His thin voice cracked.

Isabella looked over Luis's shoulder. No one was behind him. Had his father hurt him? By *Díos*, if that man had laid a finger on his sweet boy, she would… She returned her focus to his crumpled face and allowed her expression to soften. If he had been injured by his father, then he did not need to witness any more anger. One more thing for her to hide.

Luis sniffed, and Isabella felt his shoulders straighten under her hands. "I must go. I cannot help him if I stand here crying like a *bebé*."

The boy scurried around her and was at the other end of the passage before his words registered in her brain.

"Luis, wait," she called after him. "Why does he need help?"

He paused, his young eyes drilling in to hers. "I think he is dying."

Chapter 10

Bahamas, Present Day

Trent had never been on a flight when the passengers all erupted in applause as soon as the wheels hit the tarmac. If it wasn't for the death grip Summer had on his arm, he'd join in the clapping. He peered down at her huddled form. Her breathing was shallow and...wait...was she quivering? Still? They were out of danger. They'd made it. Now was time to celebrate. Move on from the fright and chalk it up to a great story you could tell your friends.

Except her hold on him hadn't loosened a single degree. Her head lay buried in between his arm and the seat, and even though they were taxiing to the terminal, she still hadn't raised it an inch to peek out.

Something in his world shifted, and it wasn't the luggage in the overhead compartments.

Flyaway hairs from the crown of her head tickled his cheek, and he smoothed them down with his hand. Who was this woman, and why did she make him feel so...different?

With women it had always been the same—show them a little attention, and they returned the favor. Win-win. You had a little fun, and then you parted ways. But now? With her?

She took a shuddering breath.

"Come here." He lifted his arm and placed it around her shoulder, pulling her close. "It's going to be all right. We've landed. It's over."

The fabric of his shirt pulled taut against his back as she fisted it in a hand at his abdomen. A second later, and all too soon, she lifted her head and pulled away. Her cheeks flushed pink, and she wouldn't meet his eyes. The hand wrapped around his shirt released its hold, and she smoothed the creases.

Fire exploded in his stomach, and his skin burned where she'd touched him.

"Sorry. I don't know what came over me."

He caught her hand and held it until her eyes lifted and connected with his. Slowly he lifted her palm to his lips and pressed a kiss to its center.

He was no stranger to desire, to physical longing, but the feelings stirred by this woman...they were new, genuine. What he'd felt when he'd been with other women had been fake—cubic zirconia—and Summer, well, she was the real deal. A genuine diamond.

Summer's eyebrows knit together. She jerked her hand away, burying it in her lap.

The plane lurched to a stop, and the Fasten Seat Belt signs dinged as they turned off. The Boston marathon couldn't have contained as much motion as the cabin of the Boeing 747. Passengers from every row rocketed out of their seat, including the man beside Trent in 6C. The man's shirt had ridden up during the flight, and as he turned, Trent's vision filled with 6C's exposed flesh—his hairy lower back.

Gross. A cold shower couldn't have worked better to extinguish whatever it was that simmered in his blood at Summer's nearness. He glanced at her, but she faced the other direction as she gazed out the small window, her nails making little clicking sounds as she picked at them in her lap.

A grin spread across his lips. Nervous? Had the little kiss on her hand unsettled her so much? His brain leapt at the next obvious question. How would she react if he kissed her for real?

———

Summer massaged her palm. The spot tingled where Trent's warm lips had grazed. She squashed her hands to her stomach. Her palm wasn't the only thing that tingled.

Traitorous body.

She couldn't possibly be reacting to him this way. He was a love 'em and leave 'em kind of guy. The way that he shamelessly flirted with her and expected women to fawn all over him just because of his good looks. Oh, she'd seen how the flight attendant looked at him. She'd been extra solicitous too, right up until the turbulence, that was. Well, Summer wasn't that kind of woman. She wasn't going to fall for his crooked grin and dancing eyes. Not when she knew what lay beneath. Arrogance and conceit. The two key elements of all players.

Definitely not the type of man she was looking for. Not that she was looking. But if she *were* looking, she wanted a man that was in it for the long haul. Not a one-night stand.

Trent leaned forward to retrieve his bag from under the

seat, and his leg brushed against hers. The percussion section of a high school marching band wouldn't have been able to keep pace with her heart rate right then. She jerked her leg away and severed contact. A self-imposed restraining order was what was needed. A restraining order and a chaperone. Golly, she missed Jonathan.

Trent stepped into the aisle and motioned for her to go in front of him. As she passed, she caught a whiff of his soap. Old Spice. How had she not noticed before? It was her favorite. Masculine, but not overpowering. It was what she imagined her father wore. A twinge of loss and her step faltered. If her dad was around now, what would he say? Would he warn her that guys only had one thing on their minds? Would he encourage her to follow her dreams and not let any distractions—especially one in the form of a Norse god who couldn't be trusted—get in her way?

She pushed those thoughts back. What was the point in dwelling on them? The mother-father-daughter family dynamic had never been a part of her life. It was time to grow up. Adult women didn't need their daddies.

She stepped out of the Jetway and into the Nassau airport, immediately moving to the side. Trent followed. Electric currents zinged, although she tried to ignore them. Impossible, since she'd never been so aware of another person in all her life. She squeezed her eyes shut and shook out her hands at her sides. Opening her eyes, she channeled her focus on the faces of the people pouring out of the Jetway. Finally, she spotted Jonathan's tall frame above the crowd.

"Jonathan." She reached out and touched his arm before he walked too far past them.

He turned, eyes wide. "Summer, thank God." His large

hands reached up and cupped her upper arms. They were warm against her bare skin.

His eyes darted over her face as if he was making sure she was in one piece, then glanced at Trent and gave a curt nod. "Excuse us a minute."

Without waiting for a response from anyone, Jonathan gently pushed Summer toward the wall, her feet taking quick, small strides backward.

Her mind worked to catch up. Why was he acting so weird?

Jonathan stopped after a few feet, giving them a semblance of privacy in the public venue.

Summer's head tilted to one side, and she could feel her brow wrinkle. "What's going on?"

The Adam's apple in his throat bobbed. "I promised myself that if we survived that flight I would do something I've wanted to do for a long time."

"Which is?"

His eyes dropped to her lips. "This."

Before she knew what was happening, Summer was crushed against his body. One hand wrapped around her waist, and the other supported the base of her head as he tilted her back. His moist lips didn't hover or linger above hers, nor were they timid or shy. They moved over hers with the assurance of a man who knew what he wanted and was going after it.

Chapter 11

Atlantic Ocean, 1689

Isabella's pulse throbbed as she hurried after little Luis down the dark passageways of the ship. Why did he think his father was dying? Did it have anything to do with what she had overheard in the hold? Fear ran its icy-cold fingers up her spine. She had left Spain hoping to leave the danger behind on its shores, never realizing a new threat may await her.

"Calm down, Luis." The deep voice of Captain Montoya stopped her in her tracks, and she shuffled back a few steps into an alcove.

Staying in the shadows had kept her safe thus far. Except for the sword fight the day before, she had been nearly invisible. No one paid much attention to a small errand boy without rank or responsibility.

Peeking around the wooden frame, the captain filled her vision. He knelt in front of Luis, a hand on the boy's shoulder. What were they saying? If only their hushed voices would carry. The captain stood, and Luis hurried back the way he'd come, the captain's long stride easily keeping pace.

Isabella pressed her back against the rough wood as they passed. When they rounded a corner, she let out a breath. She took a step and stopped, rubbing the long linen shirt between her fingers. Indecision twisted her gut.

Sunlight seeped through the open doorway that led to the outer decks. She could walk right through it and be about her duties. No eyebrows would be raised, and no attention would be directed to her. She'd be safe.

Her eyes swung to the opposite direction, following the path the two had trod. If she followed them and offered to help, then she would lose her anonymity. She could be placing herself in a situation where her secret would be found out.

The sunlight beckoned. *I do not even know Luis's father and surely do not owe him anything. Besides, the captain is quite capable. I am sure there is nothing I could do that he himself would not be able to see to.*

Isabella took a step toward the light, then stopped. The weight of her conscious anchored her feet. There may not be anything she could do to help, and it may lead to her undoing, but she could not turn away. Even if it was to stand beside the boy, she would do it. *Goodness knows the uncouth sailors do not possess an ounce of compassion to offer him.* Shoulders back, she marched back into the belly of the galleon.

The sound of coughing reached her before she stepped through to the gun deck. A few hammocks were slung across the space, with more mats littering the floor. This was where the crew slept. Those not officers privileged with their own private cabins, anyway. Isabella sidestepped the prone form of a sailor not on duty and shuffled closer to the small group of people clustered not fifteen feet away. She kept to the wall, her ears strained for any information that may pass the lips of someone who knew what was going on.

The elder Luis lay on his mat, his skin pallid and glistening with sweat. His eyes were sunken, making his already sharp cheekbones look like the peaks of the Andalusian Mountains. A thin arm draped across his midsection. Suddenly, his whole body convulsed, a deep cough racking his slight frame. He pressed a square of cloth to his mouth. Isabella didn't have to keep watching to know that when he pulled the cloth away, it would be red with his blood. She had seen it before. Wasting disease. Young Luis was right. His father was dying.

Isabella's focus had been so consumed with the sick man that she hadn't noticed the large form of the captain approaching, until he was right upon her. He regarded her, and she balled her fists behind her back in an effort to keep from fidgeting. A normal boy aboard the ship would have no reason to cower in the man's presence, and that was all she was to him.

"I can see in your eyes that you have rightly judged the situation."

The situation? Was he talking about...

A loud sniff drew her attention to the sagging body of a scared boy.

Right. The situation.

"I do not wish for the sickness to spread among the crew. We must try to contain it." He stroked his fingers along his pointed goatee. "Luis will be moved into my cabin."

She could feel her eyes widen. "What about you, *señor*?"

"The quartermaster will be receiving a bunkmate until... well, until the need for my quarters is no longer there."

He stepped even closer, filling her line of vision and blocking the huddled group not far away. Unlike the rest of the men on board whose stench welcomed a swarm of flies, the captain smelled of sweet ocean breezes and the promise of adventure. A thrill shot through her, tickling her senses.

"Benito."

Benito? Why is he calling me—

Realization dawned. So few of the men besides Pepe talked to her that she had forgotten the false name she had taken as part of her disguise.

"I will need you to care for Luis until his time comes." His eyes searched her own. "I do not wish for his son to shoulder that burden. Can I trust you in this?"

He was the captain. He could be ordering her to this new duty as nursemaid instead of asking. But he knew. He knew this latest assignment could lead to death. *Tío* Pepe was correct. Captain Montoya was a good man.

———

A warm hand on her shoulder tugged Isabella from her slumber. She jerked to the side, her hand going instinctively to her chest and *Abuela's* jewels. Safe, but she would need to sneak away for a moment later to rewrap her bindings. They were loosening and beginning to slip again.

"I did not mean to startle you."

Isabella looked up, her eyes colliding with the dark orbs of Captain Montoya's. She scurried to her feet, her numb backside protesting against the few hours' rest she'd received while propped up against the wall. The night had been long. Luis had suffered greatly with a raging fever, his wasted body convulsing violently with coughing fits. There was not much she could do besides pray and bathe his feverish body with a cool cloth. She had done both without ceasing until he had finally drifted off, his breathing labored yet even, his body warm, not scalding.

"How is he this morning?" A voice that could boom across the quarterdeck to the main deck was restrained in respect for his inferior.

"A difficult night, but he is resting now."

He nodded and turned his attention to Luis's sleeping form. The slashed leather jerkin the captain wore over a woolen shirt pulled taut across his chest as he took in a deep breath. He pulled off his broad-brimmed hat and ran a hand through his inky hair.

"If only…"

The captain did not have to finish that thought. How many times had the same two words skipped through her own mind? If only Mother had never married Hernando. If only Isabella had been able to convince her mother to run away before it was too late. If only *Tío* Pepe had been at port. If only *Dios* had answered her prayers.

And now, here they were again. So many *if onlys*, and God was going to let another of his children suffer and die.

Captain Montoya pointed to his bed along the wall. "Luis would be more comfortable on the mattress instead of the floor." He tugged her elbow. "Come, let us move him."

"No."

He turned, his eyebrows raised. "No?"

Heat crawled up her neck. "Pardon. But this illness, you know it spreads quickly and spares no man. I fear Luis may leave the illness behind on whatever he touches."

"Superstition." He placed his hat back on his head. "But we will do it your way."

Isabella dipped her head in recognition.

"Now, I must speak with the pilot and review the charts

for the day." Without a backward glance, he exited and shut the door behind him.

Her grandmother's necklace slipped, a jewel scratching at her navel. She swung her gaze from the door to Luis, still fitfully sleeping, back to the door again. There did not appear to be a lock or a way to bar it. Would anyone enter knowing the room was filled with sickness? Luis wheezed on the other side. Did she have enough time to rewrap the jewelry in her bindings before he awoke?

She chewed on her lower lip. There did not seem to be much choice. She had to take the chance and be quick about it or risk the necklace slipping farther. Grabbing fistfuls of the oversized shirt, she tugged the tails out of her breeches and bunched them under her arms and chin to hold them up. Her fingers worked to untie the knot, her frustration and anxiety growing with each second the stubborn material would not give. Finally, it loosened, and the strip of cloth unwound around her.

Coughing interrupted the silence, and Isabella whirled around, dropping the ends of her long shirt. Sunken eyes wide with shock and rimmed in black bore into her.

"Y-y-you are a woman."

Chapter 12

Bahamas, Present Day

So Jonathan finally decided to find his *cojones*. Good for him. Trent folded his arms across his chest. That didn't mean he was going to back off though. If a woman didn't have a ring on her finger, she was fair game.

His foot tapped the thin carpeted airport floor. Of course it would be nice if he knew what was going through Summer's mind as she was getting kissed so soundly. Not that he wouldn't try to persuade her if her thoughts had suddenly changed for the man previously concreted in the friend zone. She wasn't kissing Jonathan back, but she wasn't pushing him away either. If he were a gentleman, he'd look the other way and give them some privacy, but where was the fun in that?

Seconds ticked by.

Okay, that was long enough.

He cleared his throat. Jonathan raised his head, a goofy grin on his face. Summer dabbed at her pink lips with the back of her hand. She dipped her head, fidgeting with the bottom of her tank top.

"Are we ready, Casanova?" Trent mentally berated himself for the edge he let creep into his voice.

Jonathan smirked. "After you, Lupo."

No way was Trent some silly sidekick. The muscles in his jaw tightened. The boy might have found his cojones, but he'd stumbled upon a bucket of stupid as well.

"I don't think anyone checked a bag, so let's just go get the rental car." Summer's subdued voice was more effective than a pair of scissors at cutting the invisible cord tying his focus to Jonathan's answering glare.

Trent blinked, wisps of red hair moving past and then ahead of him. Summer walked on, not looking back to see if he or Jonathan followed. Her back was rigid, her movement not as fluid as usual. The kiss had affected her, but was that good or bad news for him?

Jonathan slowed and bent his body toward Trent as he passed. "Game on." Without stopping, he pulled his navy-blue carry-on behind him.

How many times had he thought of women as a piece in an epic game? He'd been wrong. Oh, so very wrong.

———

"I'm driving." Summer snatched the keys out of Trent's hand. The Chevy Impala might've been rented under his name, but she needed to be behind the wheel, needed her hands to be busy at *something*. If the sun wasn't already starting to set on the horizon, she'd suggest going to the marina, getting their boat, and beginning their search for that blasted ship right now.

She cursed the day she let Jonathan talk her into getting in that shark cage. Two little letters would've been all she needed to get past her lips to keep her world from turning upside down.

N-O. That was it.

But she'd said yes, and now look where she was. How had everything gotten so mixed up?

Jonathan had been her friend since freshman year. They'd shared laughs. They'd shared angry words. But had never, ever shared kisses.

Until now.

She felt like banging her head against the steering wheel. What was she going to do? She loved Jonathan, just...not like that. He was her best friend. She didn't want to hurt him, and she didn't want to lose his friendship. Ugh. Why'd he have to go and ruin everything?

The trunk slammed shut, and the car rocked as Jonathan slid into the front, leaving Tent in the back. Seat belts clicked, and Summer turned the key in the ignition. She looked in the review mirror. Trent winked in the reflection.

No, no, no. If only she could clip the wings of the butterflies fluttering around in her stomach. Nothing was going right. Jonathan wasn't supposed to kiss her, and God help her, she wasn't supposed to be wishing it had been Trent's lips pressed against hers. He wasn't good for her. He wouldn't stick around, not like... Her eyes slid to the passenger seat. A groan lodged in her throat. What was she going to do?

One thing was for sure—she wasn't going to be able to figure it all out in the parking lot. She looked back to the review mirror. "Did you happen to get directions to the hotel, Trent?"

He wiggled his cell phone. "Already programmed in the

GPS. Once you pull out of the parking lot, you're going to want to take a right."

It didn't take long to pull up to the resort. The Bahamas were nice, but the islands weren't all that different from Florida. Two buildings roughly ten stories tall stood on either side of the one-story lobby. Palm trees lined the asphalt, and as Summer opened the car door, the salty spray of the ocean filled her senses. Seagulls cawed overhead, and the sun warmed her skin.

Car doors slammed, redirecting her focus. The key fob fumbled in her hand before she pressed the button to unlatch the trunk. Trent pulled out her purple zebra-print luggage while Jonathan leaned in to grab his small case.

Frigid air blasted them as the automatic doors of the hotel slid open. A middle-aged woman stood behind the desk, her wide smile showing lipstick on her teeth. Summer reflexively ran her tongue across her own incisors.

Trent leaned against the desk. "We have reservations. I booked them under the name Trent Carrington."

"Very good, Mr. Carrington." The woman flashed another smile, then turned to type on her computer. "It looks like your suite is on the seventh floor. The room is ocean facing, so you'll have some lovely views as you enjoy your stay with us."

Red flags waved. The woman had said *room*. As in singular. One. No way was Summer going to be able to survive this trip without a space to decompress. The walls of her mind already closed in on her. There was just too much to deal with.

"Here are your keys." The front desk worker handed over three card keys. "Our complimentary breakfast is served from six to ten. If you need anything, please don't hesitate to let us know."

Trent thanked her and stepped back the few feet to where

Summer and Jonathan waited out the transaction. He jerked his head to the left. "Come on. Elevator should be this way."

Summer reached out her hand and placed it on his arm. "You only booked one room?" Her harsh whisper echoed off the travertine floors. Good thing the lobby was empty. She didn't want to make a scene, but if she needed to march back to the front desk and book her own room, she would.

Trent's eyebrows wiggled. "I thought it'd be more fun this way."

Sure. She knew just the kind of *fun* he had in mind. Hotel rooms were pretty standard. You either got a room with one king-sized bed or two queens. Even if every room in the resort was full, there was no way she was crawling in between the sheets with either Trent or Jonathan.

Trent's finger traced a line down her nose. "Better watch out, or your face is going to freeze that way."

Summer swatted away his hand.

He laughed, and she squashed the thought of how handsome he was with his eyes shinning like that. Or she tried to, anyway.

"Relax. It's a suite. There are two separate rooms connected by a common area. I'll even let you assign sleeping arrangements." He leaned down to whisper in her ear. "Although my vote is that you and I share, and we let the Jolly Green Giant over there have a room to himself. I bet he snores."

The color in Jonathan's face mounted. Much redder and she'd think he'd been out all day without sunscreen. Better diffuse the situation before more than verbal punches were thrown.

"You boys can play nice together. I'll room by myself. A girl needs her privacy, after all."

Trent's lips turned up in a lopsided grin. What had she said that was so funny? Then again, maybe she didn't want to know the secret thoughts churning in his head. They might prove dangerous.

The elevator was located down a long corridor, and they waited a few minutes before the doors dinged and opened. The three stepped in, and Summer pushed the button for their floor. She stood in the middle and felt eyes on her from both sides. She glanced to her right. Trent looked down, his grin still in place, his eyes sparking with fun and adventure. An indiscernible feeling caused bubbles in the pit of her stomach. She moved her gaze to the left. Jonathan's eyes bore through hers, then darted behind her and back again. An aura as stormy as a hurricane clung to him. She squeezed her eyes shut, then checked her watch. Only 7:30. Would either of them believe her if she feigned a headache and went to bed early? Maybe when she woke up, everything would magically be right again.

The elevator jerked to a stop, and they wordlessly exited. Summer watched the numbers on the doors go up as they walked along the hallway. Trent stopped and fished one of the card keys out of his pocket. The door clicked, and he turned the handle.

She was speechless. Her mom's hotel was nice, but this... nope...she still didn't have any words to describe it. Floor-to-ceiling glass doors beckoned from the opposite end of the room, the full moon shimmering off the tropical crystal waters below. She ran a hand along the main wall as she entered. Glossy, flat, glossy, flat. Painted stripes of the same color in different finishes. She moved in a circle, taking it all in. A tall, dark armoire. A kitchenette with granite countertops. An overstuffed white linen love seat. She looked at Trent. How could he afford this?

Jonathan walked around her and opened the doors on either wall. She stepped behind him and peeked around his tall form. The bedrooms. He looked over his shoulder at her. "You pick which one you want."

Why did she have this sudden urge to squirm? Okay, so Jonathan had kissed her, and that had changed their entire dynamic, but she shouldn't suddenly feel self-conscious around him. He was still Jonathan.

She pointed past him. "I'll take that one."

He nodded and went to retrieve her small luggage.

"Thanks."

The tenderness in his eyes as they swept over her face broke her heart. Why, oh why, couldn't she return his feelings?

There was no point in lying to herself either. She'd known Jonathan for a good part of her life. If there was ever a chance that she'd develop any feelings beyond friendship, it would have happened already. No way was she going to string him along with maybes and uncertainties. He was too good a guy. Too good a friend.

Was it wishful thinking to hope the situation would resolve itself? That they could pretend the kiss never happened and avoid having "the talk?"

Summer plunked down on the duvet-covered bed. It swallowed her in its softness.

What would she even say if he brought it up? *It's not you— it's me?* True, but a dagger to the heart nonetheless. *Let's just be friends?* The cry of her soul to be sure, but she doubted it would soften the blow.

She had nothing. Absolute avoidance was her only survival.

A knock sounded at the door.

It took a second to roll out of the cocoon she'd made for herself in the blankets. Opening the door, Jonathan stared down at her.

"Want to grab a bite to eat?"

Her stomach gurgled. More from anxiety than hunger, but she pasted on a smile anyway. "Sure. Let me grab my purse."

After lifting the beaded clutch off the small desk, she shut the door behind her. Where was Trent? She looked around.

"Trent isn't coming?" He had to come. He was her buffer.

Jonathan shook his head. "He's taking a shower. Besides, I think we need to talk."

We need to talk. Nothing good ever came out of those four little words.

Chapter 13

The elevator doors couldn't open fast enough for Summer. She was suffocating from the tension in the small space, which hung in the air heavier than the humidity, if that were possible. Where had the easy comfort and camaraderie gone with her best friend? The man who could make her laugh in any situation silently tortured her now.

The doors dinged open, and Jonathan cupped her elbow to lead her out and down the hall toward the exit.

What were the rules for physical contact with someone who wanted more from you than you were willing to give? She didn't want to give him false hope, but jerking away almost seemed an overreaction. She'd had tickle fights and wrestling matches with this guy when pimples dotted her face and braces covered her teeth. A hand to the elbow was a lot less touching than either of those had been.

But that was before.

Summer swallowed the lump in her throat. "So where are we headed?"

Jonathan looked down at her. His blue eyes were hopeful,

which made her feel completely rotten. "There's a restaurant across the street I noticed when we were checking in."

The traffic was minimal, and they had no trouble crossing the four-lane road. Vines trailed up the brick facade of the restaurant, lending the establishment an ambience of romance. This was the kind of place guys took their girl-friends to pop the question. And there she was, about to stick a needle in his bubble of romantic notions. Pop!

Summer longingly looked back across the street. If not for Jonathan's hand still at her elbow, she would have turned around. Hmmm... She looked up at him, his profile visible in the light of the moon. He'd known her for over a decade. He probably knew this whole thing was scaring her out of her mind and working up a knot of dread in the pit of her stomach. Maybe that was the reason for the gentle guidance at her arm.

A teenaged hostess smiled at them from behind a podium as they entered the doors of the restaurant.

"Just two for tonight?"

Jonathan's hand moved from her elbow to the small of her back. "Yes, thank you."

The hostess gathered a couple of menus and moved from behind the podium. "Right this way."

She led Summer and Jonathan to a small table in the corner of the dining room. "How's this?"

"Perfect. Thank you very much." Jonathan pulled out a chair for Summer. Her stomach rose to her throat as her backside descended into the chair.

He sat and then smiled at her from across the table. "This is nice."

More like awkward. No way she'd say that out loud. She gave him a small smile, then reached to unroll her silverware.

The cutlery rattled on the table, and she pressed the cloth napkin into her lap.

A waiter in black pants, white shirt, and black tie approached the table. "Can I start you folks off with a glass of wine? A Bordeaux perhaps?"

Jonathan looked across the table, his eyebrows raised in question.

Tempting. Something to help relax the jumble of anxiety tying her up in knots would be great. But on the other hand, her brain was already zinging this way and that, trying to keep track of the situation at hand.

She gave a small shake of her head. "Just water for me, thank you."

The waiter turned to Jonathan. "And for you, sir."

"Water is fine."

"Are you two ready to order, or do you need a few moments?"

Summer's stomach quavered. An earthquake had already shaken her world. Now she was awaiting the aftershocks. *Best go for something light.* "I'll have a bowl of the house soup."

The waiter wrote on his small pad before his head came up again, his eyes on Jonathan.

"I'll have the chicken parmesan."

"Very good." The waiter collected the menus, turned, and headed back to the kitchen.

Wait! Don't go! A desperation to call the waiter, a complete stranger, back overtook her. Which was crazy. Yesterday she would have thought nothing about sharing a meal with Jonathan, even in a cute, romantic Italian restaurant. Because she knew they were just friends. But now she frantically wished for a third party.

"Summer." Jonathan spoke low, his voice entreating her to look at him.

How could she do this and hurt her best friend? And why? Dear heavens, why did he have to go and change the parameters of their relationship?

She forced her eyes up and looked into his familiar face. Would he hate her? Could they still be friends?

"We've been friends for a long time now. Good friends."

"The best," she whispered. If only they could stay that way.

"And friends don't keep secrets from each other, do they?" He leaned forward and rested his arm on the table, his hand stretching across its surface toward her.

You can keep this secret. She bit the inside of her bottom lip.

"I've been wanting to tell you for a long time now just how I feel."

She squeezed her eyes shut. "Jonathan." Her heart was breaking. *I can't do this.*

"I love you, Summer. I've always loved you."

A tear slid down her cheek. "Please...don't..."

His hand retracted and returned to his lap. He looked away a second and took a deep breath before looking back at her. His eyes were dull with pain but he met her gaze. "It's okay. Really. But I had to take the chance. Just in case..."

She swallowed hard. "Please tell me we can still be friends."

His lips twitched. "Of course."

―――――

The towel hugged Trent's hips as he opened the bathroom door and walked to his suitcase laying open on the hotel bed. He pulled out a pair of sweatpants and a Harley T-shirt. Hunger gnawed at his stomach. Maybe he could talk Jonathan and Summer into ordering a pizza. Or Chinese. Whatever was close and would deliver.

He opened the door to the common area. "Hey, guys, do you want to..." Where were they?

His eyes landed on the door straight across from him. Summer's room. They wouldn't...would they? Dread left a nasty taste in his mouth. He stepped close and listened. Nothing. Knocked. Nothing. He cracked the door and peeked inside. Empty.

Relief made him feel a little unsteady. Seriously, he needed to get ahold of himself. She was a woman. A dime a dozen. Except he knew that wasn't true. She was special. And by all that was holy, he wanted her for himself.

A piece of white paper stood out on the black granite countertop of the kitchenette. The hotel logo boldly stamped on top, boxed print written underneath.

Took Summer to grab a bite to eat.

Jonathan. Of course he did. Trent couldn't really blame him. He'd have done the same thing in his shoes. Had done the same thing, actually. Another guy in the mix hadn't stopped him from pursuing an attractive woman and a night of fun in the past. This was the first time he'd been the one left behind though. The experience wasn't one he relished.

His stomach grumbled. Guess he'd be eating by himself. It took a minute to flip through the folder listing eateries in the vicinity. He dialed and ordered a small pepperoni pizza, hoping they'd be quicker than the promised thirty minutes.

An armoire along the wall housed a large flat-screen TV. Maybe there was something good playing he could zone out on. Sandra Bullock in a formal dress flashed on the screen. *Miss Congeniality*. Definitely not. He'd sit through chick flicks if there was a pay out in the end, but he wasn't going to torture himself for no good reason.

Next.

The Weather Channel. Not exactly mind-numbing fare, but wouldn't hurt to see what the weather was going to be like the next couple of days.

A knock sounded on the door. He grabbed his wallet and paid the delivery guy. The spicy scent of pepperoni, melted cheese, and tangy tomato sauce mingled and filled his nostrils. Since he was eating alone, there was no need for plates. The box plunked onto the coffee table, and he lifted the lid. Cheese stretched from the sides as he pulled out a slice.

"Next up, *Local on the 8s*." The station cut to commercials.

Click. Trent's head swiveled to the door as it opened.

Jonathan stepped into the room, his shoulders drooping and pain etching his face. Trent wasn't an idiot. He knew what'd happened. His heart pumped in victory, but he tried to keep the elation from showing.

"Pizza?" He held up a slice.

"No thanks." Jonathan scrubbed a hand down his face, then dropped onto the seat next to Trent. He let out a long breath. "I love her, you know." His voice was raw.

Trent nodded slowly. He'd suspected the guy's feelings ran that deep. A passing fancy wouldn't have rocked him so much.

"She doesn't love me though. At least, not in the same way."

The dude was hurting. Trent felt for him, even if he had been annoying. "Wanna get a drink?"

"No." Jonathan held his head in his hands. "No. I think I'm just going to head to bed."

He stood, and Trent watched him trudge to the door of the room before stopping and facing him again. "She's walking along the beach, by the way. In case you wanted to know." The door clicked behind him.

Trent sat there, a slice held in midair. Should he go to her? His instincts said yes, but could he trust them? Before, he'd have considered this a perfect opportunity. Sad women were forever looking for strong shoulders to cry on, and he'd always been more than willing to offer all the comfort they needed.

He set the slice of pizza back in the box and wiped his greasy fingers on a paper napkin. Maybe he could offer his shoulder and a listening ear. Just because things had progressed one way in the past didn't mean the situation had to repeat itself. Although if it did... He shook his head. He'd be the gentleman and not take advantage of Summer's distressed state.

The card key pressed in his palm as he walked out the door. Hopefully he'd be able to find her. Considering they were on an island, there was a lot of beach for her to be walking along. The elevator doors dinged open, and he stepped in and rode it down to the lobby. His fingers fidgeted with the rectangular piece of plastic before he shoved it into a pocket in his sweatpants. The elevator doors slid open, and he stepped out.

Should he bring something to Summer? A good, stiff drink might help, but he doubted the hotel bar would let him take glasses out to the beach. A couple bottles of beer? The tsking sound his mother made with her tongue whenever she didn't approve rang in his ears. *Agh!* He was a grown man. How could his mother still take up residence in his head?

The hum of a soda machine in the corner of the lobby drew his attention. Water was probably a better idea anyway. He didn't need alcohol clouding his resolve to remain a gentleman. Two bottles of water landed with a thud at the bottom of the machine, and he scooped them up.

The temperature rose twenty degrees as he walked out of the hotel and into the night. The farther he walked from the lights of the hotel, the brighter the stars shone from the black sky. Soon the planked walkway ended, and his feet sank into soft sand. Waves crashed onto the shore, then rose and receded in their liquid dance. A lone figure sat silhouetted against the picturesque backdrop, knees drawn up to her chest, long hair twirling as the wind teased the tresses. His feet crunched beneath him, the shifting sand making it difficult to walk. When he reached Summer, he sat beside her without a word, holding out a bottle of water between them. She took the water and unscrewed the lid, lifting the bottle to her lips. Wispy clouds drifted near the moon, its luminescence turning hazy.

"I'm blaming you."

The accusation slapped him. "Me? What did I do?"

"Everything was fine until you showed up looking like some kind of motorcycle-riding Norse god flirting with me."

His cheeks spread wide in a grin. "You think I look like a god?"

A low, inarticulate sound tore from her throat, and she jumped to her feet. "So not the point. Before you came along, everything was great. Now that you're here, everything is screwed up."

"It's not so screwed up." He rose to his feet.

She arched a brow and crossed her arms over her chest.

"Okay, so your relationship with Jonathan is a little… rearranged. But now you know the truth. Isn't that a good thing?"

"No."

"No?" Now it was his turn to raise his eyebrows.

"It wasn't good to watch hurt creep into one of my best friend's eyes and know I was the cause of it. To see him wither when I had to tell him I didn't return his feelings."

The moon reflected in her eyes, bright with unshed tears.

"Summer..." He cupped her upper arm. Now he could offer his shoulder.

She jerked her arm back, flinging his comforting hand aside. "Don't touch me. You've ruined everything." She turned and stormed down the beach.

Seriously? *He* ruined everything?

Blood rushed to his face. Time for the girl to get some perspective.

Long strides brought him to her side. She kept walking toward the pier.

"You're being a bit unfair, don't you think?"

A huff, but they were still moving.

"If you have to blame someone, why not blame Jonathan? He's the one who opened his big mouth."

Eyes straight ahead.

They were at the pier now. He reached out and spun her around. "Look, if you wish Jonathan had kept pretending, then why don't you try it?" He stepped forward, and Summer stepped back. He advanced, and she retreated. Until she backed into a piling.

Her eyes widened.

"You think you could do it? Could you look into his eyes and pretend your heart quickens at his nearness?"

The wind picked up and blew hair across Summer's face. Trent traced a finger over her forehead and tucked the hair behind her ear.

"Could you pretend that a single touch of his fingers sent shivers up your spine?"

He took a half step closer and ran the back of his knuckles down her arm. His voice lowered. "Could you imagine that your breath hitches every time he's near?"

His pulse drummed in his neck. Her skin was buttery soft. What had he been thinking? Her presence was intoxicating. Her tongue darted across full lips. How could he remain a gentleman when those lips were calling to him like a siren?

"And when he kissed you, could you pretend—"

Her arms reached up and wrapped around his neck. She lifted up on tiptoes and—heavenly—her lips were on his. Passion surged between them. Her lips parted, and his head swam. With one hand he cradled the back of her head; with the other he caressed her hip. Her body pressed against his. They fit together, a puzzle complete with every piece. Lips never separating, he lowered her to the sand. His hand roamed. He'd never felt skin so soft, tasted a mouth so sweet. Blood pumped, every nerve ending on fire. Hands clutched at his shirt, pulling him closer.

And then...pushing. "Stop." Her voice was breathy, her hands on his chest, pushing him away. She squirmed under him. Had she said stop? Surely not. Just hearing things in the sound of the surf. He nibbled her neck.

"Trent. Stop."

The fog in his head began to clear. He pushed himself up, and she wiggled up as well. She pulled on the bottom of her shirt.

What had happened?

She wouldn't look at him. "I'm sorry."

Nervous energy showed in the way she picked at her fingertips. He covered her hand with his. "You okay?"

She nodded but swiped at a tear.

Crying? Boy, did he feel like a heel.

"Look, I'm sorry. I didn't mean for..." He ran a hand through his long hair.

"It's not your fault."

True. She had kissed him.

That was right! She had kissed him! So why the tears?

"I just can't...I'm not that kind of...I like you, but..."

A couple of scoots and he was right beside her. He wrapped an arm around her shoulder and pressed her head to his chest.

She took a shuddering breath. "I made a promise to myself a long time ago."

An abstinence pledge. His baby sister had signed one two years ago. Amber had even gotten a fancy ring to signify her commitment to remain pure until she got married. Summer's finger bore no such ring.

"I don't know my father."

Whoa. Gear shift.

"My mom had a fling with this guy when she was twenty. They used protection, but she still got pregnant. I promised myself no child of mine would grow up without knowing their father." She drew her legs up to her chest and wrapped her arms around them.

Trent twirled a piece of her hair around his finger. "My sister made an abstinence pledge a couple of years ago."

Her temple rested on her knees as she turned her green eyes on him. That cute button nose of hers scrunched. "Abstinence pledge?"

"A promise to save sex until marriage. It's a religious thing. My whole family is big into religion and Jesus. I'm the black sheep."

"You don't believe in Jesus?"

How was he supposed to answer that? In his mind, God was definitely not the compassionate and loving personal Savior that his parents claimed. If He did exist at all, it was in the capacity of arbitrary judge. And who wanted to put stock in a deity like that?

Trent stood and brushed off his backside, then offered his hand to help Summer up. "Come on. It's getting late, and we've got a long day in the water tomorrow."

They walked back to the hotel together, the crash of the waves nature's serenade. When they reached the door to their room, Trent stopped Summer with a hand to her arm. She turned to face him.

"I like you, Summer Arnet, marine photographer, and I'd like to see where this goes. What d'ya say? Will you go on a grand adventure with me?"

She looked down at her feet, which left him staring at the top of her head. He willed her to turn those big green eyes on him, to give him a smile and say she was ready for thrills with him. Seconds ticked by, and with each one his confidence dripped like a leaky faucet, until he was more sure she was about to say no rather than yes.

He reached out and stroked a finger down her cheek and around to her chin, lifting it gently. There was a connection between them. She had to feel it too. If she couldn't hear it with his words, maybe she'd see it in his eyes.

She looked at him, finally, and he put all his feeling into his gaze.

See my heart.

Her lip caught in her teeth, her internal struggle clearly written on her face. What was holding her back?

He lifted her hands and placed them on his chest. Surely

she could feel how affected he was. How his pulse raced at her nearness.

"I can't, Trent." She didn't retreat but stared at her hands on his chest. "You drive me crazy, both good and bad, but you aren't a staying type of guy. You're the guy mothers warn their daughters about, and Mama knows best." She looked up at him and shrugged her slender shoulders. "I'm sorry. I'm sorry I kissed you—"

He stopped her with a finger to her lips. "Don't ever apologize for a kiss, love." He traced the outline of her mouth. Its sweetness would haunt him, but he'd rather be driven mad by the memory than remain sane without knowing its tender touch.

Slowly he lowered his forehead until it rested on hers. "I'm going to have to prove you wrong, you know."

She pulled back her head and looked into his eyes. "I hope you do."

Chapter 14

"I can't believe you didn't check the weather forecast. How moronic can you be?"

"For the hundredth time, I did check. The storm was supposed to hit Jamaica."

"Everyone knows that storms can change direction. You should have waited till everything was clear. This is such a waste."

"I don't know why you're so upset. I'm the one out money."

Angry voices seeped through the closed door and into Summer's subconscious. She rolled over and groaned, pressing the heels of her palms to her temples. *Make them stop.* Her head throbbed, and she didn't want to deal with anything right now.

"Maybe the storm will pass and we can dive tomorrow."

Grogginess clouded her mind. Had they said storm? Summer pulled the covers down from over her head. Rain slapped the window. Not the pitter-patter of an early morning shower, but the pelting of a major gale. The howl of wind whistled low on the other side of the wall. She flung her arm across her face and buried her eyes in the hollow of her elbow. What was the date? Right, June 21. Hurricane season had officially started three weeks ago.

Apparently Mother Nature was toying with Trent's—and by extension, her—plans. She burrowed deeper into the pillow-top mattress. No point in getting up.

"No, you can't go diving tomorrow or any time before we leave. You'd know that if you were a real diver."

"I'm going to continue to ignore your insults, but I'm warning you. My patience only goes so far."

Summer groaned. Maybe there was a point to getting up after all. She didn't know how far either Jonathan or Trent would go before testosterone cut off their brain waves.

She pushed back the covers and sat up. Too fast. What evil hands of hell gripped her head in a sadistic vice? She needed coffee. Fast.

Her feet padded under her as she trudged to the door. She glanced at the mirror as she passed but felt too horrible to care that a flock of birds had made a nest in her hair as she'd slept or that under eyes were circles the size of quarters.

The door creaked open, and the angry voices stopped midargument. Two pairs of eyes stared at her.

"Coffee."

Jonathan looked away first and pointed to a pot on the kitchenette counter. "I know how you need a cup—or four—first thing in the morning, so I made a pot when I woke up."

Sweet, sweet man.

Steam rose as she poured the rich elixir of life into an absurdly small hotel mug. She inhaled deeply, the demon's fingers loosening his grip.

"You look awful."

Her eyes snapped up. Trent's face held a look of horror.

She glanced past him to the glass balcony doors and the storm raging outside. All was an ominous gray. Rain swept sideways, palm trees bent, their fronds flapping like flags on a flagpole. She looked back at the absurdly handsome man. No one should look that good first thing in the morning. "Looks like I have all day to rectify that."

Trent stepped forward, hands outstretched. "I didn't mean that. You look cute."

Keep backpedaling, dude.

Jonathan snorted from the couch.

"I meant you look like you've had a rough night. You okay?"

"Save it." She'd need at least two more of these minuscule cups of coffee before she started to care.

Trent scooped up the remote from the coffee table. "The weather should be on TV soon. Maybe the storm is moving quickly and will clear up later today."

Jonathan scoffed. "Summer, please, talk some sense into this guy."

The screen buzzed to life. A commercial blared before Trent turned it down.

Summer rubbed her forehead. "A big storm like this, I'm guessing a tropical storm or tropical depression at least, is going to leave the ocean churned up for days."

A woman with a pixie cut standing in front of a green screen flashed on the TV. "Tropical storm Marie surprised us all during the night. Those in Louisiana can take a big sigh of relief. The eastern seaboard, be prepared to pull up your boot-straps. Currently over the Bahamas, people in Florida should expect to see Marie around six tomorrow morning."

"See there. We may have lost today to Marie, but she'll be someone else's problem tomorrow. We still have two more days we can dive." Trent's brows lifted high on his forehead, his eyes wide and expectant.

She hated to disappoint him, especially since he looked like a little boy pleading not to have his toy taken away. "I'm afraid that's not how it works. The rains may stop, but we'd all be in need of heavy doses of Dramamine to survive the choppy waters. Not to mention that once we got in the water, we'd be swimming around with nothing to show for it. Visibility is going to be lousy for days. No way we'd be able to spot your ship." She walked to where he sat on the love seat and squeezed his shoulder. "I'm sorry."

He turned his head and pressed a kiss to the top of her hand. A thrill shot through her arm, but she tried to suppress it. Might as well have tried to put a pot lid over Old Faithful. If only her body would react in a sensible manner and follow the logic in her head. A girl could lose her heart to a guy like Trent, and she'd never get it back again.

She glanced at Jonathan, who sat on the loveseat beside Trent. Had he seen the romantic gesture? Yep. He'd seen it all right. His face held a mixture of shock and hurt. A guillotine sliced through her heart. She wanted to assure him that it wasn't what it looked like. She'd done the smart thing and turned Trent down. Of course that came after a kiss that left her senseless, but that wasn't the point. She'd made the rational decision in the end.

Lightning flashed in the darkened sky, followed by the rumble of thunder.

Summer realized her hand still lay on Trent's shoulder, and she let it fall to her side. She'd need to be more careful in the future. For all their sakes. Trent didn't need any encouragement, Jonathan didn't need to get the wrong impression, and she didn't need any more confusion in her tumbled emotions.

How many cups of coffee had she had? One more wouldn't hurt. She turned, but her wrist was caught in a tight grip, and Trent hauled her down to his lap.

What was he thinking? Damage control kicked in, and she cast a quick glance to Jonathan. He looked anywhere but at them.

She tried to stand, but Trent refused to release his grip. "Jonathan, it's not what you—" Jonathan turned sad blue eyes toward her. "Don't worry about it, Summer. How'd you think he knew where to find you last night?"

"You..." So many questions. Not an hour after he'd declared his love and she'd told him they would only remain friends, he'd sent Trent out to find her? Why? And what was wrong with her that she couldn't conjure feelings for such a wonderful guy?

He grabbed a bottle of water from the coffee table and stood. "I'm going to head to the weight room. I'll catch you guys later."

The air grew heavy as he passed, and Summer felt the weight of it on her shoulders. Guilt sat like an anchor in her stomach.

Why couldn't Trent have pretended nothing had happened between them? Or at the very least respect the he wasn't the right guy for her. The insensitive jerk. She reached down and pinched the inside of his thigh.

He jumped sideways. "Hey! What was that for?" Knocked off balance by his hasty movement, her back now rested against the arm of the chair, her legs draped over his lap. Trent rubbed at his thigh, his brows pulled down in a scowl.

He should feel lucky all she'd done was pinch him. "You made Jonathan think we're a couple, when we're not."

"Is that what I did?" His eyes were wide and clear, and he wore innocence like a mask. Only his twitching lips gave him away.

She crossed her arms over her chest and looked out the glass doors, grinding her teeth.

Trent's finger trailing up and down her shin immediately drew her attention back. An internal shiver ran up her spine. "You're adorable when you're mad—did you know that?"

His voice was thick, husky, and low, and he regarded her with a magnetic gaze, pulling her in by a force she couldn't resist. Like a strong rip current, if she didn't find shore and kick hard, she'd drown in the ocean of his sweet talking.

Sweet talking. He'd probably used that line on a number of girls. Besides, no way she could look adorable in—she glanced down—cotton pajama shorts and a Minnie Mouse T-shirt. Shoot, she hadn't even...oh goodness, she hadn't even brushed her hair!

Mortification rushed to her cheeks, and she wished the couch would swallow her up. How could she have stepped out of the room without at least brushing her hair? She ran her tongue over her top teeth. Gritty. *Someone kill me now.* Her only hope was if the coffee had masked her morning breath. Not that coffee breath was any better.

She slid her legs from his lap, stood, and began to walk backward. "I'm just going to...umm...uh...I'll be right back." She turned and rushed into her room, shutting the door firmly behind her.

———

Trent chuckled to himself. Life would never be boring around Summer. Not that his life had ever been boring, but still. She was...refreshing.

Thunder cracked like a whip outside the glass doors, and he could almost feel its sting. He hung his head in his hands. So close to the sunken galleon and yet he might as well be on Mars, the good it would do him. This was supposed to be his time, his moment. Surfing the highs and thrills of adventure, not hiding away in a hotel room waiting out foul weather. If only he could get a tank on his back, fins on his feet, and a regulator in his mouth.

Of course, he'd need the winds to not be fifty-seven miles an hour and the rain to stop pouring—what was it his sister called it? Right—pouring calicos and collies. Cute kid. Stupid meteorologists. Couldn't even predict a major storm they saw miles away.

Don't you believe in Jesus? He rubbed a hand across the back of his neck. He hadn't answered Summer's question the night before, and he wasn't inclined to answer it now. If he did, he'd be tempted to say God had pursed His divine lips and blew the storm to hit the Bahamas. He had the whole world in His hands, after all, didn't He?

Trent stood and walked to the tall glass doors. Raindrops fell like tiny waterfalls along its clear surface. No way this was all some sort of divine plan. It was natural science. Pressure in the atmosphere directing Marie's course. That was all.

Now to plan his own course of action. He'd nearly maxed out his credit card to pay for the three airline tickets, the hotel suite, and to reserve the boat and diving equipment. Maybe he could get his deposit back on the rentals. That would at least make the minimum payments on his credit card for a bit while he figured out his next step.

What he needed was cash. Fast. A way to get back on the island when there wasn't a tropical storm ruining his plans. After he got his hands on the pieces of eight sure to be in the galleon's hold, he could pay off his debts. But what could he do to earn money until then?

His mind flipped like the old-time rolodex his dad still kept in his office.

Dad.

He felt the color drain from his face. There had to be other options besides *that* one. Survival and sanity weren't guaranteed if he spent too much time around his family. They'd all be laying hands on him, trying to get the Devil out. One corner of his mouth lifted in a grin. They were crazy Jesus people, but they weren't *that* crazy. More like drove him crazy, was all.

He looked past the rain-smattered glass, past the bent and flapping palm trees, to the white-capped waves rising and falling in an angry torrent. Out there somewhere was everything he'd been looking for. He couldn't give up the hunt just because he was afraid to spend any real time with his family.

It wasn't like they were going to convert him.

Chapter 15

Atlantic Ocean, 1689

Isabella's heart leapt to her throat and choked her as she clutched her hands to her chest. The strips of material she'd used to bind herself unraveled at her feet. Would Luis call out and reveal her secret to all the ungodly men on board? What would they do when they discovered she wasn't a boy after all?

"Y-y-you are woman," Luis repeated, his fever-glazed eyes wide in shock.

Isabella took a step forward, the tails of her bindings trailing behind. "Luis, please."

The sick man blinked a few times, then turned his head to the side. "I will not look so you can..." He lifted his hand slightly and waved it around.

So she could rewrap herself. Relief made her knees weak. He wasn't going to call out for the captain or another sailor. Isabella turned her back and hurried to lift the long cotton shirt back up, bunching the hem under her chin. Grandmother's necklace was once again secure, and she wound the long strip of material around her bosom. Her ribs were constricted, but less than she was used to in a corset. She pulled the ends of the material taut and tucked in the knot. With her shirt back in place, she was once more the image of a mere cabin boy.

Luis's body convulsed with a deep cough. Blood dripped from the corner of his mouth. Isabella rushed forward and wrung out the cloth lying in a basin of water. She dabbed at the crimson liquid and pushed sweat-soaked hair out of the man's eyes. When the spasm of coughing ceased, Luis lay back on his pallet, exhaustion etching creases on his brow.

"Will you tell Captain Montoya?" She didn't want to add to his burden, but she had to know. Her life depended on it.

Bloodshot eyes regarded her, and she held her breath. Everything hinged on what he would say next.

"I will keep your secret."

Gracias Díos.

"But you need to do something for me."

The knot in her stomach that had begun to loosen clenched once again. What could he possibly ask? Her mind jumped back to the two men in the hold the day before. Luis hadn't been one of the traitors, but was he a part of whatever they were scheming?

"My son—" A cough cut off his words. "When I die, my son will be alone. I do not wish for him to spend his entire life on the sea with only the influence of hardened sailors about him. You must take him. Watch over him. Be a mama to him. You must promise."

How could she be responsible for another human being? Once the ship landed in the New World, she had no idea where she would go. There was no one waiting to take her in. No warm bed or house in which she was certain a residence. The only protection from starvation was the hard metal of *Abuela's* necklace rubbing sores on her chest.

Little Luis's face took shape in her mind. How could she leave him alone, orphaned? "I promise, *señor.*"

"*Bien.*" He settled more fully into his pallet. "Now, I am hungry. Could you please bring me something to eat?"

Her face relaxed, and she gave a small smile. "I will see what I can find."

Loud snores sounded behind her as she exited the captain's cabin. Luis needed nourishing beef broth and fresh milk. Too bad the ship stocked neither. Not even fresh water. He'd have to settle for wine and salted pork like the rest of them.

First she'd need to find the quartermaster. As second-in-command aboard the ship, the man controlled all the supplies. Nothing left the hold or passed a man's lips without the quartermaster's approval. If rumors were true, he tended toward the tyrannical when someone helped themselves, before consulting him, to whatever was on board.

The galleon dipped, and Isabella stumbled. Weeks at sea and she still had trouble staying upright at all times. Thankfully her stomach was steadier than her legs.

When she stepped onto the main deck, she shielded her eyes with her hand. The bright sun rested high in the sky, its light refracting off the water's surface. Midmorning. Her stomach growled. She'd have to request rations for herself as well. Her stepfather's clothes already swallowed her. If she continued to lose weight due to lack of nourishment, the garments might fall right off.

She looked around and drew in a deep breath of fresh air.

The captain's cabin might be large compared to the quarters most of the crew called home while out to sea, but the air was stagnant and the walls confining.

The sails flew high, the wind blowing and causing them to curve. It reminded her of a time she'd filched one of her mama's petticoats as a child. She'd gathered sticks around the pond by her house, latched them together, and then tied the petticoat to a makeshift mast in the center of her crudely built raft. Her mama's undergarments were much too large for the size of her vessel, and nary a breeze. No wonder the thing had sunk in under two seconds. So far, it seemed her sailing expertise had improved with age, to God be praised.

"I did not expect to see you above deck today."

Isabella turned, the soft lines around her uncle's eyes welcoming. "I am looking for the quartermaster. Luis is hungry, and I thought it good to keep up his strength with a bit of nourishment."

Juan's lips drew to a thin line as he looked around the main deck. "I have just come from a meeting with the pilot and the captain on the quarterdeck, in which he was to have attended." He looked at her, his brow furrowed. "The captain was not pleased with his absence, but I predict the man will have a satisfying excuse. He always does. Somehow the captain overlooks his many flaws."

"Have they sailed together often?" She'd seen loyalty cloud many people's judgments.

"Sí. There is some history there, I think." Juan stared out into the horizon, deep in unspoken thoughts. He blinked hard, then turned back toward her. "No matter. If he is not to be found, then of course you must tend to your charge and provide him with something to eat. The captain would expect this."

His eyes softened once more as he gazed upon her. "Everything is well with you? Your secret is still secure?"

"Luis—"

"Juan! I need you here with me." Captain Montoya loomed from the quarterdeck. Power emanated from his tall form. His eyes dark serious, no laugh lines softening his features. Did the man never smile? She'd seen his gentleness with little Luis, but mostly he was a man given to the burden of his responsibilities. Her skin flushed as she took him in.

Strange.

Isabella's stomach growled. She turned on her heel and once more entered the darkened belly of the ship. It was a maze she had finally learned to navigate, and after descending its layers, she found herself in the hold. Voices carried and echoed off wooden barrels and crates.

"The men are ready. We put the plan to action in three days."

She froze. A mouse had once attempted to cross the street in her town, and when the little thing noticed a carriage rumbling toward it, it too had stopped in its tracks. She had silently encouraged it to either go back or continue forward, but it hadn't moved a muscle. The poor creature became flattened on the dirt lane.

Move, or your fate will be that of the rodent's.

On tiptoes, she stepped down the remaining stairs. She hunched her body and squeezed behind a large crate.

"What will be the signal?"

She closed her eyes. Every sense strained to form a complete picture, to try to put the pieces of the puzzle together. If only she hadn't been committed to keeping as far away from the rest of the crew as she could. Maybe then she would be able to recognize the high-pitched nasally voice of the speaker.

"A mighty roar and an upraised fist. We are men. We will take what we want by force."

Her hands shook. Whereas the first voice lacked confidence and conviction—a mere pawn—this man caused her to quake. His voice was hard. Vengeful? Perhaps. But without a doubt steadfast to whatever plan his evil mind had concocted.

She reached out her hand to steady herself, her legs going to mush like undercooked porridge. The crate shifted. She could feel her eyes bulge and was unable to blink.

Move! Do something! Catch it!

Paralyzing fear kept her immobile.

The crate *thunked* to the floor.

She envisioned herself getting crushed under a carriage wheel like the rat.

Torch light swung in her direction. "Who is there? Show yourself," the evil voice demanded.

Her hands grew clammy, and she rubbed them on her breeches. Time to be brave. Act like nothing was amiss. Live another lie.

She shuffled a few of the other crates around before popping her head over one. "Oh, is someone else down here? I came for provisions for Luis. He is sick, and Captain Montoya wishes him to have the best of care."

Had it been a good idea to mention the captain?

The two men advanced toward her, their boots smacking the wooden floor beneath them. She swallowed hard but met their gaze. Built like Spain's prized Lipizzaners, the leader towered over her. Fire sparked from his eyes, and she fought the urge to cower.

"What did you hear?"

Sweat gathered in the pits of her arms, and her pulse throbbed in her ears. "Hear? I heard nothing, *señor*. I have just arrived and was not aware of anyone else's presence. My mind was preoccupied with Luis's care."

The bulky man took another step forward. "I am the quartermaster. All requests for provisions must come to me."

He was the quartermaster? "I looked for you, *señor*, but was unable to find you. Luis is sick, you see, and needs to keep up his strength. He needs food if he is to recover."

His eyes bore holes in her head. "I do not believe you."

"I assure you, *señor*. Luis is very sick."

"I do not care if Saint Peter himself has come to issue Luis into heaven. I do not believe you did not hear our conversation."

Her eyes flicked to the man behind the quartermaster as terror threatened to strangle her. "I do not—"

A large hand darted out and clamped onto her shoulder. Shards of pain rippled down her arm. "Not a word, you hear? Not a word to anyone unless you wish to be the shark's next meal. *Comprende?*"

The pressure increased until Isabella was sure he'd snap her bone. Against her will, tears watered her eyes, and she nodded her head.

———

By the time she made it back to the captain's cabin, Isabella's heart returned to its normal rhythm. She would have to apologize to Luis about not getting him the food he had requested. Perhaps later she would be able to locate her uncle and persuade him to bring them a few morsels. Starvation seemed a better course than running into the quartermaster again.

The knob turned in her hand, and she pushed the heavy wooden door open. Silence met her ears. If not for the lump on the floor, she would have thought it vacant. No matter. At least with him sleeping, she would not have to tell him she had returned empty handed and he would have to remain hungry a little while longer.

She walked to the far end of the room and pushed back one of the heavy, dark curtains. They had remained drawn to give Luis every opportunity to rest. A glance behind her affirmed the small shaft of light did not disturb his current slumber.

A gray film covered the large panes of glass. Even so, she could see out. Having grown up near the seaside, the sight of the ocean was nothing new. It was, however, the first time the ocean had been the *only* thing in sight. A feeling of loneliness crept in her soul. Odd, considering the number of people who made up the galleon's crew. Finding oneself alone proved nearly impossible, so how could she be feeling lonely?

Melancholia was a fool's friend and *Diablo's* tool. Idle hands had turned her thoughts introspective. Time to get back to work.

She let the curtain fall once more and tiptoed toward Luis. Strange that she couldn't hear him at all. The hours she'd spent with him the day and night before were full of wheezing and coughing.

His head lay to the side, his eyes closed. Her stomach churned.

Please no.

A useless plea. The knowledge of the truth sank like a rock thrown in a lake.

Luis was dead.

His pallid skin had taken on a gray hue, and his chest no longer rose and fell with signs of life.

With shaking fingers, Isabella stretched out her hand and placed it in front of Luis's nose and mouth. Not a puff of breath touched her palm. She rocked back on her heels and covered her face with her hands. How would she tell little Luis he was now an orphan?

First, she must report the news to Captain Montoya. The man would not be surprised. Few recovered from wasting disease.

Squaring her shoulders, she made her way to the main deck.

"Place the end of the rope through the loop, and pull tight." A familiar, deep voice pulled her attention to a pair seated upon a crate in the corner.

Little Luis's small form hunched over a short length of rope. His tongue jutted past thin lips in concentration. He lifted the rope, a knot secure in the middle.

"I did it!" The boy's eyes shone.

Captain Montoya laid a hand on Luis's head. *"Muy bien.* Soon you will be a skillful sailor like your papa."

Isabella's throat closed. How she wished her tidings could be different.

The captain lifted his head, and his piercing black eyes bore into hers. She read his question there and sadly gave a small shake of her head.

He turned back to the young charge beside him. "I want you to take this piece of rope and practice the three knots I have taught you today. When you can do them all perfectly, come back and find me, and I will teach you three more."

Luis bounded to his feet. *"Si, señor."*

As he trotted past her, he held up his knot with a grin.

If only his days could remain so carefree.

Captain Montoya stood, his height blocking the setting sun and casting a long shadow across the planks of the deck. A halo of light shone around him, making him seem unworldly—her pulse quickened—and imposing.

"Luis?"

His voice brought her thoughts back to earth. She blinked hard. "Has breathed his last, I am sorry to say."

Had his shoulders drooped at the news? "I am sorry to hear it, though not surprised." He stepped forward, his stride full of purpose. "Come, we must prepare his body."

She followed, her own steps leaden. Emotions frayed and head slightly dizzy from lack of proper sleep, she was ready to find a quiet corner, have a nice cry, and sleep for two days straight. Her skin crawled, and she resisted the urge to scrape her nails all over her body. If she were dreaming of things she'd rather be doing, soaking in a warm bath of clean water with a new bar of soap would be at the top of the list. Temptation to jump into the frothy ocean had nearly overcome her a number of times. Maybe the quartermaster's threat to feed her to the sharks wasn't so bad. Countless vermin already considered her a meal.

The captain's cabin door swung open, and she followed Captain Montoya inside. Luis lay as she had left him. If only she had been able nurse him back to health. How was she going to keep her promise and raise his son?

The heels of Captain Montoya's boots thunked on the floor, the sound deafening in the quiet room. He bent over Luis a moment before gathering an edge of the blanket his body lay upon.

"I do not wish for his son to see him thus. It would leave a mark he would not soon forget."

Arguments to the contrary rose in her belly. She had been denied a final farewell to her own beloved mother. Hernando had seen to it. But to have been able to hold her hand or kiss her cheek...to tell her how much she loved her one last time. Even if Mama couldn't have heard.

She pushed her feet forward, past the memories and pain of regret. Bending, she clutched the end of the rough wool blanket.

"Let us wrap him in the blanket and hide his face."

Like *frijoles* in a tortilla. Her stomach soured.

The feeling continued as Captain Montoya studied her. He took her measure and found her lacking. Why did that bother her so much?

"I do not believe you are strong enough to even carry half his weight." He bent and scooped the lifeless body into his arms. "Sword practice begins again tomorrow. You must gain strength for the rigors of sea life if you wish to remain a sailor."

Good thing she did not wish to remain a sailor.

A crowd gathered as the captain carried Luis's body onto the main deck. Some of the men even removed their hats out of respect.

"*Capitan*, I have learned the knots you showed me and am ready—" The small voice skidded to a stop.

Isabella stepped behind Luis and laid a hand on his shoulder. How she wished to kneel down and embrace him. But only a woman would show such compassion, and she was supposed to be a man.

"Papa?" His little voice broke.

"I am so sorry, Luis." Isabella pushed back tears.

Captain Montoya stopped near the side of the vessel and turned to look over the gathered crowd. "Luis Rodriguiz was a good man"—he looked toward the man's son—"and a good father. *Dios*, to you we commend his body and soul." Without another word he turned and tossed the blanket-wrapped body overboard.

"No!" The one word tore from the ten-year-old's lips and echoed in Isabella's heart.

No matter the boy was nearly her height, no matter that she was supposed to pretend to be a heartless man, she wrapped her arms around his shoulders and ushered him away from the scene.

Chapter 16

Modern-Day Florida

Spending all of her twenty-six years living in the Sunshine State should have been enough to teach Summer not to leave the sunscreen at home. And having red hair meant a double layer, not go without. Even if she wore a rash guard. Her skin was painful to look at, but even more painful to touch.

Gingerly she sliced off a leaf from an aloe plant and peeled back the outer layer. The pharmacy sold aloe in bottles for sunburns, but straight from the source worked best. The juice oozed, its cool, sticky center an immediate relief from the burn. The gel of the aloe dried in seconds, leaving her skin hot and tight.

From her closet she pulled out a chevron-printed strapless dress with a stretchy top. Her back and shoulders were the most lobster-esque, so instead of slipping the dress on over her head, she stepped into it and shimmied it up over her hips. She pulled the fabric wide and carefully tugged the dress over the most sensitive areas and into place. A messy bun would have to do for her hair.

How was she doing on time? A glance to the clock on the wall showed she had at least ten more minutes before it was time to leave.

Her camera case lay open on her desk, and she scooped the Sony NEX out and turned it on. Maybe the burn would be worth it if she'd gotten a money shot. Clicking through the images, her hopes fell flat. Parrot fish, a large school of jacks, a few barracuda. Decent shots, but nothing new or edgy. More likely to be sold at the city's arts and crafts festival than to be featured in *Our World*.

Had her only chance to see her name among photo credits in the glossy pages of the prestigious magazine slipped through her fingers? They'd been back from the Bahamas a week now, and Trent had yet to call with new plans. He'd yet to call period, as a matter of fact.

Which was good.

Really.

She'd gotten caught up in the moment, pulled in by his magnetic gaze and cheap flattery. Chalk it up to a moment of weakness. That was all the kiss was—a moment of weakness. Thankfully she'd had a few days for her head to clear, and she was finally thinking straight again. Every mama warned her daughter about men like Trent. Smooth talkers, devil-may-care attitude, and sexier than anyone had a right to be.

On second thought, why did she need Trent to find the galleon? He needed her, not the other way around. She knew where it was. *If* it was there at all. All she needed to do was sell a few prints to raise money for a plane ticket. That and figure out who could go with her. Number one rule—always have a diving buddy. Jonathan was usually hers, but after what had happened last week, the thought of asking him felt awkward.

She chewed her bottom lip. Mark perhaps? Although he preferred to ferry the boat and stay out of the water. Oh well. She'd have to think about it later. It was time to head to Mom's for dinner.

———

Summer pulled her PT Cruiser through the entrance of Cyprus Grove Estates. The housing community may have given it a fancy suffix like *estates*, but it was still a trailer park. Nothing glamorous about it. She drove past the nicer modular double-wides and turned down a street of older tin-sided single-wides.

Her eyebrows rose at the sight of Mark's Chevy pickup. Guess it wasn't a mother-daughter meal after all. Maybe Mom was trying to thank him for fixing her roof. Fortunately he'd been able to get to it before tropical storm Marie had hit. Her torrential rains and heavy winds would have spelled disaster on the roof that had been a blue tarp held down by old tires.

Summer threw the vehicle into park and turned off the ignition. Hanging baskets of purple wave petunias spun in the breeze from a swivel clasp. Wind chimes tinkled in the evening air. The small porch Mom had built six years ago really did add a homey feel to the place. Even so, her heart ached. Mom deserved better. She'd worked hard her whole life and had nothing to show for it. Minimum wage wouldn't get her into a safe and comfortable subdivision. Those were for married couples with 2.5 kids. Not single working moms who sacrificed their own comforts for their daughters' dreams—like buying Summer her first Nikon as a high school graduation present.

Too bad the odds of winning the lottery weren't more in Summer's favor. Of course, one had to play to win. As it was, she barely scraped enough together to pay for her own studio-slash-apartment.

She opened the door. The pungent smell of sautéed garlic and onions filled her nostrils. Heavenly. Mom must be making her famous lasagna.

Giggles erupted, but the opened door blocked her view of the kitchen. She closed the door, and the smile on her face froze. It wasn't her mother's back she saw standing in front of the stove, but that of a man. The white Chevy, the blue Hawaiian shirt hanging from broad shoulders. It didn't take Sherlock Holmes to deduce this one. But why was Mark standing behind her mom, his arms wrapped around her middle, and, oh dear, bending down and nibbling on her neck?

Summer's body involuntarily convulsed as she imagined his scratchy beard on sensitive skin. Another shiver. If only she could banish that image forever.

More giggles.

Summer looked around uncomfortably. What should she do? Clear her throat? Open and close the door more loudly? Melt into a puddle right there on the spot?

Mark raised his head. Drat. Caught with her hand halfway to the door handle.

"Hey, girlie, are ya comin' or goin'?"

If it were possible for her burned skin to feel hotter or turn redder, it would have. "Coming. I just got here, in fact."

Mom turned around, a hand to her mussed hair. Her

cheeks had color to them, and her eyes sparkled. She looked happy.

Which made Summer feel even more guilty about the churning in her stomach. The aroma in the tiny trailer was mouthwatering, so why was she feeling nauseous all of a sudden? It couldn't be because of Mark. She liked Mark. He was a good friend. One she'd looked up to and considered a father figure. Then why did she have such a difficult time catching her breath? And what was that ringing in her ears?

She managed to push her wobbly lips up into what she hoped looked like a smile. "It smells good in here, Mom. Lasagna?"

Mom nodded, but clouds of concern rolled in and dimmed the shine of her eyes. "Yes, but look at you! Your face! Your arms! You're burned to a crisp."

Summer winced. "Four hours in the water with no sunscreen will do that."

Mom punched her hands to her hips and opened her mouth.

Uh-oh. Here comes the lecture.

But no lecture came. Mom simply shrugged her shoulder and shook her head.

Mark opened a cabinet and pulled out three plates. "Want to help me set the table?"

He knew where the plates were? She watched, stunned, as he pulled out a drawer and removed the silverware, then another drawer and brought out napkins. It was like he was at home here. In her house. No. In her mom's house. Just how much time had he been spending here anyway?

Her feet moved on their own past the brown sofa with a neatly folded hot-pink afghan draping the back and past the peninsula of blue laminate countertop. She watched as her hand reached for the glasses as if unattached to her body. All her real focus was trying to wrap her mind around what was happening and picking at the knot that had coiled tightly in her chest.

The small round table in the eat-in kitchen was soon set. Now what? Summer sat down and fiddled with the edge of the off-white lace tablecloth. She didn't know where to look. How could two people that meant so much to her make her feel so uncomfortable? And why did she nearly cringe when Mark ran a hand down Mom's arm as he passed her in the kitchen on the way to grab the salad?

Stop it, Summer. Get ahold of yourself.

Mom approached the table, a steaming casserole dish in her oven-mitted hands. After she set the lasagna on the table, her eyes darted up and fastened on to Summer's.

Summer read the message there. *Please be okay with this.*

She gave a small smile and pushed down the coiled knot. Ignoring the budding relationship in front of her was not an option, but ignoring the roiling in her stomach and the tightness in her chest was.

Mark sat down beside her, and Mom sat across from Summer. He grabbed the spatula that lay across the dish and rocked it into the bubbly cheese, oozing sauce, and al dente noodles. Everyone passed their plates and was served hearty portions.

Summer slid her fork through the lasagna layers. "So," she said, then waved her fork between Mark and her mom. "How long has this been going on?"

Ouch. She meant for the question to be playful, but must have forgotten to add a smile to her voice. Instead the question sounded accusatory. Real smooth.

Mom patted her lips with a napkin, then took time

arranging it back in her lap. She looked up, her eyes guarded. "We've been seeing each other for a while now."

Summer watched as Mark reached over, her view of his hand hindered by the table. He either held Mom's hand or put his hand on her leg. Both supportive gestures.

A strand in the knot loosened the same time a knife nicked her heart.

"Awhile? Why didn't you tell me sooner?"

Mom's gaze pierced her. "I wasn't sure how you'd react."

Like a petulant child, apparently. Surely it was just the shock. Once it wore off, her equilibrium would return to normal.

"I'm happy for you."

Mark threw his head back and roared. "Woo-wee, girlie. Do I need to grab a fire extinguisher for your pants?"

Liar, liar, pants on fire.

Summer grinned, the knot loosening by degrees.

"I'm just surprised, is all. I love you both, so I *am* happy for you." Or at least she would be.

Mom's face relaxed. "We love you too, sweetheart."

Maybe she could throw Mark off as much as they'd thrown her. "Does that mean you're my new daddy?" This time her grin wasn't forced.

Mom's face blanched. "Summer!"

Mark didn't blink an eye. He reached out, his warm hand gentle on her burned shoulder. The lines around his eyes softened as his gaze bore into her. "You've always been like a daughter to me."

Her eyes moistened. She was twenty-six. Too old to need a father, and yet the father-sized hole in her heart ached. Could Mark fill the emptiness she'd been carrying around all her life? What would that even look like? Feel like? She'd spent a lifetime imagining what it would have been like to be tossed up in the air and caught in strong arms that wrapped around her in comfort and safety. To be hoisted onto steady shoulders and carried when she was too weak to continue on her own. She'd had to pretend no interest in fancy dresses and father-daughter dances. That she didn't care there wasn't an imposing male in her life to scare boyfriends into treating her right.

The air grew thick around them as the weight of the conversation hung on every molecule. Mark sat back, the intensity in his gaze lessening. His mustache twitched.

"So, Jonathan tells me something happened between you and Trent on your little trip to the Bahamas."

Mom's head swiveled in Summer's direction, her eyebrows raised.

Okay, so not having an overprotective male figure in her life might have been a good thing. She squirmed in her chair.

"I'm not sure I'd go that far." Would she? A few kisses and meaningful looks didn't add up to *something*. Besides, she'd told him no when he offered a relationship. Trent was a player. She was sure he'd done a lot more *somethings* with other women without it meaning anything to him. The fact that he hadn't called since they got back proved she was right about it. He didn't have the staying power.

Mom passed the breadbasket but retained her grip on the end of it. "Just be careful with him. From what Jonathan says—"

What Jonathan says? What'd he do, come back and tattle on her to her mom and Mark like she'd been a naughty little girl? Her defenses rose higher than mercury on a ther-mometer in July.

"And what exactly did good ol' Jonathan say?" Sarcasm

dripped from her voice like the tomato sauce oozing from the tines of her fork.

Pain flashed in Mom's eyes. "Nothing to bite my head off about, that's for sure."

Summer squeezed her eyes shut. What was wrong with her? "Sorry, Mom, but you don't need to worry. Trent and I might have had a...moment...but we haven't talked since we got back so, as I said, it was nothing. You have nothing to worry about."

Of course, if that were true, then why were her eyes burning with unshed tears?

Chapter 17

Bam, bam, bam. Trent pounded the nails through the two-by-sixes covering the space that would become his parents' deck. The sun baked his bare back as he knelt along the rough-hewn planks. If only he could drive out his rolling thoughts with force. He was a man of action, not contemplation. Soul searching? A snort vibrated his chest. Not something he wasted time on. So what explanation was there for the past week? Body snatchers? Obviously the real Trent Carrington had been replaced by a wimpy, sniveling, tender-footed, sorry excuse for a man. Otherwise the week wouldn't have passed without him having picked up the phone and calling the woman who haunted his nights and days.

He still didn't know why he hadn't called. He wanted to—couldn't get her feisty green eyes out of his mind. Torturously, he replayed the heated moments they'd shared on the beach. But every time he picked up the phone, his heart started to race. Every suave pickup line, every piece of alluring dialogue he'd used to make a woman turn putty in his hands flew from his mind. Truth be told, he didn't want to say those things to Summer anyway. But the things he did want to say? That he couldn't stop thinking about her. That he loved the way she looked first thing in the morning, hair wild about her head. That she'd had him captivated from the first moment they'd met when she hadn't fallen for his smiles and charms. That he wanted to taste her sweet lips and feel her body melded to his again.

"Can't say as I've ever seen you work so hard."

Trent welcomed the interruption and peered over his shoulder. His older brother, Adam, leaned against the door-jamb, a smirk on his face.

Trent shrugged and smiled. "You know my motto, work smarter, not harder."

Adam pushed off the doorframe and held out a glass, jiggling it so the ice cubes floating around tinkled against the sides.

Arching his back, Trent stretched sore muscles, then stood from his kneeling position and slid the hammer through the loop in his tool belt. He took the proffered drink, the glass wet and cool, condensation beading along the outside. He downed the liquid in one gulp and wiped his mouth with the back of his hand.

Handing the glass back, he found his brother watching him.

"I'd ask who the woman was, but I know you better than that."

Trent tried to look as if his brother's words hadn't hit their mark. "What's that supposed to mean?"

Adam held his gaze. "You know exactly what it means."

Trent bent down and retrieved his balled-up shirt he'd tossed over an hour ago. He wiped it along the back of his neck and across his chest. A cool cloth would feel better, but the shirt would work to wipe away some of the sweat and grime. Buying time hadn't worked. He still didn't have a clever dodge from his brother's line of questioning. "You forget that I don't have a fancy law degree like you. I'm just an ignorant treasure hunter."

"Oh please." His brother rolled his eyes. "Fine, I'll spell it out for you. You're wound up. Inside your own head. You're doing manual labor, for crying out loud."

Well, that was mildly offensive. "Don't sound so surprised. I'm not some suit who works in air-conditioning all day." Trent looked pointedly from the top of his brother's perfectly gelled hair, over his expensive tailored gray suit, down to his black patent leather shoes. "Besides"—he shrugged—"I need the money for an upcoming exploration."

"I'm just saying that you're acting different. And for most guys, that usually means a woman has him all tied up. But I've never seen you react in such a way to any woman. So I guess you're just inside your head thinking through the logistics for your next hunt."

Trent looked away and followed a passing car with his eyes. Logistics for the galleon dive had been figured out a while ago. True, he needed to reschedule, but that couldn't happen until he had money in his pocket. Better to let Adam believe that was the reason for his preoccupation though. The car turned the corner, and Trent pulled his gaze back to his brother.

"Naturally."

Adam stared at him, his eyes narrowing. "You're lying." A grin spread across his face before he barked out a laugh. "There is a woman involved."

"I don't know what you're—"

"Trent, I'm a defense attorney. I can tell when someone is

lying, and you, my brother, are *so* not telling the truth." His smile lightened every word.

Trent crossed his arms over his chest.

Adam looked like a kid in a candy store. "So, who is she?"

"I'm not talking about this with you." No way, no how.

A smirk lifted one corner of Adam's mouth. "Would you rather I go tell Mom?"

Trent unfolded his arms and huffed out a breath. "Oh, grow up, why don't you."

"Why? This is too much fun."

"Ha-ha."

Adam leaned back against the doorframe again. He wasn't going anywhere. The gleeful sparkle in his eye didn't diminish, but he managed to temper his wide grin. "Who is she? Someone we know?"

Trent looked past his brother's shoulders and watched as Mom passed through the living room and down the hall. This wasn't something he wanted her to hear about...yet. He'd never brought a girl home to meet the family before. Had never discussed any woman with them, really. If she overheard, she'd start making a big deal about it, and he'd rather avoid that, if at all possible.

"Shut the door. You're letting all the cold air out."

Adam stepped onto the unfinished deck and closed the door behind him.

"Her name is Summer Arnet, and no, she isn't someone you know."

His brother rubbed his hands together. "When do we get to meet her?"

"Umm, how about never?"

"What? Afraid she'd take one look at me or Michael and realize you aren't the good-looking brother?"

146

"Ha! Like that would happen. You look like the backside of a horse, and Michael, while slightly less hideous, is still on his tour of duty."

Adam punched his shoulder. "So what's stopping you? You like this girl, right? I mean, really like her. You're not just messing around?"

It would be a lot easier if he were just messing around. Then he'd know what to do. How to act. With Summer he was in uncharted waters. He looked his brother in the eye. "I really like her." He'd even told her so, and she...well, she'd said he wasn't the type of guy for her. So far he hadn't done anything to prove her wrong either. What a putz he was.

Adam pumped his fist in the air. "Finally! I know you don't want to hear it, but we've all been praying for you. Hoping you'd settle down, realize God isn't your enemy, and find a good woman."

Trent held out his hands. "Whoa, dude. She isn't some Bible thumper like y'all are. She's nice, but I know what you guys consider 'good.'"

His brother waved away the comment. "You should bring her to the Fourth of July picnic this weekend."

Hmmm. There was an idea. "You don't think that move is too...I don't know...serious?"

Adam frowned. "I thought you said you weren't just messing around with her."

"I'm not, but meeting the family is a big deal."

"Now who needs to grow up?" Adam pierced him with a look. "You're twenty-seven, not seventeen. Start acting like it."

Maybe Adam had a point. If he showed Summer that she was different, that he was taking what they had between them with grave intention, then maybe that would prove he was the kind of man she needed in her life.

"Okay, Mr. Defense Attorney, you can stop staring me down like you do the jury. You've won your case. But the thing is"—he pulled a hand across the back of his neck—"even if I invited her, I don't think she'd come."

Adam's eyed narrowed. "Why not?"

Pride was a hard pill to swallow. He hated admitting his unmanly behavior the previous seven days where Summer was concerned. Especially to his older brother. "It's possible I haven't called her since I saw her last week."

"And she was expecting your call? You didn't...you know... and then not call?"

"No, I didn't have sex with her. And again, no, she probably wasn't waiting for my call. But I should have, to prove her wrong." He looked down at his feet. "Instead I only proved her right."

Adam gave a small shrug of his shoulders. "Better late than never."

"I doubt she'll see it that way. She has this idea in her head about the type of guy I am, and she's determined to say no to me at every turn."

His brother grinned. "Since when have you ever taken no for an answer?"

Chapter 18

The white sand burned Summer's feet as she half walked, half skipped her way down the beach toward the surf. Once she reached the packed, moist shore where the tide had touched, she ceased her manic maneuvers and walked like a sane person again. Finding a spot not too crowded, she unrolled her beach towel and tossed a book and bottle of Gatorade on top. She pulled her bathing suit cover over her head, then unscrewed the lid to her sunscreen and applied a thick layer across her skin. No need for another sunburn. She stretched out over the towel on her tummy and wiggled until the sand contoured to her shape. Perfect. Now for her book. She opened it at the bookmark.

In vain have I struggled. It will not do. My feelings will not be repressed. You must allow me to tell you how ardently I admire and love you.

Sigh. It didn't matter that she'd read *Pride and Prejudice* a thousand times, those words would forever be swoon worthy. Okay, so Mr. Darcy hadn't been the most eloquent of men in his first proposal to Elizabeth Bennett, but anyone could see how much he loved her. Even though he didn't want to admit it, when he struggled against the feelings he had...

Whoa. Better stop that gravy train before it left the station. Any second she'd start to see similarities between herself and Austen's timeless characters. Like how first impressions could color one's view of a person. Or how feelings for a specific person could develop whether one willed them to or not. Chugga-chugga-no-no.

Unlike Darcy, her struggle would not be in vain. She would suppress her feelings. Most keenly the feeling of disappointment that she still hadn't heard from Trent. Even her sense of vindication couldn't lift her spirit. Then of course there was the humiliation that she had thrown herself into his arms under the pier. She'd let the smooth talking of an obvious womanizer get to her.

She turned the page in her book and resumed reading— the best way to escape reality for a few precious moments.

A shadow cast over the page of her book, darkening the words of Elizabeth's retort. A regency version of a modern tell-off, in Summer's opinion. The shadow didn't continue on but stayed in place. Summer rolled to her side and looked up, her hand a visor over her eyes.

Trent. Her stomach rolled like a crashing wave. What was he doing here? A week of silence after a shared kiss and a promise that he wasn't what she thought. Well, he had turned out to be exactly what she'd thought, hadn't he. If only she could feel triumphant. She should be jumping up and shouting "I told you so" in his face. Instead she found herself being pulled in by the undertow of his presence.

She pressed her lips into a thin line. No way was she going to let him affect her again. She'd had a hiccup in her mental faculties when she'd kissed him, but now she was in control.

They'd be civil, possibly even friends, but she couldn't trust him with her heart to be any more than that.

She stared up at him, carefully wiping away any expression from her face. "I'm beginning to think you don't own a phone."

"The bill I get every month from my cell provider would beg to differ." He pointed to her towel. "Mind if I sit?"

Her gaze flicked to where he pointed. An electric current shot through her body, and her stomach rippled with awareness. She needed to keep a safe distance—more than a measly three inches. The thin material of her bathing suit cover balled in her hand as she sat up. Shoving her arms through holes, she scooted to the far side of the towel and waved her hand at the other end.

Trent sat in the middle. Right next to her. The strong scent of his soap filled her nostrils and made her squeeze her eyes shut tight instead of rolling them into the back of her head from the deliciousness. But, man! He smelled so good.

Get it together.

She opened her eyes and stared...at his boots? Seriously? Who wore clunky black biker boots on the beach? Her gaze traveled up to his signature ripped jeans and V-neck T-shirt. Up to his lopsided grin and dangerously blue eyes. Her pulse quickened. She tore her gaze away, looking out across the ocean to the horizon. Better get her heartbeat back to a normal rhythm, or he'd never believe she was indifferent to him. And she had to be. For her sake.

With a deep breath she turned back toward him. "Why are you here? Wait, better yet, how did you know *I* was here?"

He propped his hands behind him at an angle to support his weight as he leaned back, his arm brushing and resting against hers. She sucked in a breath but refused to move away.

It was all a part of the game. Only this time she wouldn't play along.

"I'm a treasure hunter, remember?" He winked. "It's my job to find precious things."

A line. He'd used a line on her. Her nostrils flared as anger boiled in the pit of her stomach. Sure, he'd been charming before. He'd flirted and smiled past her defenses, but he'd never made her feel cheap. She sniffed. Precious indeed. As precious as all the other women he'd used lines on to pick up in the past. The backs of her eyes burned.

She jumped to her feet and ripped off her suit cover once more. Glaring down into Trent's stunned face, she cut her hand through the air. "You know what? I don't care why you're here. Next time you want to talk to me, pick up your phone and call. That's what you pay for, after all, isn't it?"

Dropping the light fabric, she turned on her heal and marched to the water. When she was in to her knees, she shallow-dove beneath the surface and let the water wash over her.

———

Trent flinched. So that hadn't gone well at all. He'd barely been able to get three sentences across before she'd stormed off. Hadn't even had the opportunity to invite her to the family picnic yet. What had he said that she'd found so offensive? He searched his mind and replayed the conversation but came up empty. Shrugging his shoulders, he shook his head. Even with all his experience with women, he still didn't understand them.

Summer's head resurfaced, the sun glinting off strands of her red hair. His muscles began to relax, and he grinned. She was all spit and fire, hypnotizing him like a pyromaniac to a flame. One thing he knew for sure—there was definite heat between them.

He sat up, bent his knees, and leaned his chest against his thigh, his fingers working on the knot in his shoelaces. A few tugs and the boots slid off his feet. He peeled off his socks and wiggled his toes. What to do about his jeans? If he hadn't been in such a hurry to get down here, he would have thought to bring appropriate swimwear. Too late now. He rolled up the hem to over his calves. Glancing back out to the surf, he spotted Summer bobbing with the waves. Should've just left the pants rolled down. They were going to get wet anyway.

The water lapped at his feet as he neared the shoreline. A bit cooler on the Atlantic side than the gulf, but still warmer than some of the deeper dives he'd been on with the archeology department. Of course, with those he'd worn a wet suit.

Frothy water churned about his shins as he walked farther into the ocean. He pressed on past the push and pull of the waves, and stopped once he reached Summer's side. She didn't turn to look at him, but continued to stand in the surf, her hands out to her sides, palms down, rising and falling with the motion of the water.

While he was sure her ignoring him was meant as a rebuff, he could've stared at her profile all day. The smattering of freckles across her nose and cheeks were too darn cute. He'd play connect-the-dots with them if he didn't think she'd drown him for it.

His gaze followed the curve of her neck and stopped short at her shoulders. Her very stiff shoulders. The thought that he was making her uncomfortable didn't sit well with him. This wasn't the *your attention is making me blush* uncomfortable he was used to making women feel. No. This was a *your very presence is making every muscle in my body tense* uncomfortable.

He scrubbed a hand down his face, the saltwater stinging his eyes. "Look, Summer, I came here to tell you I'm sorry for not calling."

No cracks in the stone profile. "I hadn't expected you to."

No, she probably hadn't, and that was the problem, wasn't it? "I wanted to. You don't know how much I wanted to. I know you don't think I can stick around, be true to only one woman, be true to you. That's not the problem. Every time I picked up the phone...I just...I don't know..." *Where are all your smooth words now, Trent?* He squeezed his eyes shut. Never before had he experienced such difficulty talking to a woman, and yet here he was, the woman he actually had feelings for right beside him, and he sounded like an idiot. He pulled a hand across the back of his neck. "You scare me."

That got her attention. She looked at him, her eyes boring into his. "I scare you?"

He reached out and cupped her upper arm, his hand gently sliding down and grazing her skin until her hand was in his. He pressed her fingers. "I'm scared of the way you make me feel." His shoulders rose in a weak attempt at a shrug. "I've never felt like this with anyone before."

Her eyes searched his, and the moment lengthened. He held his breath. Should he have laid it all out on the table like that? Why wasn't she answering? Vulnerability ate away at an already record-low self-confidence.

Blessedly, she returned the pressure to his fingers, her muscles relaxing and the hard set to her face softening. "I believe you."

His breath whooshed out as laughter tickled his throat. Was she going to give him a shot now?

"But, Trent..."

Uh-oh. Not a *but*.

"You've only proven my point. You don't know how to stick around, how to talk about your feelings with a woman the way you have to, to be in a relationship. Maybe it's because you don't have the experience or maybe because it's just not who you are." She let go of his hand. "I can't risk taking the chance of finding out which one of those is true."

And he couldn't risk letting her go without a fight. She'd see that he wasn't going to walk away. All he needed was time. Time to prove to them both that he wasn't the type of man she thought he was. That he could love her like no other man could.

"Do you have any plans for Fourth of July?"

She shook her head. "Not really. I'll probably just watch the fireworks on TV."

"My family is having a big Fourth of July picnic this weekend. Please say you'll come with me."

She visibly swallowed, and he could imagine how her mind must be racing. "But I just said—" Disbelief covered her face as she cocked her head. "You want me to meet your family?"

A wave beat against their legs and caused Summer to stumble to the side. Trent reached out and caught her around the waist. He left his hand there as he stared down into her eyes. "I know what you said. But we can be friends, right? Friends celebrate holidays together. Besides, you'll love my folks. My mom's a great cook, and you've never tasted an apple pie until you've had hers."

She took a step back, and he let his hand fall to his side. Her fingers intertwined in front of her, and her shoulders rose until they almost touched her ears. "I guess it couldn't hurt. I mean, a family picnic. Should be fun, right?"

Chapter 19

Atlantic Ocean, 1689

Rough hands tore Isabella from a fitful sleep. Her heart pounded from the violent awakening, her mind slow to grasp her newfound reality.

"What are you doing? Where are you taking me?" She clawed at the vice grip on her arm, her feet stumbling to keep up with the fast pace of her captor.

Silence answered her questioning.

Díos, what is happening? Had someone found out she was a woman and had come to steal her virtue?

Fear shredded sanity from her mind until her actions were as crazed as a madman. She thrashed about, jerking her arm in every which direction to try and free it from its prison. Her foot kicked out and connected with the back of the man's calf.

Fast as the strike of an adder, the man turned and slammed her into the rough wood of the ship's bulkhead. Pain shot through her skull and reverberated down her neck and back.

She squeezed her eyes against the pulsating ache and sudden wave of dizziness and nausea that overcame her.

"You should not have meddled in other people's business." Hot, foul breath fanned her face.

Her eyes opened to slits, then widened. She pressed her body back more fully to the wall, taking every millimeter available to distance herself from the evil in front of her. She did not have to ask why any longer. The quartermaster had not believed her word that she hadn't overheard his conversation in the hold. But where was he taking her? And what would he do with her once they got there?

He jerked her forward once more, and she stumbled behind him. Her pleas fell on deaf ears, and no amount of prying could release her arm from his iron grip.

Early morning twilight cast the sky in varying hues as the quartermaster dragged her onto the main deck. The stars still shone bright directly above her, but the horizon lightened with the first golden rays of the day. Would this be the last time she would witness the wonders of the firmament?

"I do not trust you to keep your mouth shut. Therefore I must make it so you cannot have a wagging tongue." He shoved her against the main mast and tied her hands around the pole. The tight knot cut off the circulation at her wrists. He leaned down until his mouth was near her ear. "One of benefits of my position aboard ship is that I may discipline the crew. And since I caught you stealing this"—he held out a golden ring, which Isabella recognized as the captain's signet —"even the tenderhearted captain will not object if he happens upon your flogging."

Flogging. She winced. Forty lashes save one, with a cat-o'-nine-tails. Her stepfather had once forced her to watch a public flogging in the square. His sadistic thrill at violence and anguish had gorged on the scene, while she'd had to stumble away and lose the contents of her stomach. The skin of the man's back had been shredded, blood spraying the onlookers with each lash of the whip. His screams of pain had haunted her for weeks.

"What is going on here?"

Isabella raised her eyes and noticed the crew had begun to congregate. One man stood a step closer than the rest, his face curious, his eyes...eager? She would not find help among these brutes.

Where was *Tío* Pepe when she needed him most? If ever she needed rescuing, it was now.

"I found this boy stealing Captain Montoya's signet ring." The quartermaster lifted the piece of jewelry up for all to see. "He shall be punished. Let this be a lesson to you all."

Sharp, needlelike pain stabbed her hands over and over from lack of blood flow. Her eyes darted to each face, searching for one that would help her. "Please, I did not steal anything! I am innocent—"

Four large knuckles smashed into her cheek and jaw, cutting off her entreaty. Her head swam and ears rang.

The quartermaster's large presence registered behind her. Before her mind could catalogue what was happening, a ripping sound interrupted the low tones of the men's voices and the cool morning air embraced her bare back—that not covered by her bindings.

The evil man behind her swore, then laughed outright. "Mayhap I should change the manner of your punishment, *señorita*."

"What is the meaning of this?" Captain Montoya's stern voice from the quarterdeck ripped through the murmurs of the men around her.

The quartermaster took a step to the side, and Isabella turned her head in the captain's direction. His eyes narrowed, and his lips pressed into a thin line. His scrutiny traveled the length of her until their gazes met. Hot flames ignited her cheeks, and she struggled against the bindings at her wrists so she could cover her nakedness.

His eyes flicked to the quartermaster. "I asked a question, and I demand an answer."

"I caught this cabin *boy* stealing from you, *el capitán*." He pulled out the signet ring from his doublet.

Isabella shrank under Captain Montoya's burning scrutiny. She tried to shout a denial against the false accusations, but her throat closed and refused to allow any words to escape.

"Bring her to my quarters. Now." Captain Montoya turned on his heel and marched away.

The quartermaster grumbled under his breath. He unsheathed a small dagger at his waist, the sun glinting off the metal. Isabella sucked in a breath as he brought the blade to her throat. "Do not think for a moment that I will not cut the tongue out of your very head if you so much as utter a word of what you heard yesterday."

She swallowed hard and gave a small shake of her head. If need be, she'd never utter another word again.

The tip of the dagger moved away from her neck, and he stepped in front of her. One quick swipe of the blade, and the ropes around her wrists fell free. Her hands exploded in pain, as if a thousand bees continuously stung her palms and fingers. She rubbed her wrists and massaged her hands. With a jerk, the quartermaster once again seized her arm and pulled her along behind him.

Her split shirt fell from her hunched shoulders and slipped

down her arms. Frantically, she pulled the torn material back up to cover her bare skin. She'd never been so exposed.

But more than her body lay bared. Her secret was in the open. Every man aboard the vessel now knew that a woman was among their numbers. What would they do? What would the captain do? Would he protect her or punish her for her treachery? Surely he would demand answers, but what should she tell him? Malevolence seeped from the man yanking her about, and he'd already issued threats were she to confess her knowledge to the captain.

The quartermaster opened the door to the captain's cabin and shoved her into the room. She stumbled, but caught herself before landing face first in a heap upon the floor.

"That will be all." Captain Montoya's hardened voice caused her to cringe. That he was upset was apparent.

"Remember what I said." The quartermaster spoke his threat in low tones meant for her ears only.

With a click behind her, the door closed, and she was alone with the captain. Her eyes remained fastened to the floor, but she could feel his firm gaze upon her. Disappointment filled the room, and she shrank into herself. Silence stretched, but her ears drummed with the echo of her heartbeat.

Blue velvet entered her vision as material was thrust beneath her gaze. "Here. Put this on. *Señora* Cruz will be vexed if you ruin her new gown, so take measure not to stain or rip it."

Confusion furrowed her brow. He was giving her a gown to wear? No lecture? No punishment? She glanced up. Captain Montoya faced the opposite direction, his wide shoulders square and his stance firm. Undressing in the presence of a man was highly improper. Although given the fact she had masqueraded as a man aboard the ship for the last month, it didn't seem as though she could complain about impropriety. Turning her back, she allowed her stepfather's oversized shirt to fall to the ground. She brushed her fingers along her bindings, the lump in the middle of her torso a comfort. While her gender may have been discovered, her grandmother's necklace had not. Hope still flickered for her future.

With great difficulty, she pulled the dress over her head and into place. She hoped *Señora* Cruz had servants to help her with the yards of material, for it was kin to wrestling a bear, getting into the gown. The fabric hung from her frame, the lack of petticoats apparent in the limp skirt. She craned her neck to peer at her back. Servants would be needed to fasten the gown as well. She reached around, contorting her body to try and reach to secure the dress. Impossible on her own. Her eyes flicked to the man across the room, and she chewed her lip.

"Are you clothed?" His deep voice vibrated the air.

"*Sí*...except...umm..."

"Except?" He turned and stopped short at her still-exposed back. "I see." In three strides he stood behind her.

It took all her strength not to dart when the heat of his hands warmed her skin. A finger traced the ridge of her bindings. "These dirty things are no longer needed. Discard them."

They were needed if she wanted to keep the necklace safe and concealed. "This dress requires certain undergarments of which I do not possess." Namely a corset, although she could probably still fit in the gown without one. She shuffled her feet, discomfort making it impossible to remain still. Never before had she used the word "undergarments" in a conversation with a man.

Captain Montoya cleared his throat and tugged on the

dress. She planted her feet against the pull of the fabric, her body warming from the combination of the man's close proximity, mortifying embarrassment, and anxiety over what would be her fate.

With one last tug, the captain stepped back. "There. Too much trouble, if you ask me."

Her, women in general, or the gown itself? Isabella turned, the sway of the fabric about her ankles strangely foreign. Odd, for she would have thought the opposite to be true. That the return of feminine attire would bring a comfort. If nothing else, however, she was thankful the yards of material hid her trembling legs.

Memories flashed in her mind faster than the matador's cape. Her mother's horror-filled eyes, Hernando's cackling laughter in response. The eagerness of the men in the crowd at the town floggings. The quartermaster's sneer and echoing threats.

Fear fueled the bellies of men until they devoured their victims.

All men? Doubt niggled her mind. *Tío* was a good man. And the captain? She'd seen his kindness to Luis. But Hernando had seemed a gentleman at first as well.

What should she do? What should she say?

Pushing down trepidation, she schooled her features into a mask she'd worn whenever in her stepfather's presence. She'd allow a curtain to fall over her eyes so no one could see her thoughts, her feelings. Power would remain hers.

She lifted her chin and met the captain's eyes in an unwavering stare. Her muscles bunched to flee, but she refused them the movement.

Captain Montoya stood firm in front of her. "Why are you aboard my ship?"

Tightness bunched in her chest. "I needed the passage to the New World."

The dark eyes in front of her narrowed, threatened. "Speak the truth and all of the truth, *señorita*, for I know that is not the whole of the story. If passage was all you had sought, there are many other vessels you could have simply hired, and not have put forth such great effort in this ruse."

She swallowed hard, his intense stare causing her nonchalant mask to slip. "I had neither the funds to pay for said passage nor the time to wait to procure another vessel."

He took a step forward. "I only ask once more, *señorita*, for my patience is growing thin. The whole story, now, if you please."

Isabella rocked back on her heel to put as much distance between them without making it obvious. Her eyes darted to the exit. If she made a dash for it, he would be upon her before she could pull the door open. Besides, where would she run? There was no escape.

Truth? So be it. There seemed no other recourse for her now.

Chapter 20

Florida, Present Day

Fun was the last thing Summer was having. Her stomach clenched. It was wound up in more knots than the yarn she'd used the year her mom had tried to teach her to crochet. No amount of tugging had unraveled that monstrosity. In fact, the more she'd pulled, the tighter it had gotten.

Why had she agreed to spend the holiday with Trent and his family? It's not like they were dating—she couldn't be in a relationship with him. He was a man-child and only thought of women as his playthings. She'd never let herself become some toy for his amusement and then cast aside when he got bored.

It was his eyes. The pleading look in them that had swayed her when common sense had said to keep her distance.

Either way she was committed now.

The soles of her gladiator sandals pushed down on the accelerator. Maybe it wouldn't be so bad. Picnics were fun, right? At least there'd be good food. And it wasn't like she'd be alone with Trent. His whole family was supposed to be there. What were the chances he'd flirt and try to charm her while his parents watched? A groan vibrated in the back of her throat. They were probably pretty high.

No more time to analyze. She pulled into a short driveway and parked her car behind a Porsche. A low whistle blew past her lips. Someone had some money. She opened her car door and moved toward the house, but her eyes stayed on the clean lines of the little roadster. The muscles in her neck pulled taut until she was forced to turn her head and look where she was going. Trent and another man approached in long strides, both their faces stretched in wide grins.

The man with dark hair clapped Trent on the shoulder. "Look at that, little brother. I've already managed to turn her head."

Heat didn't creep up to her cheeks—it sprinted. These two were brothers? Both were good looking—another flush to her skin—but they were as different as night and day. Well, at least the color of their hair and eyes. Obviously they both had that charming flirtatious thing going on.

Trent laughed and met her eyes with a wink. That knot in her stomach? Dissolved in a second. Much more and she'd melt into a puddle of goo right there on the hot concrete driveway.

Way to shore up your defenses there, Summer.

"Sorry to break it to you, Adam, but you didn't turn her head. Your car did. You"—he poked his brother's collar bone —"couldn't make a mosquito do a double take."

Summer grinned.

Trent's brother—he'd called him Adam, right?—play-stumbled backward and clutched his hand to his heart. "You wound me." He fastened his chocolate eyes on her. "Come on, Summer. What d'ya say? Is my brother here right? Am I so unattractive that not even the most annoying of insects would want to take another look at me?"

She opened her mouth, but Trent cut her off. "It's okay. You can tell him the truth. Rip it like a Band-Aid. Say, 'Adam, you're nowhere near as handsome as your brother Trent.'"

That was true. Adam was handsome all right, but his perfectly gelled hair and designer slacks didn't make her pulse race...not the way Trent did with his wild and carefree attitude. Even when she tried to slow it down. Of course, she'd already accidentally admitted she found him hunkier than a Norse god. No need to go inflating his ego again.

She cocked her hip and placed a hand on it, then tapped her chin with the index finger of her other hand and scrunched up her lips. "I think..." Pause for effect. "If I had to choose..." Another pause. She dropped her hands and clasped them in front of her, trying to hide her smile behind a look of innocence. "I'll take the Porsche."

"What?"

"Aww. Come on!"

Manly protests rent the air, and Summer covered her mouth as giggles escaped through her fingers.

"All right you two, enough tomfoolery." A woman in her midfifties with a short bob haircut stepped down the drive. The fabric of her coral-colored capris made a soft swooshing sound as she walked. "Go make sure your father didn't burn all his eyebrows off when he lit the grill."

"Sure thing, Mom." Both men turned and walked around the side of the house toward the back.

"I'm Anita Carrington." She extended her hand, and the skin around her eyes crinkled as she smiled. The woman exuded warmth and friendliness. "Welcome to our home. We're simply thrilled you could join us."

Summer slipped her hand into Anita's and gave a little squeeze. "Thank you for having me."

"Our pleasure, dear. Now, why don't we go around back, and I'll introduce you to everyone."

Anita followed the same path her sons had taken moments ago, and Summer trailed her. A small green lizard darted in front of her, then scurried up one of the oak trees shading the Carrington property. When they rounded the back corner of the house, Summer instinctively groped for her camera hanging around her neck. Only it wasn't there. She'd left it at home, thinking the family wouldn't want a stranger taking pictures of them. Too bad, because the scene before her was picture perfect.

Patriotic red, white, and blue bunting covered the deck railing. A giant red bow topped each of the gathered swags. Bulb lights zigzagged overhead, just waiting for the sun to go down to be turned on. Dear ol' dad stood behind a smoking grill, a *Kiss the Cook* apron hanging from his neck and a metal spatula waving from his hand. A teenaged girl stepped through the French doors, carrying a large glass bowl of cubed watermelon, followed by Trent and Adam, hands also full with trays of food.

Anita pulled Summer along in her wake until they stopped beside the grill. "George, I want you to meet Summer. Summer, this is my husband, George."

George looked up from the sizzling meat and speared Summer with a broad smile. She no longer need wonder where Trent got his dancing blue eyes from. "Trent's girl, right?"

Uh-oh. How was she supposed to answer that? She looked

to where Trent was setting down a plate of hamburger trimmings. He raised his head and winked again. Is that what he'd told his family? That she was his girl?

She forced a smile to her lips. "We're just friends."

George poked around the food on the grill. "Looks like these burgers are ready. I hope you're hungry, Summer."

"Famished."

Burgers deposited on a nearby platter, everyone gathered around the picnic table on the other side of the deck. Trent stepped over the bench and sat beside her.

Summer eyed the food in front of her, but no one moved to put any of it on their plates. No way would she reach first.

George cleared his throat from a folding chair at the head of the table. "Should we say grace?" He extended his hands palms up to Anita on his right and Trent on his left.

Surreptitiously, Summer looked around. Heads bowed and hands clasped around the table. She'd never prayed before in her life. Didn't know the right protocol. Good thing she could just follow everyone else's example.

She placed one hand in Amber's, Trent's little sister. The smooth palm similar in size and shape to her own. Trent covered her other hand. His fingertips started in the middle of her palm and spread out, separating and then intertwining with her fingers. Strength radiated from his grip, and she found herself hoping he would remain as steady as his hold was on her at that moment.

"Heavenly Father, we thank you for the gathering of family on this day of Independence. For the sacrifice of men and women who make it possible for this country to remain the land of the free. Especially for Michael, who is out fighting as we speak. Keep him safe. May we remember the ultimate sacrifice of your Son, who died on the cross so that all may be liberated from the chains of sin and call you our heavenly Father. Bless the food on our table and the people around it. Amen."

A soft echo of "amen" and Amber released her hand. Trent hung on a moment longer and gave a gentle squeeze until she looked at him. He gave her a crooked grin, and she returned his smile despite herself. Activity buzzed around them as the Carrington family piled food on their plates, but she was pulled into Trent's gaze until Amber bumped her shoulder, reaching for the bowl in front of her.

"Excuse me, but can you pass the potato salad, please?" Amber grinned.

Heat burned her cheeks. She extricated her hand from Trent's and smoothed down the front of her sundress before lifting the bowl and passing it down the table. "Sorry," she mumbled. Could she hide under the table now? Trent's whole family must think she was like every other ditz that had gone weak in the knees over his golden looks and flattering speeches.

"So, Trent tells us that you are a photographer." This from Anita across the table.

Summer swallowed. "That's right. I specialize in marine photography."

"That sounds fascinating. I've never been diving myself. Too scared. What if there was a shark in the water with me?" Anita shuddered. "No, thank you. These boys made me sit through enough *Shark Week* episodes to have a healthy dose of respect for the creatures."

Images of the great white with his mouth open and coming at her flashed through her mind. Her muscles stiffened. If she never encountered another shark in her career, it would be too soon.

"I suppose I am missing out on other amazing things though." Anita shook her head. "The coral reefs must be absolutely beautiful."

Summer picked up her burger with both hands. "They really are. More color than you could imagine, and teeming with life." She bit into the sandwich, and her eyes rolled into the back of her head. Goodness. This might be the best burger she'd had in her life.

"Reminds you of our heavenly Father's love, no doubt." George's deep voice addressed her. "The intricacies of His creation never cease to amaze me."

Burger lodged in her throat, and she reached for her glass of lemonade. Creation? A heavenly Father's love? What were they talking about?

Trent shifted his weight beside her. "So, Dad, the deck turned out pretty well, wouldn't you say?"

George looked at his son, pride evident in his expression. "You did a great job, Trent. Thank you for helping us out."

Summer looked around, and her eyes widened before she fastened them on Trent. "You built this?"

"Which means we should hurry and eat before the whole thing comes crashing down." Adam shoveled three forkfuls of baked beans in his mouth in quick succession.

"Has anyone heard from Michael lately?" Amber's question darkened the mood around the table.

Summer's gaze flicked from family member to family member. Concern etched each face. Who was Michael?

Trent leaned toward her. "Michael is my little brother. He's a navy pilot out on deployment."

"Some top-secret mission," Adam said. "I don't think he'll be able to contact us until the mission is over."

"But we can pray." George met the eyes of his family, infusing strength in one look.

Except for Trent. He stared at his plate, his jaw clenched. What was the story there?

Anita took a deep breath and used the table to push herself to her feet. "Everyone finished? I'll clear away the food and get the apple pie from the kitchen."

Summer stood as well. "Here, let me help." She scooped up the half-empty bowl of potato salad into the crook of one arm and lifted the baked beans bowl with the other hand. Brown juice pooled at the bottom and sloshed as she walked into the house.

"The food was delicious, Anita. Thank you for letting me join your family."

The woman smiled. "You're more than welcome."

"Is there anything I can do to help clean up?"

Anita peered at the dishes now littering the counter. "How about I put the leftovers in some containers? Then you can rinse out the dishes so none of the food sticks too badly."

"Sounds good."

Summer turned on the water and let it run through her fingers, waiting for it to warm. She stared out the large picture window that hung above the kitchen sink. Amber sat on a homemade swing beneath a giant oak. The cords of the rope suspending the wooden seat seemed a bit frayed from time and weather. George stepped up behind Amber, and she leaned back and grinned into her dad's face.

A pang of loss pierced Summer's heart. Strange. One would first have to possess something in order to feel its loss. She'd never had a loving relationship with her father. Never had a father.

George pushed Amber on the swing, and Summer felt an

unwanted sting at the back of her eyes. The sweet picture before her should make her smile, not fall into a hole of hurt and self-pity.

She became aware of Anita's presence behind her, and she mashed her eyes closed, willing the unshed tears back into her sockets and not down her cheeks.

"Daddy's girl, that one. Always has been."

Summer didn't trust her voice, so she merely nodded. She grabbed the closest dish on the counter and swirled it under the water.

A warm hand encased her shoulder. "Are you okay, dear?" Worry laced Anita's words.

"Fine," she squeaked.

"*Fine* doesn't make one's eyes leak." The pad of Anita's finger brushed away a stray tear.

Summer cast a quick glance at Anita's face. The soft lines around the woman's eyes and her open expression spoke of genuine concern. Should she try to explain? It *would* be nice to talk to someone about it. She bit her lip, unsure.

"Did my son do something to hurt you?" Steel edged her voice.

Summer turned swiftly then. "Oh no, nothing like that. It's just..." She looked back out the window at Amber and George. "I was having a little pity party, is all."

Anita followed her gaze. "Not a good relationship with your own father?"

A half shrug lifted Summer's shoulders. "I don't know my father. Never met him." She hung her head. "He doesn't even know I exist."

"Oh, honey." Anita pressed Summer's head to her shoulder and caressed her hair.

Feelings Summer had spent a lifetime suppressing swelled

faster than a puffer fish on the defensive. Anger, loss, insecurity, pain—they all mingled and threatened to suffocate her. She struggled for breath, her shoulders shaking with dry sobs.

"Shh. There, there, sweet girl." Anita soothed, alternating smoothing Summer's hair and patting her back.

Spent, Summer took a shuddering breath and lifted her head. A wobbly smile tilted her lips, and she wiped at her cheeks. "That's life, right?"

Anita clucked with sympathy. "Unfortunately, yes. But you know, you aren't completely fatherless."

Summer supposed not. The man *was* out there somewhere. But she'd never know where, and she'd never know him. Besides, if by some miracle she *did* happen upon him, the time she needed him the most had passed.

"You will always have your heavenly Father." Anita patted Summer's cheek.

There it was again. This reference to a heavenly Father. Was that some name George and Anita called God?

"I can see I've confused you." Anita reached past Summer and turned off the water. "Come here. I want to show you something." She took Summer's hand and pulled her along into the living room, then pressed her into a brown leather sofa.

Anita leaned forward and picked up a worn book from the coffee table. The cracked leather binding bespoke of the times the tome had been opened and read. Pages crinkled as Anita flipped through the book. "Here it is." Anita turned the book toward Summer, her eyes excited. "Read this."

Summer glanced down and found it hard to focus. A rainbow had thrown up on Anita's Bible. Every word had been highlighted in some color—yellow, orange, blue, green.

They were all there. She narrowed her eyes and focused on the verse Anita was pointing to.

"See what love the Father has lavished on us, that we may be called the children of God." Summer looked back up into Anita's eager face.

"Don't you see? Even though you may not know your earthly father, your heavenly Father has always been there, calling you His precious daughter. He's waiting for you with open arms to have that relationship you've always longed for."

Summer closed her eyes. Was God like a father? She didn't know much about God, but she'd never heard Him called a father before. Images of what fathers and daughters did together formed in her mind. Being pushed on swings, riding tall on broad shoulders, father-daughter dances. Those things required flesh and blood, not some ghostlike deity. She opened her eyes.

"It may be a hard concept to wrap your head around now, but trust me—I know." Anita took a wobbly breath. "I don't talk about this very often, but I want to share my story with you because I think it will help you understand.

"That picture of a perfect father that you have in your head? It's beautiful. George is that kind of father with our kids. But not every man is that way. My dad..." Anita's eyes squeezed shut, and blotches dotted her face. She shook her head. "My dad was abusive. He used me and my sister in ways that no daughter should ever be used by their father."

Summer's heart twisted as Anita stared at her hands in her lap, her thumb rubbing hard, manic strokes across the inside of her wrist. Why was she putting herself through so much pain from the retelling? "You don't have to tell me—"

Anita looked up and gave a sad smile. "I want you to know, Summer. You need to know."

Why did she need to know? Why was this sweet woman swimming through years of hurt to divulge life stories to a stranger?

"I hated him, my father. Hated the word *father*. I was so filled with bitterness that it ate away at me. A friend of mine in college 'got saved'"—she used air quotes—"and started telling me how God was a heavenly Father. Well, I thought, if God was a Father, then I wanted nothing to do with Him. I'd had enough fatherly experience to last me a lifetime."

Summer nodded. More than enough. Men like that shouldn't just go to jail—they should be castrated.

Anita's expression cleared. "But I was wrong. I needed a father more than girls whose dads doted on them, it seemed. All the places in my heart, the empty, scarred places, filled and healed when I accepted Jesus as my Savior and became a child of God. God is called many things, you know. Healer, Teacher, Lion, Lamb, but my favorite, the way I will always think of Him, is as my Father."

Empty and scarred. Summer could relate. Longing wrung her out until her heart ached.

Could God fill the empty places? Was He the Father she'd been desiring all along?

Chapter 21

How had they gotten here? Fourth of July family picnics used to consist of legendary squirt gun wars and watermelon-seed spitting contests. Now they played at the trendy version of horseshoes. Corn hole. Trent snorted. They couldn't have picked a more redneck name for the game.

Adam tossed his bag. If it made it into the hole one more time, Trent was toast. Who knew a defense attorney could have such a good arm? Of course, it really shouldn't have surprised him. Adam had played baseball in high school. Then again, that was over a decade ago.

The bag landed, half in the hole, half on the platform. Beans shifted, and in slow motion the bag disappeared.

Adam turned, his face split in a triumphant grin. "Your turn."

Trent looked at his watch. Sure was taking Mom and Summer a long time to grab that pie. He chucked his remaining bag at Adam's chest. "I'm going to investigate what's taking so long with dessert."

"You forfeit the game, so I win." Adam's words hit his back.

He called over his shoulder, "No one wins until the game is finished."

"Then get back here so I can whoop—" Trent closed the glass-paneled door, cutting off his brother's trash talk.

An empty kitchen, half-full dishes still littered the counter. Where had they gone? Murmurings drifted from the other side of the wall that partitioned the living room from the kitchen and dining combo. Trent popped his head around the corner, then stepped into the room.

Summer's long red hair contrasted brightly beside Mom's dark-gray bob. He'd hoped the two would hit it off, but he never thought they'd get this close…literally. Bodies angled toward each other, knees touching, hands clasped together. Growing up in a religious family, he was more than familiar with this posture. They were praying. And if there were any doubt, the open Bible lying on the coffee table wiped it away.

Surprise punched him in the gut. She was a Jesus freak too? *You don't believe in Jesus?* Her question rang in his ear, and he tried to recall her tone. There hadn't been any accusation or shock or sadness. She hadn't recoiled or started to evangelize him. There hadn't been any signs that she was of the Bible thumper variety. Usually he could spot them a mile away… enough time to run in the opposite direction.

Summer sniffed and wiped at her eyes.

She'd been crying? His lips twitched. He was horrible, the way his heart lifted at the revelation. Maybe she wasn't brainwashed like the rest of his family. More than likely Mom had cornered her and Summer had felt obligated to pray out of politeness.

"Everything okay?"

Summer turned toward him, her eyes bloodshot and puffy, her lips tilted up in a wobbly smile, but her face…it radiated.

"Your mom is a gem—I hope you know that."

What in the world had happened while he'd been out playing corn hole with Adam? He looked at his mom. Her eyes shone, and she sent him an unspoken message as she nodded her head toward Summer and then himself, her mouth parting in a toothy smile. She didn't need to say anything—he heard it loud and clear. *I like her. Be a good boy and treat her right.*

He raised his brows, silently communicating back. *What's going on?*

Mom's smile only widened, and she nodded in Summer's direction again.

Trent lowered himself onto the couch beside Summer and tucked a piece of her hair behind her ear. "Why the tears, beautiful?"

She shook her head and rolled her eyes. "Just being silly."

"Silly makes people laugh, not cry."

Mom stood and poked a thumb behind her. "I'm going to go so you two can talk."

Thank you, he mouthed as she walked past.

He looked back to Summer. Her chin trembled, but she didn't look sad. Opposite of sad, really. Had Mom welcomed her to the family? That would make him happy, but he wasn't too sure about Summer.

The open Bible glared at him from the coffee table. Hmmm...maybe it wasn't the Carrington family Mom had welcomed her into.

He took a closer look at Summer. Was it too late? The concrete of propaganda had been poured, but maybe it hadn't set yet. Maybe he could set her straight on how his parents' God really worked.

Standing, he extended his hand. "Walk with me?"

Her small hand fit snugly in his, and he resisted the urge to tug her closer, to feel the rest of her meld to his body so perfectly.

Patience. He needed to prove that what he wanted with her was more than stolen moments of pleasure. If that meant keeping his hands to himself, so be it. It was torture being near her but not touching her soft skin, but it was also pure contentment.

They walked out the front door and down the drive without a word spoken between them. He didn't want his family overhearing this particular conversation. He might not agree with them or their religion, but he loved them and knew his prodigal status upset them. Besides, Mom might intervene if she heard him un-evangelizing her new convert.

"Your parents live on a really pretty street." Summer's words brought his attention back around.

The canopy of trees arched over the two-lane road, Spanish moss dangling down like nature's version of summer icicle lights. Wild ferns grew along the base of the trees as well as some small purple flowers. It was quite nice, possibly even romantic. Another time he'd *make* it romantic, but right now damage control had him in tunnel vision.

How to broach the subject? "So...uh...what were you and my mom doing when I interrupted?" He cringed. Not exactly suave, and a bit accusatory sounding. Great start.

Summer stopped walking and looked up at him with her nose wrinkled. "You've been acting strange on and off all day. Is something wrong?"

What was wrong was that she didn't trust him. That she kept him at arm's length. That she'd been talking with his mom and a Bible had been involved. "Yes. I mean, no. I mean—"

Her eyes narrowed, and she crossed her arms over her chest. "What *do* you mean?"

This wasn't going right at all. "Were you guys praying or not?"

Her hands fell to her sides. "That's what this is about? What's the big deal? Your mom prayed with me...for me. It was nice."

He pulled a hand across the back of his neck and squeezed his eyes shut. *Deep breath.* This wasn't going to go away with a simple warning. If Mom had led her in a prayer to accept Jesus as her Savior, then she was likely experiencing the warm fuzzies new faith brought. He'd seen it a million times. Until the harsh reality of the world threw a bucket of ice water on your head that left you gasping for air.

Time for some harsh reality. Maybe he could break it to her easy, shield her from some of the pain. He started walking again, and she followed beside him. "Do you remember when we were in the Bahamas and you asked me if I believed in Jesus?"

"I remember." He felt her eyes on his profile, and she whispered, "You don't, do you."

He glanced down at her. "Actually, I do."

"Then..."

"Then why my extreme reaction to my parents' religious behavior?" One side of his mouth tipped up, and he shook his head. "I believe there is a God, but I don't think He is the loving Father my parents claim Him to be."

She stopped walking, and he took another step before turning back to her.

"Why?"

He knew it was coming. Knew that if he wanted to save her from future disillusionment, he'd have to allow her to see the emptiness that the *loving father* had left him. His fists curled at his side.

"Because God, the one my parents claim, is supposed to make you whole, to fill all the empty spaces. He's not supposed to rip people out of your life and leave you feeling lost and broken, only half of who you were supposed to be."

Had he really said all that? Sure, he'd thought it, felt it every second of every day, but he'd never admitted it out loud before. The confession left him breathless. Like he'd been punched in the gut, doubled over, gasping but not able to draw a breath.

She reached out and encircled his wrist with her fingers, drawing it up close to her middle. Small strokes of her thumb across the back of his hand loosened the tension. He stared at the top of her bent head.

"Who was it?" Her soft voice held compassion, and he was glad she hadn't looked at him.

He turned his arm a little until the underside of his forearm was in full view, and he tapped on the ink there. "You see this tattoo? It's the Celtic knot that symbolizes brother-hood. I got it as a memorial for my twin brother."

She did look up then, the strokes to his hand stopping but the pressure of her grip increasing. "You had a twin?"

He nodded. "Trevor. We were identical."

"Were you close?"

How could he explain the bond of twins? It sounded crazy to say that a connection occurred before birth, even if it was the truth. He raked his hand through his hair and tried to cut off the ache. A phantom pain, like when an amputee complained that his leg hurt, but he didn't have the leg anymore. Of course, he hadn't known why he felt something missing until he was older...

He shook his head. "My brother died of SIDS when he was three months old. Mom didn't even tell me I'd had a twin brother until I was eight. I guess she saw me struggling and thought knowing might help. I did some research and learned about twin bonding. It explained why I always felt something was missing." His jaw ticked. "It didn't explain how the loving God my parents always clung to could take a child for no reason and leave the other to flounder though."

Loving. Gracious. Merciful. Just. Supposed character traits of the Almighty. He suppressed his lips to keep them from curling in a sneer. Was it loving or just to allow an innocent baby to die before he even had a chance to live? Had God shown grace or mercy to Mom and Dad, who mourned the loss of their child? Or to him? No. Thief would be a better title. Like a burglar, He came and stole the most precious and valuable things, except the things God stole could never be replaced.

Summer brought his hand up to her cheek. "I'm so sorry."

Lifting his other hand, he framed her face. He had to make her see, to save her from a heart full of hurt. "It's all a fairy tale, Summer. Whatever it is my mom told you, it's not real. My family lives in a dream world."

She bit her lip and looked to the side. "I don't know, Trent." She looked back and searched his eyes. "What your mom said, what I felt as we prayed, it was real. And the whole feeling you said people are supposed to get after they accept Jesus in their life? I feel it. I've lived my entire life with something missing too. I thought what was missing was my dad, maybe like you feel what's missing is your brother, but after I prayed with your mom...I don't know...that missing piece isn't there anymore."

Trent leaned his head down until his forehead rested

against hers. It hadn't been enough. He'd shared with her something he'd never discussed with anyone, all to enlighten her on how *loving* God really was, and it hadn't been enough. She'd cling to the fairy tale because she thought she needed a father and didn't know who her dad was.

What if he found her dad for her? Then she wouldn't have to accept a false reality when she had flesh and blood right in front of her. He'd never been able to find anything to fill his own emptiness, but he'd use all his skills to find her dad and fill hers.

Chapter 22

Atlantic Ocean, 1689

Isabella licked her lips. With which truth should she start? How she happened upon this ship, or the danger that currently threatened them all? Sudden weariness swept through her until she feared her knees would buckle.

The captain's eyes narrowed. "Do not feign a gentle constitution with me, *señorita*. You have not been on a leisure cruise these past months. The sailor I knew as Benito..." He shook his head. "No. I suppose that is not your name after all."

His eyebrows rose as he pierced her with a gaze of steel. The silence spoke what his words had not. He wanted her name.

She lifted her chin. "I am Isabella Castellano."

Not a flicker in his countenance as he continued to stare at her.

She stared back. The captain's cabin shrank as the rising tension corded between them. The desk in the center of the room, the bed alongside the wall, the trunk in the corner all faded as their eyes continued to lock in a silent battle.

Nostrils flaring, he jutted his chin to the rumpled pile on the floor. "And the clothes?"

Her lips curled. "A gift from my stepfather."

If she hadn't been looking, she would've missed the slight jerk of his head. "Your stepfather gave you clothes to impersonate a boy?"

"No." Fingers bit into her palms. "But it was small repayment for all he took from me."

Gazes held fast a second longer, and then the captain turned and strode to the large window on the far side of the cabin. He pushed back the heavy drapes, one long finger tapping his thigh.

No longer under scrutiny, Isabella withered like a plucked flower. How much longer could she meet his accusing scowl?

He turned, and she straightened her spine. No good could come from a weak display. A lesson learned well, thanks to her stepfather.

Three steps and he towered over her with a face of thunder. Black eyes flashed as his breath fanned her face. What real courage she possessed retreated. Now not only must she convince him that he did not intimidate her, but she must also convince herself. Pushing her shoulders back, she returned his glare measure for measure.

The muscle alongside his jaw ticked. "You guard your words for a man I perceive does not deserve such protection."

A hand touched her arm, and she flinched. An involuntary movement, but one that cost her.

"As I suspected." He took a step back.

Isabella filled her lungs from the added space between them. Some of the tension dissipated with the distance...until she ventured another look at his face. Still etched in stone. Still harboring a brewing storm. If he suspected mistreatment, had he no compassion for her plight?

"My ship became your refuge then. A poor choice, but perhaps your only option?"

Loathing soured her stomach. "My stepfather is *Diablo* himself. He killed my mother and then turned his eyes on me." She pounded her chest with a closed fist. "If you are looking for repentance for my deception, then you will be sorely disappointed."

His eyes sparked, and his lips pressed thin.

Boldness expanded her chest, and she sneered. "And now my fate goes from one man's hands to another. What is to become of me? A prisoner in the hold of the ship? Thrown into the sea to feed the sharks? Although that is an end to which I have already been threatened."

A muscle in his cheek twitched. "Who threatened you?"

She could taste the quartermaster's name on her lips, but caught herself before spitting it out. Even in anger one must exhibit self-control.

Isabella studied the man before her. Danger lurked in Captain Montoya's eyes. His muscles bunched, ready to charge like a raging bull, yet her heart rate remained steady, the palms of her hands dry. Despite all of his intimidation, she was unafraid. He would not harm her.

Certainly the man was angry. But if not with her, then whom?

It is man's God-given responsibility to protect and care for His creation—including the beautiful culmination of His creation—woman. How she had forgotten the priest's words? Though not spoken to her, she had overheard them as the priest talked to a man given to too much wine and mistreating his wife.

Was Captain Montoya's temper ignited by the injustice done her? If she revealed who had threatened her, would he storm out to seek restitution? She must measure her words carefully, for even if the quartermaster were under lock and key, there were others who'd conspired against the captain.

"There is much going on aboard this ship of which you are not aware."

His feet squared. "No more riddles, Isabella. Speak plainly. Who has threatened you?"

Isabella. Her heart thrilled. Besides the few times *Tío* had spoken to her in private, weeks had passed since she'd heard her *nombre.* Even if the captain had said it in a low, warning manner.

A small lock of black hair curled on Captain Montoya's stern brow. Hard lines framed his mouth, and his strong jaw clamped together. She had thought him intimidating and more than a little dangerous, but of a sudden her perception shifted. Instead of hiding behind a facade of bravado, her fingers itched to smooth his forehead and trace the deep grooves along his mouth. His stance, the muscles bunched beneath his jerkin, the truth hidden in the depths of his black eyes. Was it true that he sought to protect her from a threat of harm?

But it was she that needed to protect him. Rather, she needed to warn him so he could protect them all. As his shoulders widened, she had no doubt he could navigate the winds of peril blowing their way.

She took a step forward and laid a hand on his forearm. They both stared at the point of connection until she dropped her hand and lifter her eyes back to his. "Mutiny is on the lips of your crew."

"Mutiny." Incredulity coated the word.

Díos, help me convince him of the truth. "While in the hold I overheard a plot. Some of your crew plan to take the ship from you."

Suspicion clouded his face. "What were you doing in the hold?"

Heat creeped up her neck, but she refused to avert her gaze. "Securing my disguise."

His eyes lowered to her bosom, and she squirmed. Unfortunately, the bodice of *Señora* Cruz's gown dipped low and pressed tight, revealing creamy flesh better left hidden behind fabric.

Was that a twitch of his lips? She wanted to cover herself with her arms. Or slap his cheek.

Her skin flushed hot as he looked back into her eyes. "Who threatened you, Isabella?"

She held his gaze. "The same man threatening you."

He was in her space again in an instant. She took a step back, but he caught her shoulders and held her in place. Inches separated their faces. "I will have a name."

She lifted her chin. "After you hear all I have to say."

His grip tightened before he released her. He crossed his arms over his chest. "I am listening."

Pressing a hand to her stomach, she swallowed hard. "I do not know when the attack is planned, nor everyone involved. Those bent on treason will take over the ship, and I fear many lives will be lost in the fight. The sign will be a raised fist and a mighty roar."

Face hardening once more, he regarded her. "And the leader?"

"'Tis your quartermaster."

Captain Montoya swore under his breath.

A burden lifted from Isabella. "You believe me?"

"*Sí.*" He caressed the hilt of the sword strapped to his side. "Though you have deceived us all, in this I judge your words to be truth."

Hurt nicked her at his words. True, she had misled them, but it had been necessary. She hadn't had any other choice. That she would now be deemed untrustworthy sat like an anchor in her stomach.

"What will you do?"

Without shame he deliberately looked from the top of her shorn head to the hem skimming the wood floor. Fabric bunched in her hands as she squeezed the sides of her skirt.

"That is not your concern, Isabella."

He continued to use her name. To remind her that she was a mere woman? That these matters were beyond her sensibilities?

Her teeth clenched. "I disagree."

One brow rose.

"The quartermaster is aware that I am privy to his plans. He has warned me against speaking the truth and exposing him. Do you not think he will take measures to secure my silence? Has he not already promised what end I will face if I do speak against him?"

His hand curled around the hilt of his sword. "That will not happen."

She eyed the length of his sheathed weapon. "Do you plan to stay by my side the remainder of this voyage? To forgo sleep in order to protect me? 'Tis not possible."

He shook his head. "Juan and a few of my other men that I trust with my life will rotate to guard—"

"To the detriment of everyone's duties and the safety of all. What of the mutiny? True, *Tío*—"

Captain Montoya's head jerked back. "*Tío?* Juan is your uncle?"

She pressed her lips together. Already she had said too much. Had she jeopardized *Tío's* position by revealing their relationship?

His eyes glinted. "Juan knew you were aboard the entire time?"

There was no need to reply. Silence confirmed his question.

"You worry about treason, but already I have been betrayed." He shook his head. "How could Juan have allowed his niece to do all you have done?"

Accusation cooled her blood. "He did not know until I was already aboard the ship. I would not be dissuaded."

The captain turned and paced the length of the cabin, muttering under his breath. His sword bounced against his leg as he walked like a caged animal. The movement caught Isabella's attention, and a plan began to form in her mind. She remembered the weight of the sword in her hand. How her muscles had strained but her spirit had soared during her one and only spar. Having a man guard her at all times endangered them all. All eyes needed to be focused on the rising threat and disarming those bent on rebellion. If she could protect herself...

Without thought Isabella stepped in front of Captain Montoya and cut off his path. "Teach me to fight."

He met her gaze briefly. "No."

One word and he stepped around her like she were nothing more than a stump along the trail.

Lengthening her stride, she intercepted him once more. "Do not forget you have already given me one lesson. I only ask you continue what you have started."

His eyes narrowed before slipping to the decidedly feminine parts of her body. "I will not teach a woman the use of the sword."

Would men never cease to think women weak? Was it not women who bore and raised them? Had she herself not fulfilled every task set to her the last month aboard the ship, same as every other male crew member? How she wanted to stamp her foot against the injustice.

"My fate is sealed then."

The pacing ceased at the other side of the cabin, but the captain didn't turn to face her.

Isabella allowed the silence to stretch. Perhaps he would come to his senses and realize that not only did she need a way to protect herself, but she could also help defend the galleon from impending danger.

Still his back remained toward her. Would there be no more discussion? If not, there was no reason for her to stay in the cabin. She needed to find *Tío* Pepe and inform him of everything that had transpired. Little Luis would surely be looking for her as well.

Without the layers of petticoats required, the hem of her borrowed dress dragged along the floor on her way to the door. She lifted the front to ensure she wouldn't trip, but the ill-fitting clothing posed a nuisance. How would she keep her balance when the ship swayed with the ocean waves during a strong wind? Hernando's discarded garments caught her attention as she passed them. They really were more practical for life at sea. Perhaps a moment would arise when she could come back and retrieve them.

Her hand lifted to open the door.

"You have not been dismissed."

A prisoner it was to be then. Although not a cell in the

hold but within the captain's own quarters. "There is nothing left to discuss."

"I am still captain of this ship, and those on board will obey my commands."

Isabella swept a hand down the length of her. "You forget that I am no longer a member of your crew, *el capitan.*"

His eyes narrowed, and a second later he jerked the chair out from under his desk and dropped into it. He motioned to a chair on the other side. "Sit."

Her chin notched up. "I do not—"

"Sit."

The order brooked no argument. As much as she wanted to remain on her feet, to challenge his demands, she found herself moving in his direction. She lowered herself onto the seat and smoothed out her skirt, refusing to look up.

"I will teach you to fight."

Her head snapped up as a grin spread across her face.

"However, until you have mastered the weapon, you will remain here, in my cabin, at all times." His eyes bore into her.

Back to prisoner. She looked around her new cell and stopped short at the bed pushed against the wall. Her throat constricted, and she swallowed past the lump. True, she'd been sleeping among men for weeks now, but they had all believed her a man as well. Captain Montoya's demand that she stay within this room was for her own safety, surely. He wouldn't...would he?

"Now"—his voice brought her attention back around—"I need to investigate and perhaps put a stop to this mayhem before it even begins." He stood and walked around the desk, stopping at her side. Bending at the waist, his fingers slipped into his boot. When he straightened he held a small dagger in his hand. "Only use this if absolutely necessary."

She nodded as her fingers closed around the leather sheath. The blade weighed little more than air.

Captain Montoya strode toward the door, and Isabella heard the hinges creak. The sound of the door closing didn't come, and she turned. He stood there, looking at her.

"Do not open this door, no matter what." And with that he was gone.

Chapter 23

Florida, Present Day

Following the clues and going straight to the source—two basic principles for treasure hunters. First time a source was the mother of the woman who fascinated Trent. That made things…interesting. It had only taken a second to pull up Summer's Facebook profile and then a click on the About tab, click on Family and Relationships, and, voila, a thumbnail picture of Patricia Arnet appeared. He knew where Summer got her high cheekbones and creamy satin skin. The smattering of freckles across the middle-aged woman's face made him think she had been a redhead before her hair turned silver.

Trent wiped his sweaty palms on his jeans. He didn't have much experience with mothers. Not since high school anyway. Even then it was usually the glare of the fathers that kept him in line. There was his own mother, of course, but she didn't really count in this consideration.

The back of his throat tickled, and he coughed into his elbow. If only Summer knew the name of her dad, he could bypass her mom altogether. Why *didn't* Summer know her dad's name? Seemed like her mom had been up front with her about her conception and all. Why hide the man's identity? Was there something sinister or shameful about him? Doubt niggled the back of his mind, but he pushed it away.

Maybe Patricia had never told the guy that he'd knocked up his one-night stand. A fellow had a right to know if he had a long-lost daughter. Maybe she did tell him, but he'd high-tailed it out of there. It was a one-night stand after all, not a long-term relationship. Maybe…maybe he should stop stalling and go talk to Patricia himself.

———

Two hours hadn't been long enough to cruise away his jitters. If anything, the time had wound Trent up even more. Like a four-year-old on five cups of coffee. He killed the engine of his Harley and shook out his hands, flinging nervous energy from his fingertips. It was ridiculous, this jumpy feeling that had his muscles twitching and prevented his lungs from taking a complete breath.

He stared at the single-wide. Just one of dozens lined up on their tiny lots. Besides showing its age, the trailer had a homey feel about it. Hanging plants from a small covered porch, banana trees reaching to a roof that looked like it had been recently replaced, small driveway swept clean. None of it calmed the zinging inside his chest.

Move. The single-word command had its desired effect. He dismounted the motorcycle and walked to the front door. No doorbell. He opened the storm door and knocked, taking a step back as he lowered his arm. Hopefully Patricia was home. He probably should have called first, but he hadn't known what to say. *Hi, you don't know me, but can you tell me the name of the guy you hooked up with twenty-six years ago?* Pretty sure he would've been answered with a dial tone, or worse.

Footsteps sounded in the house, and the door creaked open. A man stood in the doorway.

"Oh." Trent mentally stumbled. From what Summer and his little Internet research had said, Patricia was single and lived by herself. He hadn't expected a man to answer the door. The guy looked familiar though. Had they met before?

"Trent, isn't it?" The Tom Selleck look-alike, all the way down to the mustache and Hawaiian shirt, extended his hand.

Trent shook it. "I'm sorry. I've forgotten your name."

"Mark."

Right. The other guy that had been in Summer's office that day with Jonathan.

"Are you looking for Patty?"

"Umm, yeah, is she here?"

Mark stepped to the side and opened the door wider. "She's fiddling with something in the back room. I'll get her."

Trent walked into the house and shut the door behind him as Mark disappeared. He soon emerged with a woman who looked remarkably like what Trent pictured Summer to look like in twenty-five years, only a little shorter.

"I've got some errands to run, so I'll go and let you two talk." Mark bent down and planted a kiss on Patricia's cheek. "It was good to see you again, Trent." Another handshake and then Trent was left alone with Summer's mom.

She took his measure, scanning him up, down, and up again. "So you're Trent."

There was nothing about the tone of her voice, her expression, the look in her eye, nothing to give away her thoughts. Did she approve? Disapprove? Setting aside judgment until she got to know him better?

He stepped forward and offered his hand. "It's nice to finally meet you, Ms. Arnet."

Her small hand gave his a light squeeze. "It's Patty."

First name basis. That was a good sign, wasn't it?

"Come on in and take a seat. Would you like some iced tea?"

"Uh, sure, that sounds nice, thank you." He sat on one end of a beige microfiber loveseat and scooted aside a small throw pillow decorated in geometric shapes.

Glasses clinked behind him, and Trent heard the suction of the refrigerator door as it opened, then closed. He picked at the corner of his cuticle and then buried his hand under his leg. Only females poked at their nails when they were nervous. If only he could convince himself that Patty was just another woman, he could charm her like a leprechaun with a four leaf clover. Then he could stop being nervous and doing stupid things like picking his nails.

"Here you go. I hope you like it sweet. I tend to put a bit more sugar in my tea than most people."

Trent took a sip and tried to keep his eyes from bugging out. He'd need a trip to the dentist if he drank that whole glass.

Patty sat on the opposite side of the couch and curled her legs under her. Her elbow poked the back pillow, and the side of her head rested in her hand. Every muscle relaxed.

He wished he could say the same thing.

"Now Trent, you're going to have to forgive me." She sat up straighter and folded her hands in her lap. "There's a question that keeps coming to my mind. It's archaic, and I've tried to forget it, but I can't stop thinking about it."

Trent set the tea glass on the coffee table. "What question is that?"

Her eyes lasered him. "What are your intentions with my daughter?"

Intentions? Whoa. So this was what a deer caught in the headlights of a tractor-trailer felt like.

"Uh…" Nothing. His mind was completely blank. Like a TV with the power turned off.

What had Summer told her mom? As far as he knew, she still thought he'd start chasing after other women any minute. He hadn't had enough chances to build her trust in him yet.

"Your reputation precedes you, and Summer is my little girl. I don't want to see her get hurt by someone like you."

Was it hot in here, or was it just him? He ran his finger along the inside of his collar, pulling the material slightly away from his throat.

"Are you or are you not a ladies' man? Trifling with young girls' hearts and then leaving them to pick up the broken pieces?" Patty's shaped brow arched high on her forehead.

How was he supposed to answer that? Ladies' man? Yes, that probably described his actions toward women in the past. Leaving them with broken hearts? He remembered the note left on the pillow a few weeks before. Not likely many shattered hearts. They'd all used him as much as he'd used them.

Trent met the icy blue eyes of Summer's mother. Mama bear protecting her cub. That revelation eased some of the tension collecting in his shoulders. She wasn't attacking him personally. She was only trying to protect her daughter. What could he say that would put her mind at ease?

"I'm not going to lie to you, Ms. Arnet. I've been with my

fair share of women." Patty's face pinched, and he winced. Maybe the complete truth hadn't been the way to go. No backing out now. He plowed ahead, hoping he'd say something that would douse the sparks shooting from the woman's eyes. "But there's something different with Summer. Something special. When she smiles, she lights up the room. She's feisty and fiery and we butt heads, but she's also amazingly talented and creative and sensitive."

Slowly the lines around Patty's eyes and mouth softened.

"To tell you the truth, I'm completely captivated by your daughter, ma'am."

A hint of a smile curled the corner of her lip. "That's a pretty good answer, and I'm going to choose to believe in its sincerity."

"I'm being completely sincere. I've never felt for any woman how I feel for your daughter." He laughed without humor. "I just have to convince her of that fact."

"Summer can be a bit stubborn, but persistence usually wins out in the end." She leaned over and patted his leg. "So why are you here, Trent? I doubt it's to have this particular conversation."

He chuckled. "No, not exactly." Although the topic he was about to broach would be equally uncomfortable.

Patty took a sip of her tea. "I'm listening."

Where should he start? "I want to do something for Summer, but I need your help."

"Intriguing. How can I help?"

He licked his lips. "Summer has mentioned several times how wonderful a mother you are. You two seem to have a great relationship."

"It's been just the two of us for a long time."

"And that's great. Really."

"I'm sensing a 'but' here."

He ran a hand through his hair. This was a sensitive subject—*fragile, handle with care* written all over it. "No one was meant to be both father and mother to their child, Patty. As terrific a job you did as a single mom, there's still something missing in Summer's life. A piece you can't fill by yourself."

Trent felt like a cad as Patty stared out the window of the living room, moisture collecting in the corners of her eyes. This wasn't going well. He'd insulted the woman by implying she wasn't good enough. That her daughter was somehow not whole and the fault lay at Patty's feet.

He scrubbed a hand down his face. "I'm sorry. I didn't mean to—"

She looked at him, a tear slipping over her cheek. "No, you're right. I've seen it too. The way she used to look so longingly at other dads in the neighborhood when they played with their kids."

Instinct took over at the sight of her distress, and Trent scooted over, wrapping his arm around her shoulders. "I want to find Summer's dad for her."

Patty sniffed, then pushed back so she could look at him. "Does Summer know what you're planning?"

He shook his head and let his arm fall back to his side. "I want it to be a surprise."

She seemed to be chewing the inside of her cheek. "You might want to talk to her about it first."

Why? "You don't think she wants to meet her dad?"

"I don't think she knows what she wants, besides changing the circumstances of her birth. But I can't change that. And I can't change that she didn't grow up playing catch with a daddy who adored her. As far as reality..." She shrugged. "If

Summer really wanted to meet her father, she could have. I've kept tabs on him all these years."

None of it made sense. If Summer had a dad-sized hole in her life, why wouldn't she fill it, especially since the man's location wasn't a mystery after all? "Did you ever tell the father he had a daughter?"

Patty's cheeks flushed pink. "No. We hooked up one night after a few too many drinks at the bar. When I realized I was pregnant a few months later, I did go to tell him. I never made it out of the elevator of his apartment complex."

"Lost your nerve?"

A scornful laugh ejected past her lips. "I didn't think he'd want to be interrupted. He and a blonde were going hot and heavy. Couldn't even wait to get his front door open."

Trent cringed. "I'm sorry."

She waved away his condolences. "It's not like we'd been in a serious relationship. At least this way Summer knows she wasn't rejected by her dad, because he doesn't even know she exists." Patty hung her head, and Trent squeezed her shoulder.

The picture she'd painted struck too close to home. There weren't any children running around with his genes coursing through their bodies, were there? He'd always been safe, always used protection. Had it been enough?

He clenched his eyes tight, trying to wring the uncertainty and sudden self-abhorrence from his mind. "Why do you think she's never contacted him?"

"Plain and simple? Fear."

"And if I contacted him for her?"

One thin shoulder lifted. "It could go either way."

It was his turn to stare out the window, although there wasn't much of a view—just another single-wide that had seen better days.

What should he do? He'd been certain that once Summer met her dad, she'd see the ridiculousness of the idea of a heavenly Father. There was also the possibility she'd see his grand gesture and start to take his feelings for her seriously. Was that still the case, or would he be opening her up to greater pain? He could always contact the man first, and if her father didn't want to have anything to do with Summer, then Trent could just not tell her that he'd talked with her dad. Then again, maybe the man would be thrilled to learn he had a smart, successful, daring woman as a daughter.

A fat bumblebee buzzed around the yellow blooms that hung from the porch. In his peripheral vision, a small brown bird swooped in and perched along the railing. Trent shook his head and chuckled under his breath. Ironic. Birds and bees show up at that particular time when the conversation hovered around parentage.

"Would you like Dave's information? That's his name. Dave." Patty's voice snapped his attention back around.

"Please." There were always worst-case scenarios, but he'd shield Summer from any hurt. She didn't have anything to fear, because he'd be there for her. He wasn't going anywhere. The sooner she realized that, the better. Besides, he had to show her the truth. Fathers came in flesh and blood and didn't reside on fluffy clouds or sit on golden heavenly thrones.

Patty walked to a small bookcase with two shelves and bent down to retrieve a turquoise pottery jar. She sifted around in it and brought out a folded Post-it Note. Her fingers pried open the paper, and he watched as her eyes scanned the writing. She folded the paper back over and handed it to him. "I hope you and this—what you're trying to do for her—I hope it will make my girl happy. That you both will finally make her feel full up to the top and flowing over."

And to know the love of Christ which surpasses knowledge, that you may be filled up to all the fullness of God.

Trent groaned inwardly. Twenty years later and Bible verses his mom had forced him to memorize as a kid were still lodged in his brain. Guess it was no different from knowing the story of Peter Pan, although a lot more annoying.

Trent took the paper. "I'm going to try my hardest to make your daughter happy. I promise you that." He unfolded the paper. *Dave Landstrom, 551 Juniper Rd, DeLand, FL.* Where was DeLand? Google was definitely going to have to help him with that one.

"What about that sunken treasure of yours?" Patty picked up her glass of tea and took a long drink.

Trent stuffed the paper in his back pocket. "It's been there for over three hundred years. I don't think it'll be going anywhere in the next couple of weeks."

"And then what?"

"Then we'll dive down there and see what prizes the old girl holds."

Patty gave him a pointed look. "That's not exactly what I meant, and you know it."

Were they on to mother interrogation round two?

"I guess it depends. If the galleon had been full of gold and silver and on its way back to Spain, then I'll be set for life."

"You'd be content to leave the adventurous lifestyle behind? No more hunting after shadows of the past?"

He gave her one of his charming grins. "Life is full of adventures."

"Exactly. You don't need to be off chasing new ones."

Trent laughed. Seemed the Arnet ladies were full of spitfire.

"What if that galleon of yours is emptier than my bank account?"

How he hoped that wasn't the case. "I'll be teaching history when the school year starts."

She seemed to be considering that as she nodded. "Good to hear you have a stable backup plan."

Stable was one word to describe it. He'd probably go with dull or boring. At least there would still be summers available to hunt down those *shadows of the past*, as Patty put it.

Patty's head tilted to the side. "You know, I've heard teaching can be very fulfilling."

Fulfilling. They were back to that. The verse in Ephesians jumped in his mind again. The phrase grated on his nerves. It implied that he was somehow not already filled, that there was something lacking in his life.

Wasn't there?

Yeah. There was. And he had the ink on his arm to remind himself of it every day. The missing piece's name was Trevor, and no *fulfilling* job would ever take away the hole left in his life.

Chapter 24

"Two pounds of the regular salted peanuts please." Summer let one handle of her purse fall from her shoulder, then unzipped the bag and pulled out her wallet.

"That'll be five dollars." The roadside vender rolled down the top of a brown paper bag and held it out to her.

She counted out five one dollar bills and exchanged them for the sack.

The south had a few foods that were iconic—grits, hominy, and boiled peanuts. And fried chicken, of course. But who didn't like fried chicken—with mashed potatoes and gravy followed by a warm apple pie with a lattice crust? Summer's stomach growled. No time for a decent meal, but when she'd seen the pickup truck with a posted sign on the side of the road, she hadn't thought twice about pulling over.

She slid into her PT Cruiser and cranked the AC. Steam escaped from the bag when she unscrunched the top. She took a deep breath of the briny scent. Heaven. A peanut squished between her fingers as she fished one out of the bag and placed it seam-side up between her front teeth. Salt water squirted in her mouth, and she sucked all the juice out, cheeks caving in. Sucked dry, she used her thumbnails to pry open the shell, then popped the small nuts into her mouth. Her eyes rolled into the back of her head as she chewed.

The ringtone of her phone interrupted her foraging for the next peanut. She didn't pay attention to the name that flashed on the screen. "Summer Arnet speaking."

"Summer, this is Tabitha Michaels from *Our World*."

Summer's breath hitched. Tabitha Michaels was calling her? She hadn't submitted anything new for consideration to the magazine, so why was the editor contacting her? Oh, who cared? *The* Tabitha Michaels was calling her!

"Look, one of our regular photographers is taking a leave of absence. The editors of the magazine have decided to fill the position with someone we feel has potential."

Waiting with bated breath was a real thing—not just something people said. Every nerve, every cell in Summer's body froze as anticipation rose faster than a drowning person to the surface of the water. She'd need a hyperbolic chamber after this phone call.

"There are three photographers we've had our eyes on. We've just been waiting for that perfect photo that proves at least one of you has what it takes to be an *Our World* photographer. You are one of those three, Summer."

Summer bit her lip against the squeal wanting to escape and instead stomped her feet in a sitting happy dance. This was it. Her dream was finally coming true.

"We only have the one position available, and three potential photographers. We've decided to give you each a chance to wow us. I need a sample of your work in my inbox by Friday. This has to be your best work, Summer. Don't play it safe."

Summer's face was going to split in two if her grin grew any wider. "I won't let you down, Mrs. Michaels."

"I look forward to seeing your work." A click sounded over the line.

Summer squealed and threw double-time punches into the air. "Yes! Yes! Yes!"

All she had to do was get the best picture of her life to Tabitha Michaels by Friday, and she'd be a real live *Our World* photographer. Goodness. That only gave her Wednesday, Thursday, Fri—three days. Was it even possible to arrange everything and dive off the Bahaman coast in such short time? Tickets would be expensive, but it could be done. Finding a hotel shouldn't be too difficult in the middle of the week, so really the only hurdle would be securing a boat and diving equipment. She'd scour the entire island if need be to find an oxygen tank and regulator.

The cogs of her mind shrieked to a halt. What if Trent was wrong? What if the shadows he'd seen in the great white photos were just that—shadows? If she went down there and didn't come back with *the* picture, then everything she'd worked for would be for nothing. She had one chance. One chance to prove herself and secure her spot among *Our World*'s greatest. What if she flew all the way to the Bahamas only to discover the sunken ship was a figment of Trent's imagination? The deadline was in three days. There wouldn't be any time to arrange a second dive in another location.

She needed to call Trent. Needed to hear his confident voice assure her that a three-hundred-year-old treasure really did sit at the bottom of the ocean. Her hands shook as she swiped the screen of her cell and punched in the four-digit passcode. Trent's number displayed among her recent calls. One tap and the phone rang in her ear.

She drummed her fingernail against the steering wheel. "Come on. Pick up."

"We're sorry, but your call has been forwarded to an automatic messaging system. Trent Carrington is not available…"

Summer groaned and pushed to end the call. She swiped at the screen and brought up the text messaging.

Call me ASAP.

Where could he be? She only had three days. That meant she needed to be on a plane. Pronto. As in, the next flight out. The next day would be devoted to diving and shooting pictures, and then she'd need a solid block of time to do editing. Every photo had to be perfect. She wasn't going to acquire another chance like this again.

Summer opened her contact list and typed Anita Carrington into the Search field. Maybe Trent's mom would know where he was.

"Hi, Summer. How are you doing, sweetheart?"

"I'm good, Anita, but I was trying to reach Trent, and he didn't answer his phone. Do you happen to know where he is? It's kind of important."

Anita clucked. "No, I'm sorry. I don't know where he is. Is there something I can help with?"

Make Trent materialize in the next five seconds? "If you hear from him, can you tell him to call me? I really need to talk to him."

"Sure thing."

"Thanks. I'll talk to you later."

Summer rubbed her temples. Now what? That galleon was Trent's thing. His dream. She was only along as navigator and to snap pictures, both to launch her career and to document his discovery.

If she didn't dive there, then where could she go to find the edginess that Tabitha Michaels was looking for? The Arctic and Antarctic Oceans held a number of dangers—both the elements and the animals. In fact Gloria Shupe, one of *Our World*'s most prolific photographers, had just done a layout where she'd swum with a leopard seal, a proficient and dangerous predator amid the frozen ocean. But Summer didn't have any connections in either the Arctic or Antarctic. She wasn't sure she had the guts for something like that either.

If not a creature with an element of danger, then how about one rarely seen or captured in photos? It could work. Actually, it would be great. Summer crossed her arms over the steering wheel and rested her forehead in the crook of her elbow. There was a reason those creatures were unique. They were hard to find. Time was against her. She couldn't waste a single second trying to hunt down something she might never see.

One thing was for certain—sitting in her car in front of the boiled peanut vender was getting her nowhere fast. She put the Cruiser into gear and pulled back onto the road. The phone on her thigh weighed on her leg. She glanced down at it, then picked it up, one hand still on the steering wheel. Holding the Home button for a few seconds activated the voice command.

"Call Trent Carrington."

"Calling Trent Carrington," the computerized female voice responded. Ringtones filled the inside of her car, but Trent's rich tenor voice never answered.

"We're sorry, but your call has been forwarded to the automated—"

A growl tore from Summer's throat. Where was he? She waited until after the beep, then left a short message. "Trent, I need you to call me. *Our World* is giving me three days to get them photos that will impress. This is my shot. Call me."

Hopefully he'd hear the message and call her back soon. If not… She shook her head. That wasn't a possibility.

She pulled her car into a vacant spot in front of her building and killed the engine. Purse and peanuts in hand, she shut and locked the car door. Disappointment slithered its way down her spine. It was irrational, but she'd held on to a thread of hope that Trent's Harley would be parked along the street. He'd made a habit of just showing up, and she'd so wished that would've been the case today.

The key slid into the lock, and the dead bolt turned. Summer dumped both bags in a chair by the door then walked to her desk and wiggled the mouse. She typed in the password and waited for the computer to boot up.

Where was her phone? Now wasn't the time to be leaving it on vibrate in her purse and missing Trent's call. She walked back to her purse and plucked it out. Her thumb pressed the home button, but the illuminated screen didn't show any missed calls or texts.

Sitting in the black swivel chair behind her desk, she opened the web browser on her computer, then typed in her favorite travel website. She inputted the dates and location and waited until a list of possible flights showed on the screen. The next available flight was in twenty minutes. It took longer than twenty minutes just to get to the airport. Her eyes scanned the listings as she clicked the down arrow on her keyboard. There. A flight in three hours. Her finger hovered over the left click button on her mouse.

Number one rule of diving—always bring along a buddy.

She glanced to the phone on her desk. The screen reflected

the light shining overhead but was otherwise black. She snatched it up and quickly unlocked and dialed.

"We're sorry, but your call has been forwarded—"

Seriously, how could this be happening? Why have a cell phone if you don't answer it?

The phone beeped. "Trent, I'm booking a flight that departs at 7:10 for Nassau. Delta flight A4675. If you get this message, then head to the airport and meet me there. I'm going to try to get a room at the same hotel where we stayed last time. Please, please be there. I'm"—she sighed and let her head fall forward onto the heel of her palm—"I'm going to call Jonathan after I hang up. I hope you understand."

Calling Jonathan? Not her first choice. But what else was she supposed to do? There weren't any other options available. As she slid to Jonathan's contact information, she shut her mind to the possible ramifications. A girl had to do what a girl had to do. That was all there was to it.

"Summer. What are you...I didn't expect...uh...hi." Surprise and pain filled Jonathan's voice.

Darts laced with guilt pierced her heart, and the bubble of excitement she'd been riding around on since Tabitha Michaels's phone call popped. Summer hit the ground of reality with a thud. Maybe calling Jonathan hadn't been a good idea.

She cleared her throat and tried to sound unaffected. "How have you been? I've missed you."

Jonathan moaned. "That's not fair, Summer."

Moisture built in Summer's eyes. "I know, and I'm sorry, but it's the truth. You were my best friend. *Are* my best friend. Please tell me I haven't lost you." She sucked in her bottom lip between her teeth.

Jonathan exhaled hard. "You haven't lost me."

Summer's teeth release their prisoner.

"But I need time. You can't expect me to move on in a second."

"How about three hours?" She braced herself for his answer, calling herself all kinds of heartless.

"Excuse me?"

"I need you, Jonathan. I know you said to give you time, but I need you. In three hours. Tabitha Michaels called, and *Our World* is giving me a chance, but I have to have the perfect photos in her hands by Friday. So I'm hopping on a plane tonight for Nassau, and I need you to come with me."

Silence stretched until she thought her nerves would break.

"What about Trent?"

The derision in his voice was unmistakable but not unwarranted. "It's not like that. Besides, I can't reach him. I left a message for him to meet me there, but there's no telling when he'll hear the message, and it might be too late."

"Let me get this straight. You want me to go to Nassau with you, the very place you broke my heart—"

Summer winced.

"Not only that, but there's a chance that *he'll* show up, rele-gating me to third wheel, and I'll have to sit quietly by and watch you two both realize your dreams together?"

Cruel. Insensitive. Selfish. What had she been thinking? Yes, she wanted that spot in *Our World*, but nothing was worth this. She'd find somewhere else to take the pictures. If she stayed local, then maybe she could even hook up with a group dive or something semiprivate through a company.

"I'll do it." Jonathan's voice wavered. "You're killing me, but I'll do it. This is your dream. What you've been talking about for years. I could never take that away from you."

"No. Jonathan. You don't have to do that. I shouldn't have even asked. I'll just stay local, and—"

"Summer, stop. I said I'll do it." His voice lowered. "I'd do anything for you."

Summer brought her legs up in front of her and hugged her knees. She didn't deserve his friendship. "I wish..."

"Don't say it. I know."

A tear slid down Summer's cheek.

"So..." Forced levity pushed Jonathan's words. "What's the flight info?"

———

Trent straddled his Harley, his feet planted on either side of the powerful machine. First in line at the red light, he had an unobstructed view of the car dealership catty-corner to him. Dave Landstrom hadn't returned his e-mail or his phone calls. Didn't speak well of the man's character, but Trent had determined not to jump to any premature conclusions. Of course, the lack of communication left him only one choice. Confront the guy face to face.

Conspiracy theorists were always paranoid about Big Brother knowing their every move, but a quick Google search could let any Joe off the street get a glimpse of your life. For instance, Trent now knew Dave Landstrom, a.k.a "The Storm" to his high school football team, was five foot nine inches and carried about ten extra pounds around his midsection. He had light-blue eyes, and his surfer blond hair was beginning to thin on top. The man had married a decade and a half ago and had three children—a boy, a girl, and another boy. He worked at one of the used car dealerships in town—apparently

DeLand was full of them—and even coached his youngest son's Little League team.

Dave must have changed quite a bit since Patty had hooked up with him. Now he was the family man, not the ladies' man. Which bode well for Trent...er...rather, it bode well for Summer. Summer, who desperately needed her father in her life, so much so that she substituted him for an aloof deity.

The light changed to green, and Trent turned the throttle on the bike's handlebars, zooming forward. Courtesy led him to meet Dave at his work instead of his home. It wasn't Trent's place to throw the grenade of an illegitimate child in the midst of the Landstrom family.

Trent pulled into the dealership and then cut the engine. He'd no sooner slid his helmet off than a voice spoke from behind.

"Looking to trade in your motorcycle for something with four wheels?"

Used car salesmen were like leeches—get warm bodies within their radar and they'd latch on and suck them dry.

"We get a lot of guys in here, their wives forcing them to trade in their bachelor rides for something more family friendly."

Trent scoffed. A woman would have to pry his rigor mortis hands from around the handlebars of his bike before he'd trade it in for some soccer-mom ride.

He placed his helmet on the motorcycle's seat and then turned.

"Dave Landstrom." Trent grinned. Luck was surely on his side. He'd only have to deal with the one leech instead of wading through the pond of them drifting around the dealership.

Dave started, then scrunched his face. "Do I know you?"

Trent held out his hand. "Trent Carrington."

Dave shook it, his eyebrows still pinched in confusion.

"Name doesn't ring a bell? I sent you an e-mail a couple of days ago. Left a few messages on your voice mail."

Dave's eyes widened, and he took a step back.

"Is there somewhere we can talk?"

The guy's Adam's apple jumped. He cast a quick look over his shoulder.

Trent crossed his arms over his chest, disgust souring his mouth at the middle-aged man's show of cowardice. "It's either here or at your house, Dave. You could have just returned my call or answered my e-mail, but now I'm here, and I'm not leaving until we have a few words."

Sweat beaded on Dave's forehead and above his upper lip. He dabbed at his temple with the cuff of his oxford shirt. His weight shifted to the other foot, and he scanned the line of cars opposite them. Probably wishing he could dash to one and make a mad getaway. Putz.

"Are you interested in one of our functional crossovers?"

Trent followed his line of site to a newer white Dodge Durango. "No, I'm not interested in a crossover."

"You sure you don't want to see the inside?" He inclined his head toward the vehicle.

This time Trent looked past the vehicle. A man in a suit stood watching them from behind the floor-to-ceiling glass of the showroom. Dave's boss?

"Sure. Show me the interior." At least there they'd have some sort of privacy.

Dave's posture relaxed slightly. "I'll go get the keys and be right back."

"Make sure you do." Trent watched the guy scurry into the

building. What had Patty seen in him? Granted, he could have changed quite a bit in twenty-six years, but still.

Trent shoved his hands into his pants pockets. He felt eyes on him and, sure enough, the suit was still watching. Creepy.

A few minutes later Dave returned and unlocked the Durango's doors. Trent slid behind the wheel, the leather seats crackling beneath his weight. Good thing he had the protection of his jeans, or the hot leather would have burned his legs. Already the car held the heat and humidity like a sauna. No way he was sitting in a closed vehicle in the middle of summer. They'd both boil their insides. He reached over and snatched the key from Dave's hand. The car cranked right up, instant air blasting from the vents on the dashboard. Hot, but pretty soon the Freon would work its magic.

"Look, what do you want from me?" Summer's sperm-donor father squared his body in the seat so he faced Trent. At least some backbone was beginning to show again. Maybe the guy gained a bit of his courage back now that his coworkers couldn't overhear the conversation.

"I want you to meet your daughter." Plain and simple.

"This other girl you claim is my daughter?"

"Dude." Not cool. Not surprising, but not cool.

And how would you respond if some girl showed up on your doorstep claiming you were her daddy? The thought sucker punched him in the solar plexus. He shook his head, trying to dislodge the unbidden image. He'd been careful. Used protection. Always. Besides, this wasn't about him. Not right now, anyways. It was about Summer. And Dave, of course. Sympathy for the guy wormed its way past Trent's initial dislike. He didn't want to think he could possibly be Dave in twenty years.

Dave ran a hand through his hair, making the thin strands

on top stick up. "What do you want me to say? Out of nowhere I get an e-mail and then several voice mails claiming I have a long-lost daughter who wants to meet me. Is it some kind of joke? Do you guys think you can get money out of me or something?"

Trent looked Dave up and down. His oxford shirt, no-name brand khakis, and scuffed penny loafers combined wouldn't have cost a hundred dollars. If someone wanted to target a man for child support or an inheritance or whatever, that person definitely wouldn't zoom in on Dave Landstrom.

"Summer isn't looking for a handout. She just wants to meet her father."

Dave's face skewed. "How do I even know she's my daughter? I don't remember any Patricia Arnet."

Trent sighed. "A one-night stand. I doubt you'd remember after twenty-six years."

"Still doesn't answer the question of proof. There's no way to tell if that girl is my kid or not." Dave crossed his arms over the bulge of his gut.

Had the guy never heard of DNA testing? Not that Trent wanted to go that far. He didn't want Summer to get wind that her dad was questioning his role as her father. Patty had warned Trent of Summer's fear of rejection. Asking her for some form of DNA so he could prove to her deadbeat dad he was her father could crush her. He could always steal some hair from her hairbrush without her knowing, but would some test convince Dave to step up and be the dad Summer had always longed for?

Maybe Dave would feel more comfortable easing into the role of a father of four instead of only three. Maybe if he talked with Summer over the phone first, got to know the wonderful woman she'd grown into, then he'd be proud and honored to be called her dad.

Trent slipped a hand into his pocket, but his fingers only connected with linty fabric. Where was his phone? *Don't tell me I forgot it.* Well, there went the idea of giving Dave Summer's number. He'd have to e-mail or text it.

Dave exhaled a long breath, and Trent nearly gagged on the tuna smell blowing in his face. "Look, this girl is twenty-six years old, right? She's all grown up. She doesn't need a father." He rubbed his forehead. "Even if she did, I can't be that guy for her. I have a family of my own. Three kids and a wife. It wouldn't be fair to them to dump this whole mess on their heads."

Disappointment, anger, a tightening sense of desperation —the emotions brawled it out until Trent's temper landed a knockout blow. "So that's it then? You're just going to turn your back on your own flesh and blood? Deny your kids a relationship with their sister?" He let out a humorless laugh. "You know, Patty had been afraid she'd come up short filling the shoes of a father figure. The woman had nothing to worry about." Trent exited the Durango and slammed the door.

Chapter 25

Atlantic Ocean, 1689

Isabella stood in front of the large window in Captain Montoya's cabin, cold seeping into her hand as it pressed against the glass. The view had not changed since the last time she'd stood in this spot. Still the vast ocean covered everything, no land in sight. The bow of the mighty galleon sliced through the surface like one might part a large crowd. Though the view was unaltered, she had changed immensely. No longer dressed in her stepfather's loose breeches and cotton shirt, she was now cinched in a gorgeous brocade gown, albeit also borrowed. Where before she had been a peer to the crew, free to come and go where her duties led, now she was a prisoner in these walls, a traitor to the laws of the sea.

It was easy to fall prey to the melancholy that stalked her, to allow herself a moment of pity for her circumstances. Had she not fled her home and all that she knew for a chance at a better life, a safer existence? But every step she had taken away from a danger of which she was aware had brought her to this place with more threats and perils than she could have imagined. Would she have been better off staying in Hernando's household? Or perhaps she could have used her grandmother's necklace to flee to another part of the country. Only a fool would have believed she could start a new life in the New World.

Frustration knotted her gut. What was the captain doing? Had he called his quartermaster out for the man's whispered mutiny? Could the clash of rapiers be heard on the wind? Or perhaps Captain Montoya had ordered the man to walk the plank. Not likely, as the captain was too much a gentleman for such roguish pirate behavior.

And what of *Tío* Pepe? Had he learned that her secret had been discovered? Was he even now trying to formulate some plan to rescue her? Or had the captain exacted disciplinary actions for her uncle's silence of her existence aboard the ship?

Isabella sighed and let her hand fall to her side. So many questions, and no way to obtain answers. She'd go mad if she didn't hear of any news soon.

The lock on the door jangled behind her, and she spun. So the captain had finally returned. She squared her shoulders and raised her chin. The bolt rotated, and the door creaked open.

The quartermaster. That dreadful man. What was he doing here?

Isabella took a pace back, her body colliding with the cool glass. Panic caused her heart to charge like the bulls in the annual run in Pamplona. Her eyes darted around the room. No other means of escape. The only recourse for her was to fight. She spied the small dagger Captain Montoya had left her on top of his desk.

The quartermaster shut the door and turned to bar it. Now was her chance. She sprung toward the dagger and enclosed her fingers around its white ivory hilt. It would be impossible to overpower the seasoned sailor, but perhaps a surprise attack would land her a mortal blow.

She dashed toward him, blade arced overhead.

The quartermaster pivoted, and his beefy hand caught her wrist. He swung her in front of him, slamming her body against the door. *Crack!* A sharp pain at the back of her skull shot needles through her head. Black dots danced in front of her eyes. The pressure of his forearm as he pinned her against the rough wood made it feel as if her chest would cave in on her.

Mere inches separated his face from hers, and the stench of rotten teeth rolled her stomach. He wrenched her wrist at an odd angle, and the dagger clanked to the ground. "Thought to kill me, did you?"

Isabella didn't respond. Instead she met his lewd gaze, determined not to show the fear that had her legs shaking or the pain that caused her vision to go foggy around the corners.

"When I'm done with you, it will be your blood seeping between these planks, not mine."

Díos.

It was a word. A prayer. The only coherent thought able to form in her mind.

The quartermaster lowered his arm, and Isabella drew a complete breath. Bile rose to her throat. Her free hand struck his pockmarked cheek, and the following sting upon her palm felt like a victory. She gave him a smug smile, but it slipped when he snatched the wrist of the offending hand and yanked both wrists above her head.

He leaned in close, his breath warming her ear. "A little fight will make this all the more fun."

She felt her eyes go as round as a piece of eight. Her hands were bound in his grip or she'd claw his eyes out. The only weapon left to her was her legs. He stood close, which made her target accessible. With all her strength she thrust her knee up and into her captor's groin. A curse erupted past sneering lips as his hands fell away and he doubled over.

The dagger. Isabella spied it on the ground mere feet from her. She sprang toward it but was caught around her middle and hoisted in the air, her back thudding against the vile man's chest, his arms encasing her and cinching like a corset from *el diablo*.

He cursed and began to drag her farther into the room, away from the door and the dagger.

Isabella screamed and thrashed about, kicking and frantically pushing at his thick arms. Any means of escape, of fighting back, were inching away from her. One hand clamped over her mouth, and she did the only thing she could think to do. Her teeth sank into the calloused, filth-stained flesh of his palm.

"Ah!"

Isabella was flung like a sack of rice and landed hard on her rear. The contact wasn't quite so jarring nor the descent as far as she would have thought. A quick glance down uncovered the reasons.

He'd thrown her atop the captain's cot.

Indignation rumbled low and deep in her chest. She'd not fled her stepfather's unwanted advances just to face the same fate with another man.

The quartermaster towered over her, trapping her. "What did you tell him?"

"I said not a word." *Dios* forgive her for breaking the ninth commandment, but this man would have no qualms disobeying the sixth—for he had murder in his eyes already.

"I do not believe you."

Isabella's gaze darted to the door. *Pepe, where are you?* She waited a second, but no one rushed through the door to her rescue. No one ever had, and it appeared no one ever would.

She looked back to the quartermaster, the hard planes of his face, the puckered skin of a jagged scar above his left brow, the promise of violence in his gray eyes.

All caused her insides to quake.

"If the captain had knowledge of your subterfuge, do you not think he would have done something about it? Bound you or cast you off the ship altogether?"

The quartermaster narrowed his eyes but seemed to be considering her words. She licked her lips and continued, "Your warning rang true. Besides, it is not my battle or my concern. I only want to arrive at the New World. Nothing more. The treasure, whether it is to go to the king or to you, I care not."

His lips turned up at the tips. "Maybe there is some sense in that pretty little head of yours after all."

His gaze raked over her, and a shiver raced down Isabella's spine.

"Some sense, but not much." He leaned closer, his look lusty.

She slanted away from him, trying to maintain some distance while suppressing the fear threatening to paralyze her mind.

"We have been at sea for weeks now. Too long for a man to

go without the comforts of a woman." He reached out and trailed a finger down her neck.

Reflexes moved her muscles, and she swatted his hand away.

In a blink he brought his hand and encased it around her windpipe, crushing and cutting off all oxygen. A strangled sound tore from the back of her throat as she smacked at his arm and pried at his fingers. His hold remained secure. The corners of her vision became cloudy and darkened.

"You will be taught your place, and once you have learned it, maybe I will decide to spare you your life." He let out a malicious laugh. "You can be an added bonus for the boys once the ship is rightfully in my command."

Death would be preferable, which, if she didn't fill her lungs soon, would be her fate.

The quartermaster loosened his grip around her throat and shoved his hand into her hair, grabbing a fistful and yanking her head back. Her chest expanded with an intake of breath, but there was no reveling in it. No moment to thank the good Lord for that which she'd taken for granted all her life—the ability to breathe.

Her scalp tingled from his grip on her hair, but revulsion soon covered any of her physical discomforts. His mouth, warm and wet, descended upon the exposed skin of her throat, and she felt the rumble of his moan.

Frantically she pushed against his chest, but she might as well have been pushing against a brick wall. No. A brick wall she would welcome. A brick wall stood in its place, unmoving. The quartermaster was no wall, brick or otherwise. His body moved ever closer until he was upon her, crushing her.

Bang!

The door burst open. The sudden interruption whipped

the quartermaster's head around. His eyes, dilated with desire, appeared sluggish in calculating the interference of his lascivious intent.

If only she were stronger or had a better angle—one where a large man wasn't pinning her down—she'd take advantage of his distraction. As it was she could barely wiggle beneath the man's weight. She strained against it and craned her neck to see past the quartermaster's bulky frame. Who had saved her from certain defilement?

Captain Montoya stood at the entrance, feet spread in a battle stance, the promise of a fight flashing in his black eyes. One arm crossed his body as he marched into the room, hand ready on the hilt of the sword strapped to his waist. His boots thunked against the floor, and Isabella thought she'd never heard a more blessed sound.

"Unhand the woman, Romero."

The quartermaster's jaw tightened, but he raised his hands into the air.

Slowly the crushing weight lifted off Isabella's body. She shuffled to the other side of the cot and then caught the captain's gaze. He motioned behind him with his head. Message received, although not necessary. She would happily put as much distance as possible between herself and the quartermaster as she could.

Tío stepped through the doorway, and she scurried into his outstretched arms. He ran his hand over her hair and kissed the top of her head. "Are you well, *mi sorbina?*"

She nodded into his chest. Another minute and she wouldn't have been. As it was, she felt bruised and shaken, but at least she was still whole.

"What trouble you have brought aboard my ship, Romero, and after everything I have done for you." Captain Montoya stopped a few feet in front of the quartermaster, his hand still poised on his weapon.

Hatred rolled off the quartermaster's body like steam from a boiling pot. "I would be in command of my own vessel if not for your report."

"You would be rotting in prison, or worse, swinging from a noose, if not for my intervention." He shook his head. "It seems I only prolonged your fate."

The quartermaster's lips pressed into a thin line. "I'll not do either."

Isabella would not have thought a man Romero's size could move with the speed he did. Quicker than the flick of a matador's cape, he removed a blade from his knee-length boots and lunged at Captain Montoya's middle. The captain jumped back as the sound of his sword coming free of its sheath rent the air.

Romero lunged again. *Zing*. Metal clashed against metal.

Isabella's heart raced. *Tío's* arm held tight around her shoulder, comforting but also perhaps a little restraining. Did her uncle know she thought to help the captain? It was uncertain which opponent had the upper hand. Romero's blade was short but ghastly, while Captain Montoya wielded his rapier like an extension of his arm.

Captain Montoya parried another attack, this time a slash intended to cut his face. He weaved to the side and then brought his sword up at an angle. The quartermaster hissed through his teeth and clutched his midsection. He pulled his hand away. Blood not only tinged his fingers but seeped from the long gash under his rib cage. Face already flushed, the color deepened with fury.

Isabella expected the quartermaster to roar and advance

with a volley of powerful blows. Instead he circled the captain with deliberate steps.

Captain Montoya matched Romero's stride. Footstep answered footstep. The captain's shoulders bunched under his leather jerkin, eyes alert to any movement that may need to be deflected or any opening that would provide a good attack.

There must be something she could do. Why had *Tío* Pepe not brandished his sword and joined in the foray? Surely between him and the captain they could defeat Romero in minutes. The standoff between the two men pulled her nerves so tight she thought they'd sever completely. Still they circled each other with the speed of a *tortuga*. She was not fooled, however. That turtle could turn into a tornado in any second.

As if to prove her point, Romero sprang forward. The captain didn't meet the oncoming blade with his own, but spun away from it in one fluid motion, landing his elbow in the back of the quartermaster's head. The large man stumbled forward, but Captain Montoya did not pursue.

Why didn't he slice the vile beast into pieces? If Isabella had her dagger and the skill in which to wield it, she would not hold herself back, as the captain seemed to be doing.

"Will you yet surrender?" Captain Montoya still stood in position, ready if Romero came at him again.

The quartermaster looked up and spit near the captain's boots. "Never."

For the first time since the dual began, Captain Montoya struck first.

Zing. Clash.

Romero answered the captain's first two attack maneuvers, but then Captain Montoya's sword swung down, and the quartermaster's dagger clanged to the floor. He sprang for it, but the captain kicked it across the room.

"I ask you again—will you not surrender?"

The quartermaster dove for Captain Montoya's middle. His arms reached around the commanding officer's back, and they tumbled to the ground. The captain's rapier slipped from his grip.

Isabella covered her mouth against the sharp intake of breath. With a sword fight she'd believed the captain to be the better opponent, but in an all-out brawl? His lean muscles, though strong, were no match for the brawn and power behind Romero's sheer size.

Romero pushed himself up until he straddled Captain Montoya. His fist closed and slammed into the captain's head. Again. And again.

"Do something." Isabella quaked against her uncle's side.

He squeezed her shoulder, and she looked up into his face. Regret made his eyes appear heavy. "I am. I am doing what I should have been doing while Hernando was abusing you and *mi hermana* back in Spain—protecting you." His voice wavered as he struggled with his words. "I can never get my sister back, but I will not lose you as well."

Isabella opened her mouth to offer some condolence, to assure him it wasn't his fault Mama had died, but her words were cut off by the sound of crushing bones. She turned toward the sound. Blood oozed from the captain's lip and matted the dark hair of his goatee. Already his face was beginning to swell and color.

Isabella couldn't just stand there. If she did, Captain Montoya would surely die. But what could she do? She took a step forward, thinking that if she flung herself on Romero's back, it could earn the captain a moment to regain an upper hand.

The ship dipped, and she stumbled slightly to the right.

Ouch. The slippers the captain had made her wear to accompany the dress did not protect her feet quite so well as had Hernando's boots. She glanced down at the offending object, and hope lifted her heart from its miry depths.

Her dagger.

"Isabella, don't."

But it was too late. She swooped the dagger up, then lifted the hem of her skirt and sprinted toward the quartermaster, whose large body still hunkered over Captain Montoya, now limp.

She raised the blade above her head and plunged it into Romero's back.

Instead of slumping forward, he roared like a mighty lion and turned, the hilt of her dagger still sticking from where she'd driven it.

She stumbled and landed on her rear. She continued to shuffle back across the floor and away from his murderous stare. Her back hit the wall. There was nowhere else she could flee.

He loomed before her, a sadistic grin spreading across his face.

Every muscle taut, her legs and arms growing numb, she waited. Any second he'd crush her as easily as a cochineal bug, her blood brighter than any red dye gotten from the insect.

The seconds stretched, and the grin froze on his face. Her eyes slid down and landed on the point of a rapier extending from his stomach.

Isabella gasped.

The quartermaster stumbled forward and landed in a heap at her feet.

Chapter 26

Isabella covered her mouth and turned her head away from the sight of the quartermaster's lifeless body. Already she had been witness to too much death. First her mother, then Luis, and now another corpse lay mere feet from her. Would it ever end? She'd run for safety, but it seemed the angel of death would chase her to the ends of the earth.

Footsteps shuffled across the wide-plank floor, and she managed a peek from the corner of her eye. *Tío* Pepe stepped around Romero's legs and then hunkered down in front of her. His eyes searched hers.

She squeezed them tight against his probing. Exhaustion pulled on her shoulders, on her spirit. The brave mask and unaffected attitude she'd donned was slipping, and she hadn't the strength to right them.

The weight of her uncle's warm hand lay on her shoulder, and instead of crumbling under it, she drew comfort from his presence. Was he the one who'd come to her aid? Who'd thrust the sword through Romero's middle? Her eyes flicked to the prone body, the long blade and hilt sticking from his back straight into the air.

"Are you well, *mi sorbina?*" Juan's voice held concern, and Isabella felt something shift within her. It had been so very long since someone had cared for her well-being.

The numbness that had taken over her limbs was beginning to dissipate, leaving behind a tingling sensation. Like the summer sun thawing the winter snow, her fear melted away.

Captain Montoya shifted on the ground and then sat up, his hand held to his head. A moan escaped cracked and bloodied lips.

Isabella scrambled to her feet and stepped to his side, her uncle following in her wake. She knelt in front of the captain. Her hand lifted but stopped midair. Would her touch cause him more pain? One eye was swollen shut and already turned a purple to rival a field of Spanish lavender.

He held one arm protectively about his middle as he worked his jaw back and forth. He looked up, and his eyes locked on hers. They held as if connected by some unseen cord.

A ripple of awareness stirred in Isabella's belly. It hadn't been so long ago that those same black orbs had left her feeling intimidated. Now they filled her with...something else entirely. Something new—different. And not wholly unpleasant.

"It seems I have you to thank for preventing every bone in my body from being crushed." He turned his head to the side and continued speaking at a lower volume. "Although it wounds my manly pride sorely that it was necessary for you to have done so."

Isabella smirked but then covered her mouth with her

hand. She had no wish to wound his *manly pride* further by laughing at him.

The ship rocked from side to side, and her stomach rolled, her mirth falling away. She had grown used to the different motions of the vessel. The stillness when the wind died and the ship sat in the water like a log thrown into a large lake. When the winds picked up and the sails were hoisted, the ship bounced along, much the same way her father had bounced her upon his knee. Then there was the gentle swaying when the ship was turned in such a way that the waves lapped against its side.

The movement now was none of those. More like a naughty child rocking a cradle with too much force. Any more and the baby would likely fall right out.

The ship pitched again, and Isabella lost her balance and stumbled forward onto her knee. Her uncle caught her elbow while the captain grabbed ahold of her other hand.

Captain Montoya stood and helped her to her feet. Lines formed above his brow. He looked past her but a moment and then turned without a word and rushed out of the cabin.

Isabella didn't know a lot about ships, or the sea, or the men who commanded them both, but one did not need to possess great knowledge to understand the serious nature which had befallen them. For not even after she'd informed the captain of the planned mutiny had he marched off with such haste and determination. She took a step toward the door to follow, but *Tío* stopped her with a hand to her arm. She turned, and the same look that had taken over the captain's strong face owned her uncle's as well.

She laid her hand atop his. "What is it?"

"The weather has turned foul." He tried to brighten his countenance—for her sake, she was sure—but worry dampened any forced lightness. He pressed a kiss to her forehead. "Stay here below deck. I am going above to be of service."

Before she could respond, she found herself alone once more in the captain's cabin.

Arh! She wanted to scream. Men were so infuriating. Had she not proven herself capable? Was it not she who had come to the captain's aid, attacked a man more than twice her size, and even thrust her blade into his body without a quiver of doubt? If the captain and her uncle thought to protect her genteel faculties, then they were years too late.

The galleon continued to rear and buck worse than an unbroke stallion. She spread her feet and put out her arms to balance herself against the wild movement. Once she'd seen a boy place a plank atop a small cannonball near the docks. He'd stood on the wood, legs spanning so the ball was directly underneath him. Isabella had thought it would've been fun to see if she could balance upon it as well. Turned out it wasn't so fun after all.

The floor seemed to fall out from under her, and her chest slammed up against the wall. Grandmother's necklace dug into her skin, and Isabella winced in pain. Layers of material she'd used to bind herself protected against cuts from the large jewels, but they didn't add enough cushion to prevent bruising.

Weeks of sitting in the same spot, added with the crushing weight of the quartermaster when he'd pressed himself upon her, and she was ready for a few moments of relief from the family heirloom. Surely she could find someplace within the captain's cabin to hide a necklace. There'd be time before they reached the New World when she could come back and retrieve it.

She exhaled all her breath. It would be easier if she could

undress, but the buttons in the back of her gown would make that impossible without help. This would have to do. With her shoulders hunched, she reached between her breasts and dug through the torn fabric there until she felt something hard. She pinched the chain and tugged it free.

No matter how many times she looked upon the piece of jewelry, the awe she felt when viewing it never diminished. It was a circle of fine gold with alternating emeralds and diamonds. A larger emerald pendant with a teardrop pearl hung at its apex, which lay just below the throat when worn. Isabella remembered her mother wearing it once. She couldn't recall what the occasion had been, only that her mother had looked resplendent in her black brocade gown. The arms, bodice, and hem had been embellished with small green flowers, and her ruff was an intricate lace design instead of her everyday cotton. A gold chain had hung loosely around her waist. Isabella remembered the moment her mother had asked her to help with the clasp of the necklace. As soon as she had fastened the jewelry about her mother's neck, she'd looked up, and their gazes met in the reflective glass. The emeralds complemented the flowered embroidery, but even the beautiful gown and extraordinary necklace couldn't compare with her mother's radiance.

Hot tears stung Isabella's eyes. It was good to remember, but oh, did the memories bring an ache so great she thought her heart would cease to beat.

She took a shaky breath and waded through the past until she emerged once again into the present. The task at hand was to find a nice, safe spot for the necklace. Her eyes cleared of moisture as she looked about the room, avoiding Romero's lifeless body sprawled in the center of the floor.

The captain's desk? Had she not heard that some nautical

desks were equipped with secret compartments? She ran her hand along the underside, but her fingers skimmed solid wood. No grooves, no crevices. She jiggled the drawers, but they both held fast. Without a key she would not be able to open them.

She continued her search about the room. A chest lay along the far wall. Perhaps there would be a place to conceal the necklace there. The lid lifted without protest, and Isabella caught her lip between her teeth.

A glimpse of white cotton, then dark velvet with shiny brass buttons. Neatly folded garments rested in two piles.

She released her lip from its prison and let out a huff. Hiding her grandmother's jewels among a gentleman's clothing was not an option.

Where then?

The ship plunged, and Isabella pitched forward, landing hard on her hands and knees. *Oomph.* The necklace skittered across the floor, finally stopping when it snagged on a knot in the planks.

She crawled to it, not caring how improper it was for a lady to be in such a position, with her bottom in the air and scurrying along the floor like a babe. The necklace was her only chance at a new life. She needed it either with her or secure in a concealed location, not out in the open lying upon the ground where any person could spy it should he walk into the room.

When her hand pressed down on the plank beside the heirloom, it lifted. Isabella's eyes widened. A loose board? A childhood friend had often hid sweets from her siblings under a loose panel in her room. Her four brothers had never been the wiser.

Isabella pried the beam up, the wood creaking loud in her

ears. She flattened her cheek to the ground and closed one eye, straining to see in the small opening. It was dark, and she couldn't make anything out. That was a good thing though, *verdad*? It meant there was another layer of wood between the two decks.

Dios, protect the jewels, and may we all make it to the New World alive. She pressed her lips against the hard stone before shoving it through the small opening. For good or bad, it was out of her control now.

She took a deep breath and propelled herself back onto her feet. Now that *Abuela's* necklace was safely hidden, it was time to face the storm. No one could call her a well-trained sailor, but she had learned much the months she'd been at sea. Two extra hands could be helpful, and she was willing to put them to use.

Isabella braced herself along the wall as she walked down the corridor and up the rungs that led to the main deck. Salty spray slapped her face, forcing her to blink back the sting from her eyes. The sound of the wind and the waves roaring in her ears drowned out the shouted commands of the captain. He stood on the quarterdeck, his long black hair fastened with a leather thong at the base of his neck, strands being yanked out and flying wildly about his head as the squall raged with the temper of a toddler. He held the giant pegged wheel unmoving in his hands—the only still thing in sight. Sails flapped with the gusts, untied rope at the ends snapping like the whip of a carriage driver. Men scrambled to batten down hatches and pull down sails from the masts.

It was sheer chaos.

Her intent had been to help battle the storm, but now she knew that was pure madness. The only way they'd survive was if Jesus himself were on board and uttered the words *peace be still.*

A sailor hurried past her, and her eyes followed his progress. Everyone moved with a purpose.

Did she have a purpose?

Sí.

Luis had given her one—to take care of his son. Where was he? Her eyes roamed from one person to the next. All grown men. Not a child among them. When was the last time she'd even seen little Luis? So much had happened in such a short period of time that her mind was still spinning, trying to catch up. Had it really only been that morning that she'd been yanked awake by Romero on false charges of stealing? Without a doubt little Luis would have heard Benito was really a woman—*she* was a woman. She needed to find him and explain.

Cupping her hands around her mouth, she yelled, "Luis!"

The wind caught her words and carried them away.

A lump lodged in her throat, and she struggled to swallow it down. Now was not the time to let fear win. Someone depended on her, and she would not let him down.

She shuffled to the rigging of the mainmast and fell upon the ropes when the boat shuddered from the crash of a wave. Hand over hand she pulled herself along, her feet slipping from the water pouring over the deck.

Just a little farther.

It was hard to see, the sky dark as it was, water stinging her eyes, the wind blowing wet strings of hair into her face. Again she called the boy's name, searching through the pelting rain for a glimpse of his small frame.

Nothing.

She reached the end of the rigging and eyed the distance to

the steps leading up to the quarterdeck. Without support she doubted she'd stay on her feet for long. Muscles coiled, then she sprang for the ladder. Her hands scraped the rough wood, and she pulled herself close to steps, her forehead pressed to the top rung.

The ship rolled to the side, and she lost her footing. Splinters bit her palm as she clung to the ladder.

"Ah!" A stray barrel rolled into a crewmember, knocking him to the deck. The two bounced off the mainmast and continued to roll on the deck until they disappeared over the railing.

Isabella squeezed her eyes shut and turned her face away. A tear seeped past her lids, mingling with the rain and salty spray already dampening her cheeks.

No more. I cannot take any more. There was only so much strength in her bones, so much courage in her soul. And she'd used it all. There was nothing left. She felt wrung out —used up.

A hand descended from above. "I said take my hand." The voice shouted over the roaring wind and crashing waves.

Isabella lifted her head, and the captain's face came into view. The blood had been washed from his lip, but his eye remained swollen shut, a deep gash sliced vertically over his brow. She placed her hand in his. Strength flowed into her parched spirit.

He helped her up onto the quarterdeck but didn't release her hand. If he was here with her, then who was manning the helm? She looked around him, trying not to let her gaze rest too long on the way his soaked shirt clung to his body.

Pepe held the large wheel in his hand. Strain showed in the gritting of his teeth and the bulge in base of his neck that reminded Isabella of the roots of a tree—which was fitting since his feet were planted in place. She had seen many palms fall to the ground after a strong storm. She had no wish to witness her uncle topple.

Captain Montoya pulled on her hand and effectively brought her focus back to him. "What are you doing here? Were you not ordered to stay in my cabin?"

Now was not the time to worry about whether she had obeyed his instructions. Isabella quickly scanned the quarter-deck, but the only occupants were the three of them plus two sailors attempting to lower the sails of the mizzenmast. No Luis.

"Have you seen Luis?" She had to yell in order to be heard above the storm.

"What?" He lowered his head closer to hers.

"Have you seen little Luis?"

A shake of his head had her insides plummeting. Where could the boy be?

"It is not safe for you here. You must go back below deck."

Isabella nodded and turned to go. She'd search each level of the ship until she found Luis.

"Look out!"

There was no time to react. A wall of water rose and lifted the galleon high into the air and then came crashing down, swallowing it up in one famished gulp.

Chapter 27

Florida, Present Day

A four-hour drive had never seemed so long. Memories had chased Trent every mile of I-75 until he was loathe to admit they'd caught up and now tormented him like sadistic demons. They might as well have put on a horned headband and toted around a pitchfork like some Saturday morning cartoon.

Past logic for his actions seemed no more than water through a strainer. He'd run all the justifications through his mind—the women he'd been with were consenting adults, he had to find happiness and steal moments of joy where he could, he was just following the natural and biological course of the human race—until the defenses produced the same reaction as nails on a chalkboard. That muscles-seizing, teeth-gritting, eyes-squeezing, cringe-worthy reflex. Because even if his past relationships had been consenting, and even if some of the women had used him the same way he'd used them, that was the bottom line.

He'd used them.

Which meant his mom was right. A groan rumbled through Trent's chest. No man wanted to admit his mama was right.

You can try to fit a square peg in a round hole all you want, Trent, but nothing is going to fill that Jesus-sized void in your life but the Man upstairs.

He shook his head to try and dislodge his mom's voice, but even there she wouldn't be quieted.

You're searching for treasure, for recognition, for meaning. Don't you know, son, that your treasure is already stored for you in heaven, that your recognition comes from the Creator, and that your meaning is found in your status as a child of the King?

It wasn't a Jesus-sized hole though. It was a Trevor-sized hole. One put there by God himself. Or, at the very least, one that God could have prevented.

"Why'd you take him, huh, God? Didn't you know I'd be missing a part of myself when you let him die?"

A voice whispered that it wasn't his fault. Not if that hole had been created by someone else. All his decisions, the women he'd been with to fill the hollowness, it wasn't his fault.

Even as the thought registered, he pushed it aside. Only a coward didn't take responsibility for his own actions. He was an adult, a man. The guilt lay at his own feet. And the consequences.

Consequences. He had a few phone calls he needed to make as soon as he got home and found his phone. Meeting Dave Landstrom had been like looking into a dirty mirror, and the image had sickened Trent.

His Harley rumbled the last mile down the road, and he found himself wishing the drive had been longer. These weren't going to be easy phone calls to make. He'd rather wrestle an alligator than have this conversation—multiple times.

He killed the engine and propped up the kickstand. Mrs. Wheeley waved from two houses down, and he returned the gesture as he walked to his door and unlocked it.

No searching required. His phone lay like a beacon on the coffee table.

Trent took a deep breath. *Let's get this thing done.*

He pressed the Home button, and a list of notifications filled the screen. Maybe he should check and see... No. He shook his head. No procrastination and no distractions. He swiped the screen and brought up his contacts list.

Where should he start? Chronological order? Alphabetical? He rubbed his forehead with the pads of his fingers and hung his head. Shame soured his stomach.

He ran his thumb up the screen and stopped at the *D*s. Susan Daigle. Legs as long as Florida's coastline, with a personality just as flat. She had the art of body language down with come-hither eyes and not-so-innocent touches that promised more as the night wore on. They'd met at a club, the music too loud for any proper communication. Not that he'd been there looking for a chat. She'd be as good a place to start as any.

A tap on her name, then another on the Phone icon, and ringing sounded from the receiver. He pinched the bridge of his nose as he waited for her to answer.

"Hey, sexy. Calling to have a little fun?" He'd forgotten how sultry her voice sounded.

"No, Susan, that's not why I'm calling." He paused and

swallowed hard. Old habits died hard, and his traitorous body was reacting on its own accord.

"No?" Her voice took on a pouty tone. "That's too bad, because I miss you, baby. You and me, we always have a good time."

Hot. He put the phone on speaker and set it down, then shrugged out of his leather jacket and undid his top two buttons. Maybe Susan hadn't been the best place to start. He'd forgotten how strong she came on.

"I'm calling to apologize." There. He'd said it.

Her throaty laugh rang in his ear. "Apologize? Whatever for?"

She was going to make him spell it out for her. He pressed his thumb and forefinger into his eye sockets. "For using you."

She laughed again. "Honey, you can use me anytime."

Mouth gone dry, he popped off his couch and paced to the kitchen. A half-full bottle of Dasani sat on the counter. He unscrewed the lid and took a large gulp.

Now for the really uncomfortable part. "There's one more thing, Susan. We didn't…you aren't…you haven't…there's not a baby, is there?"

"Baby! Are you nuts?"

Yeah. He just might be.

"Look, Trent, you're good for a fun time and all, but if you're looking for a baby, then you've got the wrong gal."

The line clicked, then went dead.

Trent took a deep breath, then let it out slowly. Was Russian roulette this nerve-racking? One thing was for sure—he'd dodged the first bullet. Hopefully, none of the barrels were loaded.

Straightening his spine, he slid his finger up the phone's screen again, stopping this time at the *M*s. Marissa Morgan.

Sweet girl. Too sweet to have tangoed with him. Before he lost his nerve, he rapped on her name.

"Hello?"

So, unlike Susan, she didn't have his number saved.

"Marissa, this is Trent."

Silence hung over the line, and he wondered if he needed to add his last name. Maybe she didn't remember him.

"Hi." Her voice was small. Hesitant.

He rubbed his hand across the back of his neck. "How are you?"

"I'm good, thanks. Surprised you're calling, but glad. I've been wanting to talk to you, but every time I picked up the phone, God told me it wasn't the right time."

"God?" That was new. She hadn't been a Jesus freak before. He'd made it a point never to spend *any* time with them.

Except for his family, but that was different.

A nervous giggle. "He didn't *speak to me*, speak to me. Although that would've been cool. I just kind of got this impression that it wasn't time to talk to you yet, you know?"

No, he didn't. "Uh, is it okay to talk now?"

"I think the fact that you called me means that it's the perfect time."

This conversation was weird. He'd expected it to be difficult and uncomfortable, not wacky. He took another swig from the bottle of water. "I called to apologize. I knew I wasn't looking for a serious relationship when we met, and I took advantage of you."

Another pause. Unlike Susan's instant response, Marissa seemed to need time to process.

"Thank you. That means a lot to me. I take responsibility for my own bad choices though. But, Trent, I have to tell you, a month after we spent time together, I found out I was pregnant."

Pregnant. His head spun faster than the Tilt-A-Whirl at the county fair, and left him just as unstable on his feet. He did the math in his head. He'd been with Marissa five, six, no, seven months ago. That meant in two months he'd be a father. His hand reached out and gripped the edge of the counter.

"I'm going to be a dad?" His voice sounded breathless and far away, like it was someone else speaking.

"I'll be honest. I'm not positive the baby was yours."

Was. She'd said was, not is.

"Did you…"

"I miscarried the baby at fourteen weeks."

His mind was running a relay, one thought racing by, then passing the baton to the next.

"When I first found out I was pregnant, I was scared. No one plans on being a single parent, right? And I was ashamed because I wasn't positive who the baby's daddy was. But then I felt him move. He was real, you know? A part of me. I know babies grow in the womb, but I swear they grow in the heart too." Her voice shook. "When I lost him, I lost a part of myself. He took a part of me with him."

Trent knew. He'd been living that all his life.

Marissa sniffed, and he imagined her wiping at her eyes. "It still hurts, but I've since been able to see the blessing that came from the miscarriage."

Blessing? The word chafed more than a wool sweater. "How can you say that?" Although his voice came out harsher than he'd intended, so be it. Losing someone you loved could never be a blessing.

"Because of the miscarriage, I found God."

God again. Really? "God took your child. Maybe my child too. You didn't do anything to deserve that."

"Bad things happen to good people. And it hurts. But we can't blame God."

Trent's jaw tightened. He very well could blame God.

"There's sin in this world, and death and loss are consequences of that sin. But you know what? Every pain we feel? God feels it too. Every tear we cry? God sheds it too. He hurts with us, because He loves us." Her voice grew soft. "I felt Him, Trent. When I was all alone, my shoulders shaking from grief, I felt His arms wrap around me and His peace embrace me, and I knew. I wasn't alone. He was with me."

Trent deflated like a flat tire, and he sank to the ground, his back resting against kitchen cabinets. He pulled his knees up, laid his arms across them, and hid his head in the crook of his elbow.

"Can I pray for you?"

"I don't—"

"Father, I want to put Trent in Your hands. Open his eyes to see Your mercies and his heart to Your peace. Be real to him, Jesus. Let him feel Your presence and be filled with Your grace."

As Marissa prayed, a strange breeze stirred in Trent's kitchen. He lifted his head and looked around. Odd. All the windows and doors were shut. The wind moved about the room, as if taking on an entity. It caressed his face and seeped into his skin all the way down to his bones. His blood warmed and surged, and his chest swelled until he thought he'd burst.

Then all was still.

Trent lifted his face to the ceiling. *God?*

A blanket of peace covered him. It was too much. He let his head fall, and he cried.

Chapter 28

Summer woke early Wednesday morning and turned over in the hotel bed. The sliding glass doors to the balcony allowed for a spectacular view—the sun cresting the horizon, painting the sky in vibrant warmth of yellow and orange.

This was it. Everything hinged on today. All her career dreams would either be made or broken by what she discovered under the ocean's surface. Praying was new to her, but she bowed her head and folded her hands over the white duvet covering the lower half of her body.

"God, I know we aren't too well acquainted yet, but I read last night in the Bible I found in the bedside table that all good gifts come from you. Could you, perhaps, send me a gift today? This really means a lot to me. Thank you. Amen."

Not the most eloquent of prayers, but she'd remembered the *amen* at the end. Summer grinned as she recalled a prayer she'd read as a teenager from one of her favorite books, *Anne of Green Gables*. When Anne had ended her first prayer, she'd signed off with *yours respectfully*, much to the consternation of

Marilla Cuthbert. At least Summer was one step ahead of Anne Shirley.

Her phone vibrated on the nightstand. A text from Jonathan. *Up yet?*

Thumbs moved in a response. *Yep. I'll meet you in the lobby in 10 minutes.*

She tapped out of the conversation and quickly scanned her screen. No other calls or texts. Where was Trent? She thought she would've heard from him by now. He'd made such a big deal about this being a discovery of a lifetime that she figured he'd have hightailed it out here as soon as he heard her messages.

Was he otherwise occupied? Perhaps by a tall blonde or an exotic brunette? Her stomach soured as she pictured him with a woman on each side, his arms draped across their shoulders.

She pounded her forehead a couple of times with the heel of her palm to dislodge the image. So what if that was the case? It wasn't like they were an item. He was free to pursue anyone he so desired. Of course he did say he was going to prove her wrong about his character. She sniffed. Well, he was off to a great start. Hadn't been there when she'd called. Wasn't here now when she needed him.

Stop.

Needed him? She needed him about as much as she needed brain surgery.

Maybe it was a good thing he wasn't there. Everything seemed to get confusing when he was around. This way she could focus on what was important—getting the best shots for Tabitha Michaels. No hindrances, no distractions. While she was down there, she'd check out the ship, maybe take some photos for Trent so he could inspect them and see if it was worth his while to go back *on his own* and scope things out.

They'd be even then, and their business together would be over.

She could move on with her life. Maybe meet a steady, one-woman guy and get her heart back in order.

Speaking of order, sitting around musing all morning wasn't part of the agenda. She swung her legs over the side of the bed and rummaged through her suitcase for her swimsuit and wet suit. The black neoprene was easy to find, but she had to almost dump the entire contents of her suitcase to find the small green material that was her bikini. She sat on the edge of the bed and bunched the legs of the wet suit up, then stuck her foot through the hole. Tugging, pulling, contorting, she felt like a sausage shoved into a casing. A bead of sweat gathered on her hairline by the time she had the suit on her legs and up over her hips. She allowed it to hang and then fastened her bikini top between her shoulder blades. A quick braid down her back, and she grabbed the hotel card key. She slung her camera bag and a small duffel over her shoulder and headed down to the lobby.

Jonathan was waiting for her in one of the wingback chairs adjacent to the front desk.

She did a double take because he was without his glasses—a rare occurrence. "Ready to go?"

"Aren't you going to see if Trent arrived last night?"

She followed his finger and looked at the short woman behind the Carrera marble countertop. Should she check to see if he made it in?

You don't need him, remember?

She turned her head back to Jonathan. "If he'd come, then he should have called. Let's go."

Choosing to ignore his raised eyebrows, she marched toward the door.

"Something I should know about?"

She glanced over her shoulder as the automatic doors opened. "Nope."

"Reeeally."

The way he drew out the word irritated more than a mosquito bite. She jerked to a stop and turned to face him. "What's that supposed to mean?"

He shrugged and squinted against the early morning sun.

Summer punched her hands to her hips. "Say what you have to say, Jonathan."

"I just find it interesting that there's trouble in paradise already, that's all."

Having a tiff with her best friend wasn't on the agenda for the day either. "Look, I don't know what you think is going on between Trent and me, but it looks like you've got the wrong idea."

"Reeeally."

She poked him in the chest. "Stop saying that."

"I reeeally don't want to." A grin split his face.

Summer felt her own lips lift against her will. "You're exasperating. Now let's go."

They climbed into the rental car, with Jonathan behind the wheel. He turned left out of the hotel and headed toward the marina. A George Strait song played on the radio, and Summer found herself tapping her foot along to the beat.

Jonathan reached out and turned the dial of the radio, silencing the twang. He rubbed his hands along the steering wheel a few times and then glanced upward and muttered under his breath, "Why am I going to do this?" He sighed before gripping the wheel hard. "Look, I'm going to set aside my feelings for a moment and talk to you like a friend."

"Oookay." She adjusted the AC vents. Wet suits weren't exactly light and airy.

"What are your real thoughts about Trent?" He glanced her way and then back at the road.

My real thoughts? There were too many to sort out, and every time she tried, she'd been left with a headache. "He's an egotistical, flirtatious, thrill seeker who thinks all women will swoon when he flashes a crocked grin." *But he's also persistent and patient and seems to see me for who I really am.*

"And?"

"And he drives me completely insane because he never takes no for an answer and always manages to get what he wants." *But somehow I find that I enjoy myself in his company and in the end am grateful that he fought so hard to get his way—when his way was to spend time with me.*

"And?"

She let out a long breath. It didn't look like Jonathan was going to let up until he unearthed the whole truth. "And I can't stop thinking about him no matter how hard I try."

How would he respond to that? It wasn't too long ago he'd bared his own heart to her. She chanced a look at him and watched as his jaw hardened.

"But?"

She was surprised he was able to get the word out through clenched teeth.

The linchpin *but*. "But I know it will only lead to heartache, so I've been trying to deny my attraction to him."

"You know? Psychic now, are we?" The sarcasm at least softened part of his scowl.

An unladylike snort blew out her nose. "I don't have to be a psychic to see it coming. You know the kind of guy he is."

He looked quickly at her. "So you don't think he's serious about you?"

Her shoulders lifted. "He says he is. Sometimes I think so too. He even invited me to meet his family over Fourth of July."

"But?"

She looked out the window and watched as the palm trees whizzed by. "A leopard doesn't change his spots."

The car slowed, and Jonathan turned into the marina. He parked, then turned and rested his arm against the back of the seat. "I wish I could give you some kind of advice, but I can't." He scrubbed a hand down his face. "We've been friends for a long time, and I've loved you almost as long. I thought I could be that friend who could listen to your guy problems, but I was wrong. At least I can't now, not yet anyway."

She hung her head. "I'm so sorry."

He chucked her chin with a closed fist. "I'm the one who asked, right? So see? Not your fault." He pulled the key out of the ignition. "Now let's go find you the picture of a lifetime."

They walked toward the building off the side of the dock. A red painted sign with Boat Rental in large white letters stood tall along the roof. The door jingled when they entered, and the smell of fish bait assaulted Summer. She moved her camera and duffel bags to her other shoulder.

"Can I help you folks?" An older gentleman emerged from behind the counter. His skin was beyond tanned and more leathered than cowhide. Large hibiscus flowers colored his shirt—which was only half buttoned—and tufts of curly white hair poked from his chest.

Summer cleared her throat. "We reserved a boat and diving equipment for two under the name Arnet."

The man smacked his hands together. "Right and deedy.

I've already loaded the equipment onto the boat. You guys will be taking out my twenty-five-foot Boston Whaler. Woo-ee, she's a beaut and will treat you folks real good." He turned and perused a pegboard lined with keys. "Aha, here we are." He grabbed a pair from the second row, with an orange foam buoy keychain attached.

They followed the man out the door and down the floating dock, which gently rose and fell with each wake of a passing boat. They passed a menagerie of different vessels ranging from inflatable rigid hull open boats to towering grand yachts. Finally they stopped next to a midsized cruiser with twin engines and a green canopy casting shade over the central steering console. Two mounds of gear rested in the rear of the boat.

Summer turned toward the rental guy. "I'm going to check the equipment first, if you don't mind."

He held out a hand. "Be my guest."

Jonathan knelt on the dock and reached for the boat's railing, pulling it flush with the wharf. She smiled her thanks and climbed aboard, setting her bags on the ship's deck.

The boat swayed, and she used the railing to keep her balance as she made her way to the bow. Thankfully, everything seemed to be placed in an organized manner. Two buoyancy compensators along with four tanks were easy to spot. Two sets of fins, with masks and snorkels lying on top. Regulators, pressure gauges, weight belts. Everything looked like it was there. She quickly checked the tanks. Pressure and volume—all good. She looked to the guys on the wharf and gave them a thumbs-up.

"All righty. I have your credit card and your destination coordinates on file. We'll square up as soon as you bring her back in." The rental guy gave her a salute. "Have fun out there."

"Thank you," she said to his retreating back. She turned her gaze to Jonathan. "Why don't you do the buddy check before we head out? I don't want to take any chances and have to come back to shore because of faulty equipment."

Jonathan climbed aboard and started inspecting the gear. "Looks good to me. Ready to go?"

Anticipation surged through her veins like electrical currents through a wire. She bounced from one foot to the other. Yeah, she was ready. Born ready, as they said. These were going to be the best pictures of her life and she'd show everyone at *Our World* that she deserved a spot among their prestigious photographers.

Except...

A gray cloud of doubt rained down and short-circuited her optimism. Wouldn't she have seen a ship down there last time she'd been in the water? There hadn't been anything. She was sure. How could anyone miss a large sunken vessel? Everything hinged on this expedition—all of her dreams.

What about Trent's dreams?

No one could deny that a conscience had a voice. A sinking feeling pulled her down, and she swallowed against the bile in the back of her throat. Had Benedict Arnold felt this rotten before he turned traitor against the early colonists?

She gave herself a mental slap in the face. *Stop being so dramatic. You're not being a traitor. You called him a dozen times, and he never answered or responded. You can't put your dream on hold because of him.*

Good point. She had made every effort, even going so far as to call his mom, so it wasn't like she was excluding him on purpose. Tabitha Michaels had only given her three days. She couldn't sit around and wait for him and watch her dreams dissolve into thin air just because he couldn't be bothered to pick up a phone.

"Summer?" Jonathan gently shook her shoulder.

"Hmm?"

"I asked if you were ready to go."

"Oh. Yes. Let's go."

Jonathan climbed out of the Whaler, then bent to untie the thick ropes from the cleat hitch on the dock.

"Wait! Summer, wait!" called a voice near the shore called, and Summer turned and squinted. The boats in the water rocked back and forth, and a particular mast from a neighboring yacht swayed into her line of vision. She bent sideways at the hip to see around the offending obstruction and sucked in her breath.

Trent jogged along the two-foot-wide floating walkway, fire in his eyes. He came alongside the boat and hopped down onto the deck.

When Summer had initially met Trent Carrington, her first thought had been *striking*. That description still fit as he loomed over her, his face near inches from hers. Short blond stubble shadowed the lower portion of his face but couldn't hide the strong set of his jaw—which ticked at the moment. His hair had been pulled back from his face in a man-bun at the base of his neck, letting her witness fully the depth of emotion in his sky-blue eyes. Emotion so strong that it evoked fear in her. For whatever other reason was there for her to quiver?

"I thought we had a deal."

She swallowed past the lump in her throat. "You didn't return any of my calls." Her voice cracked.

Drat. She'd have to do better.

"So you were going to go without me?"

Weak excuses marched through her head, but none of them made her feel any better or would help defuse the situation. "Tabitha Michaels only gave me three days."

He swore under his breath and turned away from her. He took three steps, muttering so low she couldn't make out any of his words. Finally he stopped and dropped into the helm seat, rubbing his fingers across his forehead. "I've been calling you all morning, but you never answered."

Strange. She bent to the duffel at her feet and unzipped it. Her phone lay on her dive booties, backside up, safe in the Otterbox and Ziploc she'd put it in that morning to protect it against liquid threats. She turned the phone over and pressed the Home button. Six missed calls and voice mails. Just as many waiting texts. The thing hadn't been turned off vibrate mode from the night before.

She looked up at Trent, an apology on her tongue.

He'd assumed his normal pose—feet crossed at the ankles, fingers clasped and resting behind his head, a lopsided grin playing upon his face. Any vestiges of anger or hurt had disappeared—in their places resided calm confidence and nonchalance.

"I recall someone once asking me why I have a phone if I never use it."

Her own words used against her. "I'm sorry. I—"

He unhooked his ankles and leaned forward until his elbows rested on his knees. "All's well that ends well, right?"

"That's awfully generous of you."

One eye closed in a wink. "What can I say? I'm a generous guy."

Summer rolled her eyes, then tossed her phone back into her duffel and zipped it up. She looked at him, one hand going to her cocked hip. "Why didn't you use your phone yesterday? I must have called a dozen times, and you never once answered or called back until this morning. What were you up to?"

Trent's grin faltered, and he broke eye contact for a second before looking back at her and lifting one corner of his mouth. "Would you believe I accidentally left my phone at home?"

Yes. She could believe it. She'd done the same thing a few times. But leaving one's phone at home didn't elicit such a faltered reaction. What was he trying to hide? The blonde and brunette she'd pictured earlier returned to her mind.

And why should that surprise her?

It didn't. Not really.

What did surprise her was the ache it caused in the middle of her chest.

Chapter 29

What had happened? Trent scratched the back of his head. One minute he and Summer were teasing, and the next a curtain closed over her expression and he was left reeling, as if he'd missed something important.

She moved to step around him, but he reached out and captured her arm. Time stood still as she peered into his eyes and then snapped her gaze to his fingers holding her. His hand fell away.

He needed a do-over. Whatever he'd said to earn the cold shoulder, he needed to turn back time and not say it. She was acting like she had when they'd first met—aloof, distant, guarded. Hadn't he already broken down some of those walls? Proven—even if slightly—he wasn't the man she thought he was? Or even if he had been, he wasn't anymore. Why couldn't she see that and give him a chance?

Jonathan tossed the ropes that tied the boat to the wharf into the Whaler, then hopped down onto the deck. The boat drifted away from the dock and rocked with the lapping water.

The man looked at him with lowered brows, then flicked his head toward Summer.

Message received. Although Jonathan would have as much of a guess at what was going on as Trent did.

He shrugged and shook his head.

Jonathan narrowed his eyes, then turned. His shoulders hunched, and he brought his hands to his mouth. Beatbox sounds rent the air as he swayed and dipped.

Summer's head swiveled.

"Bahama mama, don't ya wanna dive down under that clear blue watta." Jonathan's hands jived in the air, and then he flicked his nose with his thumb. "Come back up with picture perfect. Don't object, because with all due respect, I predict your dreams come true."

The dude was a horrible rapper. Totally embarrassing.

Summer laughed, and the sound made Trent wish he'd been the one to make a fool of himself. Then maybe she'd be looking at him with a smile and gratitude in her eyes, instead of at Sparky.

Her gaze drifted to his, and her expression cooled. "We were just about to cast off before you showed up. We can wait while you grab some gear."

"Oh, that's okay." Jonathan put the key into the ignition, the orange buoy dangling. "He can use mine. I'll stay up with the boat while you guys dive."

Trent watched as Summer's gaze oscillated between him and Jonathan, her lip caught between her teeth.

"Are you sure?"

It was déjà vu all over again. The same reason Sparky had ended up in the Bahamas the first time around—she was using him as a buffer. Which begged Trent to question, why didn't she want to be alone with him? Did she not trust him? Or maybe she didn't trust herself when she was around him.

"I'm sure. Now let's go make all your dreams come true."

The engine revved to life, and Jonathan pushed the throttle forward.

Trent gripped the railing to keep his balance and watched as Summer shuffled around the helm to sit on the seat directly in front of the steering column. The short bench could technically seat two, but she'd dropped right down in the middle and stretched out both arms along backrest.

One side of his mouth quirked up. If she thought that'd keep him away, she'd better think again.

The boat cruised at a slow speed through the no-wake zone, and Trent easily walked from the bow to where Summer sat, legs crossed.

"Is this seat taken?"

She looked up at him but otherwise didn't move a muscle. "Yes."

"That's too bad." He plopped onto the seat, half his leg on top of hers.

"Hey!" Her thigh wiggled free from under his, and she scooted over.

They passed the Slow No Wake buoy sign into open ocean, and the boat burst forward with speed. The bow rose above the horizon, white spray arching at the fiberglass sides. Twin four-stroke engines, as well as the friction and displacement of water, caused a static louder than an entire percussion section.

"Why are you mad at me?" Trent shouted over the noise.

Summer crossed her arms. "I'm not mad."

He gave her arms a pointed look.

They unfolded. "Happy?"

"Not until you tell me why you're upset."

"I already told you—I'm not mad."

The wind pulled strands of his hair from where he'd fastened them earlier and whipped them in his face. "I'm not buying it."

One slender shoulder lifted. "That's your problem, not mine."

"Is it?" He rested his elbow on the backrest. "If it were only my problem, then these muscles right here"—his thumb followed the curve of her neck, over the thin strap of her bikini top, all the way down to where her clavicle met scapula —"wouldn't be so tense now, would they?"

She sucked in a breath and held perfectly still. "I don't know what you're talking about."

"No?" He let his thumb rub back and forth along her smooth skin. Every freckle dotting her shoulder begged to be kissed.

Green eyes turned toward him, and he read vulnerability in their depths. "Where were you yesterday?"

He didn't want to hurt her. Definitely didn't want to ruin the day she finally realized her dream.

"Do you trust me?"

She bit her lip, and her gaze wavered. "I want to trust you."

It was something, but not what he wanted to hear. "Please do. I promise I'll tell you, just...not right now. Okay?"

A sigh blew from her mouth. "Fine."

Good. It gave him time to figure out how to cushion the blow when he told her about her dad. If he could avoid it at all, pretend yesterday had never happened, he would. But then he'd have to break the promise he just made, and he could never do that.

The boat slowed, and the bow dipped back down as the

hull sank deeper into the ocean. Jonathan killed the engine, and water whooshed around them. He peeked over the low windshield. "We're here."

Trent stood and looked around. Nothing in sight except endless blue sea meeting endless blue sky. And hopefully endless possibilities.

Summer leaned over and unzipped the camera case at her feet. She brought out a large black square with knobs and buttons. Definitely the most high-tech camera housing he'd ever seen. A click of a button, and the display screen lit up. She pointed the lens in his direction, then brought the viewfinder to her eye.

He ran a hand down the front of his torso. "I doubt this is what your magazine is really looking for."

"Just a test shot, I assure you."

A splash off the stern brought his attention around, but it was just Jonathan dropping anchor.

Trent turned back around. "So what kind of pictures are you hoping for today, besides phenomenal ones?"

She looked up at him while she pushed her feet into booties. "Photos of a sunken treasure ship, of course."

"No sea life?"

Her lips bowed. "It did cross my mind that a sperm whale would be cool. They're known to frequent these waters. If I could get a shot of one swimming by the ship, it would give the photos a *Moby Dick* feel."

"Your Tabitha Michaels would eat that up, I'm sure."

She grinned, then scanned him head to toe. "Aren't you going to get ready?"

He'd snagged a wet suit at the rental place and had managed to pull it up to his hips before he'd dashed down the wharf after them, but he still had his white V-neck on and needed Ato suit the rest of the way up. Gripping the bottom edge of the shirt, he tugged it up. When his head popped free of the material, he found Summer sitting very still, staring. At his abs. He lowered his arms slowly, amusement dancing a victory jig in his chest. She could act cool and nonchalant, like his presence had no effect on her at all, but she was only lying to herself.

"Enjoying the view?" He grinned. Teasing her was too much fun.

Her cheeks infused with color, and she tore her gaze away. She reached for one of the oxygen tanks and brought it between her knees. Next came the buoyancy control device, or BCD, which she slid over the tank valve and then secured the device to the tank with straps. The dust cap came off the regulator, and she slid the regulator over the yoke valve of the tank and tightened the yoke screw. She attached the low pressure inflator to the BCD, and it clicked in place.

Trent watched as she opened the tank valve and checked the pressure.

Every movement performed with precision. How many times had she gone through the ritual before? After zipping his wet suit, he followed her example by readying his gear.

Jonathan jammed the diving flag, a midsized red rectangle with a diagonal white slash through the middle, into one of the slots on top of the roof.

By the time Trent hoisted his BCD on his back, Summer had finished slipping her mask over her head. Her top lip puckered from the soft silicone rubber encasing her face. He reached and outlined the pout with a finger. "Cute."

They shuffled to the stern of the boat, the fins on their feet making it awkward to walk. On impulse he stopped Summer with a hand to her shoulder. "I know this sounds weird coming from me, but I think we should pray."

She lifted the mask from over her eyes and let it rest on her forehead. "You do?"

"There's a story there, but we don't really have the time right now."

"Later?"

He nodded. "I promise."

Her eyes twinkled. "Wow. Two Trent Carrington promises in one day. I must be a lucky girl."

Luck had nothing to do with it, and he was willing to promise a lot more than an explanation. If only she'd trust him.

He held out his hand, and she placed hers in it. He looked over his shoulder at Jonathan sitting at the helm. "Want to pray with us?"

The man stood. "I didn't take you for a praying man."

"It's new."

One eyebrow lifted. "Losing some of your spots?"

Huh? "What are you talking about?"

Jonathan looked at Summer, his other eyebrow joining the first high in his forehead. "Never mind."

Something was going on there, but Trent didn't have a clue as to what, nor the time to find out.

He cleared his throat, nervousness suddenly making him antsy. "I've heard thousands of prayers in my life, but I'm pretty new at saying them myself." His weight shifted to the other foot.

Summer leaned in and whispered, "Your mom said to talk to Him like a friend."

Friend. Right. He bowed his head. "God, uh, thanks for this opportunity...for Summer. I hope it's everything she's always imagined and the pictures she's about to take will impress everyone at *Our World*. Um, thanks. Amen."

Summer squeezed his hand, her head still bowed. "And keep us safe. Amen."

Probably still thinking of the great white. The creatures were known to travel over twelve thousand miles in less than a year, so the probability of it still being in the area was pretty slim.

Summer pulled her mask back into place and stuffed her regulator into her mouth. Trent did the same while he watched her jump into the water, legs scissored. He stepped up onto the side of the boat and looked into the water below.

For a second he stood there, searching for the part of him that had been plagued for twenty-eight years. The part that had driven him to search for…something. Anything. But had never been satisfied. Until yesterday. Sure, there was still anticipation. Excitement for the adventure and the thrill of discovery, but he knew his happiness wasn't pinned on what they found today. Peace invaded every pore.

Then he plunged.

Chapter 30

Atlantic Ocean, 1689

Isabella hit the water with a force that took her breath away. The tempestuous ocean caught her with a stinging slap of frigid fingers. It pulled her under, gripping her skirts and yanking, twirling and twisting her in a devilish dance until she didn't know which way was up. Pieces of wood sliced through the water like they had been shot from one of *Santa Rosa's* cannons. Her eyes burned, and her lungs were about to explode. She kicked hard, but her head never broke above the surface. Darkness crowded in on her, and she felt herself sinking even farther.

Something wound its way around her waist and tugged her back against a solid surface. An arm perhaps? Her foggy brain refused to cooperate as it slipped further away from the light. Just when she thought she'd succumb to the blackness, she burst out of the watery grave. Her chest heaved as she gulped in air, violent coughs seizing her body.

"Are you unharmed, Isabella?"

She turned her head and looked into the captain's eyes— eyes that matched the storm raging around them. Lightning lit up the sky, and for a second, his features. The gash above his brow looked to need stitches. Her gaze traveled down to his mouth, where it seemed the cool water had done some good for the swelling.

Captain Montoya's lips parted, and Isabella became aware of his breathing. Her own matched his shallow intakes.

The arm around her waist tightened.

A swell rose and fell to their left, reality crashing around them.

The captain, however, did not loosen his hold. "Can you swim?"

She nodded instead of shouting against the wind and rain.

The hand he had been using to tread water now extended and pulled against the current, his other arm still secure about her. She kicked her feet to help propel them forward. With a sinking heart, she noticed no additional crewmen bobbing above the surface. Where were *Tío* and little Luis?

They swam to a large board that floated from the ship a short ways away. Captain Montoya lifted her enough so she could relax her upper body on the wood while the rest of her dangled in the water below.

The rain finally died to a drizzle, and the wind blew away. The sea began to return to its normal rhythm. Isabella eyed the captain's hand on the plank, the only part of him touching the lifeline. "Do you not wish to rest as well?"

"I fear it will not hold both our weight."

She slid fully back into the water. "Then we will take turns."

His eyes narrowed before he grabbed her waist and

hoisted her back onto the wide plank. "That will not be necessary."

Teeth chattering against the cold, she tried to hold her jaw tight. "Do not let your pride be your downfall, *el capitán*."

He looked away and then peered harder toward the distance.

Isabella followed his gaze. "*Que es?* What do you see?"

"I think there's someone..."

Before he completed his sentence, he disappeared under the water and emerged again on the other side of the board. His arms arced overhead as he swam away from her.

She squinted to see whatever drove him away from her, but nothing caught her eye.

A second later she saw it. A small hand waving slightly above the ocean's surface. Little Luis? She kicked her feet behind her, but the length of her skirt hindered her movement.

With a slowness that caused her heart to ache, the distance separating them shrunk. Finally, she was near enough to make out the survivor's features, and her breath hitched. A gaunt face surrounded by a mass of scraggly hair had never looked so handsome. Luis's son, her son now, had not been lost forever.

Captain Montoya helped the boy swim as he held fast to his own sliver of the once-grand ship.

Luis's gaze combed her face, and his mouth fell open. "The other men, they said you were really a woman, but I did not believe them. I thought they must have dreamed of the mystical *sirena*."

Isabella laughed. "I am afraid I am no mermaid." She lifted a leg until a foot emerged, the silk slippers she'd been wearing long lost in the ocean's depth. "See? Ten toes." She scanned the horizon, not a speck of land in sight. "Although fins would benefit us greatly."

"How about sails?" Captain Montoya looked beyond her shoulder.

She turned and saw a ship much smaller than Captain Montoya's *Santa Rosa*, with one tall mast protruding from its middle. It drew near, and Isabella had to bite the inside of her cheek to keep from crying with relief.

Captain Montoya drew to her side and bent his head toward her ear. "I will be the one to speak."

What did it matter to her who said what to whom? The good news was, they weren't going to drown after all.

A rope ladder flew over the side of the vessel, and Isabella eyed it warily. Luis gripped the rigging first and ascended faster than one of the monkeys she'd heard about in Gibraltar.

"You next." The captain's warm breath fanned her ear when he spoke.

She swallowed hard and enclosed her fingers around the rough cords. The ladder swung with her weight, and she squeezed her eyes shut against a wave of dizziness. Warmth seeped through her wet bodice at the back, and she turned her head only to have her gaze collide with the captain's. His body arched around hers. Never had she felt so protected.

He nodded toward her. "You are doing fine. I will not let you fall."

A small smile angled her lips before she returned her focus to climbing the roped rungs.

Strong hands reached for her at the top and helped to pull her fully on board. Little Luis stood near the ship's railing, his hands clasped in front of him and his gaze held fast to his scuffed boots.

She knelt in front of the boy. "I have been wanting to do

this for a long time." Her arms wrapped around his thin shoulders, and she pulled him close. At first he stood rigid, but then he became softer than a good flan. He laid his head on her shoulder and hooked his arms under hers. After a few moments he stepped back, a shy grin playing across his mouth.

Isabella stood and surveyed her surroundings. Rough men mulled around the deck. She recognized a face here and there as some of the crew from the *Santa Rosa*.

A boy on the verge on manhood approached, splotches of hair dotting his jaw. His gaze assessed her, and she pushed back her shoulders. While his regard may not have leered, she would show no weakness.

He waved a hand behind him while not taking his eyes off her. "These men I fished out of the sea say your sunken ship carried nothing of value, but I find I have salvaged a treasure from the wreckage after all."

The captain of the ship seemed no older than she. Was it possible?

Captain Montoya moved to stand beside her. "You have an eye for beauty, my good man, for my wife is a rare gem."

Her eyes widened. Wife?

The sailor—or perhaps pirate, albeit one so young?—compressed his lips and stared hard at Captain Montoya. "Wife, you say? Why bring your woman on such a voyage?"

"We were recently married, and I could not part from her."

The man continued to stare, then flicked a glance her way again, one side of his mouth pulling. "Yes, I can see why." He reached out his hand, and the captain grasped it. "I am Daniel Abana. I will take you to Nassau, but you will need to keep an eye on your woman. The city is a den of pirates who will not think twice to steal whatever it is they want, including *señoras*."

The captain found her hand and hooked it in the crook of his elbow. "She'll never leave my side."

Captain Montoya dragged her along as he toured the deck, checking on his men who had been pulled from the wreckage. She scanned every face, searching for her beloved uncle. At her query to his fate, each man in turn shook his head. No one seemed to know what had happened to Juan de la Cruz. Until the last man.

"*Sí*, I saw Juan when the storm fought its hardest. Pedro had climbed up the rigging to cut the sails, but had frozen halfway up. Juan followed him and was able to get him back to the deck, but when the big wave tossed the ship on its side, Juan's foot caught in the ropes. I was washed away after that, but I do not think he was able to free himself before the galleon capsized."

Isabella's heart clenched, and her knees went limp. If not for the strong arms of Captain Montoya, she would have collapsed. He lifted her like a child, and she buried her face in his leather jerkin. Tears squeezed past gritted eyes. How could *Tío* Pepe be dead? He had already come back to life for her once. Would he really leave her all alone with no family? Would *Dios* take him from her when he was all she had left?

"Is there a room where I may take my wife? She has suffered a terrible shock." The captain's chest rumbled against her cheek.

Still, she jammed her eyes closed, refusing to open them. Refusing to look around her and see the truth for what it was. That among all the faces of those who'd survived, her uncle was not included.

She was aware of movement, of being carried from one

place to the next, of a door shutting. She waited, expecting the captain to set her down, perhaps on a chair or a bed. Her body lowered, not onto a soft cushion but onto a lap.

Captain Montoya cradled her back. "I am sorry about your uncle. Juan de la Cruz was a great man and a good friend to me."

Isabella couldn't find her voice, so she merely nodded her head, the soft leather covering his chest caressing her cheek.

Slowly the shock wore off, leaving a searing grief in its wake, embarrassment its companion. She slid from the captain's lap and ducked her head. "I apologize for my behavior."

He stood and placed a finger under her chin, lifting until their eyes met. "No apology is necessary, Isabella."

Her tongue hit the roof of her mouth to say thank you, when he spoke again.

"I know this is not a good time, but we have many things to discuss. Daniel Abana will dock at Nassau. Have you heard of the city?" At the shake of her head, he continued. "It is no place for a woman, especially a beautiful *señorita* such as yourself. There are Spanish, English, French, but no matter where they were born, they have all turned out the same—pirates. Thieving reprobates, the lot of them."

She kept quiet while he began to pace. "Though I do not begin to know what your plans had been when you boarded my ship, I doubt finding yourself among a den of pirates was among them." He paused his pacing and looked at her. "Have you thought about what you will do now?"

Instinctively her hand went to where *Abuela's* necklace had rested for so long. The only hope of her future lay at the bottom of the sea. Fear's talons gripped her. What would she do? In a city full of self-serving men who allowed greed and base desires to drive them, there was no place for her. No respectful job she could acquire, no cozy house to call home. The only means to provide for herself and Luis would be in the skin trade. She would rather have drowned than to end up in that fate worse than death.

"Do you wish to return to Spain? I am sure we could find a vessel to return us all."

Return to Hernando? It was like escaping a pack of wolves only to land in front of a viper. She shook her head. "I will not touch Spanish soil."

The captain rubbed the back of his neck. "I thought not." He took a step toward her, his gaze catching her eye. "Then there is only one course for you to take."

She regarded him. "What course is that, *el capitan*?"

"You will marry me."

Chapter 31

Off the Bahaman Coast, Present Day

The sound of bubbles from her regulator instantly put Summer at ease. Things with Trent might be confusing, but diving—the languid feeling of ocean all around her, the rhythmic cadence of her even breathing, the dancing of light refracting off the water—this balanced her equilibrium.

Trent came along beside her and gave her a thumbs-up. She nodded, and they continued to dive deeper at a steady pace. If Jonathan had stopped the boat at exactly the same spot as last time, they wouldn't have to search in too large a radius before they found something. If anything was even here, that was.

Summer reached up and turned on her headlamp. A twin light illuminated from Trent, and she looked over. He'd turned on his handheld flashlight. The sun still shone through at this depth, but she didn't want any shadows hiding what could be there.

The glow from Trent's flashlight oscillated back and forth. So far nothing. Not even a fish.

Then the beam beside her stopped moving. It fixated on one spot, and Summer peered toward the end of the shaft of light. Nothing there. She turned her head to look at Trent, and he jabbed his finger in the direction she'd been studying, his eyes bright with excitement.

Already he moved in that direction, finned feet propelling him forward. She followed and gripped her camera, just in case.

What she assumed were shadows on the ocean floor began to take shape...and not the shape she'd imagined.

Stupid. Stupid. Stupid. Her throat closed against the disappointment. She'd let her imagination run away with her and hadn't stopped to think about the logistics. Of course there wouldn't be a grand old ship pristinely preserved, masts still standing tall after three hundred years in the high saline waters of the Caribbean. Not to mention wood-eating shipworms and other marine life. Crustaceans and octopi were notorious for moving or breaking anything in their way.

She tried to tune out the mocking voice of defeat and erase the image she'd built up in her mind. With the deadline looming the next day, she didn't have any other option but to make this work.

Trent swam a few feet ahead of her, bubbles rising above his head. She turned off her headlamp. At only a depth of about thirty feet, they really didn't need it.

Summer stopped kicking and let her body suspend in the water. Her eyes scanned below, and a sense of awe overtook her. Clearly defined and yet still camouflaged among the silt and sand, jutting a foot or so above the ground, lay the remains of a ship.

What was the story behind those remains? She felt if she could just listen close enough, the voices from the past would whisper to her. Had this ship been among the fleet that brought riches to Spain, as Trent thought? Perhaps it had been a pirate ship. Plausible, considering Bahama's ripe history.

She brought her camera up to her face, willing the wreck to speak to her. Her finger descended on the shutter, the frame capturing Trent inspecting the discovery.

Were these photos going to be enough to convince Tabitha Michaels to take a chance on her? The editor had asked for something different, edgy. Summer was used to photographing coral reefs and the marine life that called that habitat home. In comparison, these photos were grey and colorless, but they were different.

She swam closer and took shots from all angles, then kicked her legs to propel her nearer the surface and took more. How had no one found this shipwreck before? They weren't too far from the coast, nor very deep.

Movement caught her eye, and a hawksbill sea turtle came into view. The animal's fore flippers pushed up and down like the wingbeats of a bird, soaring gracefully through the water. Each scute of his shell a tawny tie-dye of hazel, chocolate, and caramel. He glided through the water at a leisurely pace, unconcerned about the strange creatures sharing his space.

Summer snapped frame after frame of the turtle. Swimming above him, she noticed the juxtaposition of his colorful body contrasted sharply with the drab, silty background. The shipwreck's outline made an interesting backdrop—one Tabitha Michaels would hopefully appreciate.

The turtle swam off into the hazy distance, and she returned her attention to the ship remains below. Water pushed around her as she made her way to where Trent was examining a specific section. He reached out a hand and ever so gently rubbed away some of the sand and silt.

Something was different there, but she couldn't pinpoint what it was. Besides the silhouette of the ship, the only shapes within the hull were the contours of old crates. The swirly line of a distorted circle didn't look like it belonged among the rest of what they'd found.

Summer watched through her lens as Trent brushed aside a bit more sand. His thumb and index finger pinched together at the silt, then lifted, a jeweled necklace dangling from his hand. She zoomed in, and the shutter closed as it captured the photo.

Never in a million years would she have imagined she'd be a part of a discovery like this. Hidden treasures and the men who hunted them were things of Hollywood, not the mundane existence she'd lived until now. Who would have thought her reality would far outreach any of her fantasies?

She lowered the camera from her face and met Trent's eyes. The blue of his irises buzzed with excitement. He pointed up to the surface, and they both ascended until their heads bobbed out of the water.

Trent tore his mask from his face and spit the regulator out of his mouth. "We found it, Summer." He threw his head back and laughed. "I can't believe we found it."

She removed her regulator and scooted her mask high on her forehead. A smile stretched across her face, his exuberance contagious.

Their gazes pulled and locked. He brought his arms around her, and in a breath his mouth found hers. While their kiss under the pier had been carnal, full of passion and desire, this kiss—she melted against him—this kiss was different. His soft lips lingered, didn't demand and didn't rush. The sweetness of it filled her, scattering her senses until they were the only two in existence.

As all good things did, the kiss ended. He pulled back enough to look into her eyes, his hand cradling her cheek. "I've been wanting to do that for a long time."

Heaven help her. If she was honest with herself, she'd admit she'd wanted that kiss for just as long as he had. Denial and logic hadn't served her well as barriers around her heart. He'd scaled them both and found a way in.

She pressed her cheek against his hand. "What am I going to do with you?"

He leaned in and kissed the tip of her nose, and then winked, one side of his mouth lifting. "Anything you want."

She gasped, then grinned. Cupping her hands, she shot water in his direction.

Laughing, he splashed her back.

The boat sidled up to them, and the engine idled. Jonathan poked his head over the side. "Find anything?"

Trent lifted his arm from the water, the necklace clasped in his hand.

Jonathan whistled. "Blackbeard's treasure, huh?"

Summer laughed. "Hardly. Although it will be interesting to see what else is down there."

Jonathan lowered a ladder, and Trent and Summer climbed aboard the boat. Water collected at their feet on the deck, and Jonathan tossed towels at them.

"I'll report the find to the proper authorities." Trent ran the towel over his head. "There's a lot of protocol with a find like this."

Summer eyed the jewelry still hanging from Trent's hand. "May I?"

He handed it over, and the weight surprised her. Looking

closer, the quality of the gold and gems caused her jaw to unhinge. Not even three hundred years in a watery grave buried beneath layers of sand could tarnish the heirloom's beauty.

"Do you think there's a story to this necklace?" She didn't look up. Didn't direct her question to anyone in particular. Just spoke the words, her own imagination building up different scenarios.

Perhaps the necklace had been a gift from a doting husband, given to his wife on their sixtieth wedding anniversary. Nah. People didn't live that long in the seventeenth century, and what would an elderly couple be doing sailing across the ocean to the other side of the world? A gift for a fiancée then? Maybe a young navy captain had given the family heirloom to his lady love before he set sail on the seven seas. After establishing a place for her in the New World, he had sent for her. Only, the ship she'd sailed upon had encountered a great storm and she was lost to him forever.

Goose bumps sprouted across her arms. Awareness rippled through her as Trent came to stand at her back.

His breath warmed her ear and caused a shiver down her spine. He reached out a hand, his arm jacketing hers as he took the weight of the necklace in two fingers. "There is always a story."

She turned her head and immediately regretted the action. Not even inches separated their faces, their lips. Her breathing stilled, while her heart raced.

This was not a good idea.

While she admitted to being no better than the other women who'd fallen for his charms, that didn't mean she had to act on those feelings.

Memory of their shared kisses mocked her.

Fine. It didn't mean she had to act on those feelings *again*.

The boat lurched forward. Unbalanced, she fell first against Trent's chest and then into his lap. His arms encircled her, and she felt oddly protected.

As suddenly as the boat had gained momentum, it stopped. She jerked forward and then back, settling more firmly between Trent's thighs. He rested his chin on the top of her head. If it wasn't impossible, she'd suspect him of arranging that little surge just for this cozy embrace.

She extricated herself from Trent and glared at Jonathan. What had he been thinking?

Jonathan glanced away and muttered a "sorry" under his breath.

Agitation seeped away. *Uncomfortable* was the best word she could think of to label how he must feel, but she knew that probably didn't even begin to describe it.

And it was her fault.

She'd rejected him, she'd begged him to help even when he'd said he needed more time, she'd admitted to feelings for another guy, and now, on top of all that, she'd made him witness her reaction to Trent's nearness. Talk about being the worst friend ever.

She glanced in his direction to find him staring out over the horizon. Walking to his side, she bumped him with her shoulder. "I still have some oxygen in my tank. You want to go down and take a peek?"

He looked down at her, parallel lines etched along his cheeks. "Nah, that's okay. Let's head in if you're done."

"You sure? How about looking over some of the pictures I took?"

More than the steps he took to the helm's chair distanced them. "Maybe later."

Her heart strained to make it right, to fix the pieces in their friendship that had come apart like a puzzle jostled by a toddler. But he'd begged for time, said later, and no matter how much it hurt, she needed to give him the space to work it out.

Trent had no sooner finished stowing the equipment than Jonathan opened the throttle. The boat bounced, a slight wind making the water choppy. Summer gripped the white vinyl seat cushion and gritted her teeth against the jarring. Hair that had worked its way out of her braid whipped out behind her, and the sting of the wind caused her eyes to water.

They made it back to the marina in half the time it had taken to reach the dive location. Jonathan jumped from the boat. A cowboy at a rodeo couldn't have tied a calf's legs as fast as Trent secured the rope to the dock's cleat.

He pressed his hands to his thighs as he stood from his hunched position. "Did you leave anything in the rental car, Summer?"

Had she? No, everything was either back at the hotel or in her duffel. "I don't think so. Why?"

Jonathan's eyes looked past her to Trent. "I assume you're staying at the same hotel?"

"Yeah, they had a room available, even though I didn't book ahead."

"Would you mind taking Summer back to the hotel? I need to head home earlier than expected. Something came up."

"Sure."

Jonathan turned without looking at her and started walking toward shore, causing her chest to weight like the cement piling surrounding her.

"Jonathan."

He stopped but didn't turn around.

The boat rose and dipped with the waves, but she stepped over the expanse from its side to the dock. Half a dozen steps and she faced him. "I'm sorry." She touched his arm, but he seemed to look through her instead of at her. "Please...please don't be angry with me forever."

The muscle in his jaw twitched before his rock facade softened. He jammed a hand through his hair, leaving it sticking up near the front. "I'm not mad. I want you to be happy...I just wish...I just wish you could be happy with me." He cast a glance back toward the boat before settling his regard to her. "If he can make you happy..."

"Promise we're still friends?"

A sad smile bowed his lips. "We'll always be friends. But friendships aren't static, and ours can never go back, no matter how much you want it to."

She reached up on tiptoes and flung her arms around his neck. As if by sheer willpower she had the ability to make their friendship all it had been, she hung on. Would he still be the prankster who put whoopee cushions on her chair to make her laugh when she was too stressed out? Still dare her to do crazy things like stuff twenty marshmallows in her mouth and sing the national anthem? Still be her roller-coaster buddy?

A groan rumbled at the back of his throat. "You're killing me."

She lowered back on flat feet, and he chucked her chin like an older brother would to a kid sister. "I'll see ya back at home."

His flip-flops slapped his heels with each step he took away from her. Some of the heaviness in her middle lifted, and she took a full breath.

Trent stepped up beside her, her duffel bag and camera case slung over his shoulder. "Everything okay?"

Not yet, but... "It will be."

He put a hand to the small of her back, and they started walking toward the marina's office. "Hope so. I know I gave him a hard time, but he's really not so bad."

"Pretty great, actually." A couple beats passed in silence, then she stopped, brows bunched low on her forehead as she looked at him. "Why did you give him a hard time?"

One side of his mouth hiked up his face. "Isn't it obvious?"

Realization dawned in a *duh* moment. "Me?"

The other side of his mouth matched the first. "Bingo."

Heat rushed to her face, and it wasn't due to the tropical sun. She set her feet back in motion, Trent keeping stride beside her. A peek from the corner of her eye showed he still grinned ear to ear. If he weren't carrying all her equipment and things, she'd give in to the temptation to shove him off the side of the dock.

Air-conditioning inside the office cooled her heated skin. The same gentleman who'd rented them the boat that morning stood behind the counter, watching a small portable television. He turned the knob when he noticed them approaching.

"Have a fun time?"

Trent placed the boat key on the counter. "Yes, thank you."

Summer stepped up and laid her hands on the Formica. "We left all the equipment stowed on the boat. I hope that's all right."

"No problem a'tall."

She ran a finger along a faux vein in the countertop. "So we're all set?"

He nodded. "If there's nothing else I can do for you folks. I hope you come back real soon."

"Thank you very much. Have a nice day."

The man smiled, then turned the knob on his television, and the screen came to life.

She walked through the front door but halted right outside. Half a dozen cars filled the parking lot. "Which one is yours?"

Trent pointed to a small hatchback a couple spaces over. "It's unlocked. I left the keys in the glove box if you want to crank it up and turn on the AC while I put your stuff in the trunk."

"Not afraid someone would steal it?"

He looked down at his wet suit. "More like no place to put the key."

Her eyes followed his line of sight. Tight neoprene hugged his body like a second skin, outlining the strength of muscled arms and well-sculpted legs. She swallowed against a mouth suddenly gone dry and quickly ducked inside the car. The glove box popped open when she pulled the handle, the key and fob on a single ring on top of some paperwork. She leaned over the center console and turned the ignition.

Trent slid into the driver's seat and pulled the seat belt across his chest. "Back to the hotel?"

"Yeah. I want to get these pictures uploaded to my computer and start working on edits. Tabitha Michaels didn't give me a specific time tomorrow for the deadline, but I want them waiting in her inbox by the time she gets to the office."

He put the car into gear and pulled out of the parking lot and onto the road. "Sounds like a plan. Mind if I join you? I want to do some research regarding the ship and the necklace."

"Sure, as long as you aren't too distracting." Especially considering the last time he'd invaded her space while she'd been editing, he'd insisted on taking her out for coffee.

Laughter filled the car. "Distracting, huh? I can only promise not to intentionally distract you."

"And unintentionally?"

"All I know is, I find it maddeningly hard to concentrate when I'm around you." He shrugged and flicked a quick glance at her. "I was just kind of hoping my presence brought you a bit of diversion as well."

Not a line. No hook, no sinker. Although the first part sounded like it. However, the hitch in his voice betrayed vulnerability, while the small moment their gazes met she'd witnessed sincerity in their depths. And those were two things she never thought she'd see in a guy like Trent Carrington—vulnerability and sincerity. Leastwise not where women were concerned. Did that mean she'd been wrong about him? Not likely, since his past spoke for itself. But maybe he had changed, or at least was changing. Even possible? Leopards didn't change their spots.

But maybe, just maybe, people weren't leopards.

Chapter 32

"How's it going over there?" Sitting at the desk in Summer's hotel room, Trent looked over the top of his laptop. Her legs stretched out across the white duvet and crossed at the ankles, while her back leaned against the tall headboard of the queen-sized bed. The notebook rested in her lap as her eyes bore a hole into her computer screen.

"I sent it."

He closed his computer. "You did? When?"

"About five minutes ago." Lips pressed inward, she raised her eyes to meet his.

Her gaze was so uncertain that he felt the punch of it in his solar plexus. It left him momentarily paralyzed to respond with any sort of reassurance.

"What if the editors don't like my work? What if the photos aren't good enough?" Her throat rose and fell with a hard swallow. "What if I'm not good enough?"

Two strides was all it took to reach the bed. He lowered himself on the edge and gripped her hand. She didn't immediately turn her eyes to him, but slowly, like the unfolding of a flower, he peered into her sparkling emeralds. "If the editors don't see the talent in front of their faces, then they're morons."

Truly, he'd find out the magazine's home office, go there himself, and tell every single one of those editors how much sense they lacked if they didn't offer Summer the position. His jaw tensed at the thought of such a possibility, but he forced himself to relax the clench. Summer needed reassurance, not his defensive posturing. "Don't ever think you're not good enough, Summer Arnet."

His lungs filled with a deep breath to help cool the boiling of his temper. It didn't work. Heat still flushed his skin. Only maybe the fire in his blood had more to do with the small bow of her upper lip resting upon the fullness of the lower. Or that her gaze had also fallen to his mouth. Perhaps it was due to the sound of her shallow breaths or the wild racing of his heart.

"Why?" The single word came out on a breath. One that feathered his lips as the distance separating his from hers vanished.

His mouth brushed hers, then separated only enough to speak. "Because you're the best person I know." He claimed her mouth once more, the soft mewling sound that evicted from her throat driving his senses.

Her lips tore away from his. "Don't kiss me." She scooted over more into the center of the bed, distancing herself from him. "I don't want you to."

Oh, she wanted him to all right. The softness of her mouth, the response of her body, the quiet sound in the back of her throat, all contradicted her claim.

He propped his weight with a stiff arm. "You don't?"

A strand of hair fell across her temple as she shook her head.

"Care to explain why?"

She tucked the wayward lock behind her ear. "Depends."

"On?"

Both hands came around and clasped each other on her lap. "Care to explain where you were yesterday?"

She didn't trust him. Still. It hurt worse than the one time he'd had to lay down his bike to prevent a more serious accident. Then he'd been somewhat protected by a leather jacket and jeans. With this—with her—he had no protection. He jammed a hand through his hair and lowered his head, the strands falling back around his shoulders. Every action had an equal reaction. Wasn't that Newton's law? She didn't trust him, didn't think he was sincere in his feelings for her—the reaction to his past relationships with women. He couldn't blame her. Didn't. But that didn't make the ache go away.

The bed creaked as the mattress was relieved of his weight. "Take a walk with me?"

"Why?" Even as she asked it, she scooted to the far side of the bed and stood.

"Because it's good to be moving when hearing hard things."

Her eyes were wary as they regarded him. "What's going to be hard to hear?"

He palmed the hotel card key. "Come on. I'll tell you on the beach."

The walk from the room to the sandy shore didn't last long enough for Trent to figure out how he was going to tell Summer he'd talked to her dad. And that he didn't want anything to do with her.

As soon as their feet hit the sand, she sprung on him. "Well?"

"Hold on." He plopped down onto the white grains. "Let me take off my shoes."

She slipped out of her sandals and dangled them from her fingers, then cocked a hip. His boots wouldn't be so easy. Neither did they need the extra time he spent untying the laces and hefting them off. He knotted the laces together and let them hang from his shoulder.

"I'm waiting."

And none too patiently, from her pursed lips and the hands that flagged her hips.

He sighed and set a course through the soft, dry sand to the damp, packed earth in reach of the tide's caress. "I went to DeLand yesterday."

She didn't respond. Didn't ask where that was or why he went or whom he saw there, just put one foot in front of the other and remained silent.

The sun arched over the horizon. Its rays would soon be cast in a brilliance of color across the sky. A thing of beauty. Amid the ugly telling, Summer would need loveliness to remind her of the good. Maybe even the reminder of the heavenly Father she had so recently come to know.

"Dave Landstrom lives in DeLand."

Again silence, although not really. The sound of the water rushing and receding, crashing and flowing accompanied his words.

"Do you know who Dave Landstrom is, Summer?"

She stopped walking, her eyes down. He sensed her struggle, an internal warring that didn't show but which he felt. Whether she won or she lost, she looked up, the sheen of moisture in her eyes. "He's my dad." Her chin quivered as much as her voice.

"Oh, babe." His arms came around her and drew her close to his side. He tucked her there and would have liked nothing more than to shield her from this hurt. "I'm so sorry."

Her hands clung to his back as she buried her face in his chest. "He doesn't want to see me, does he?" His shirt muffled her voice, but not enough to miss the raw edge.

"Dave Landstrom isn't worthy of the title *father*." Trent cradled her cheek and thumbed an errant tear. "He isn't worth crying over."

She nodded and sniffed but didn't loosen her hold. Which was fine by him. He'd hold her, offer her his strength and whatever comfort he could, for as long as she needed it.

"Why'd you do it?"

As with many things people did, he'd had more than one reason. A grand gesture on her behalf. Women fell hard for stuff like that, and he wouldn't lie and say the thought that she might soften toward him because he had done something big for her hadn't crossed his mind. Of course, once he pushed away all the side motives, one main goal still remained—with a flesh-and-blood dad in her life she'd come to recognize she didn't need a figment father figure in the form of God Almighty.

Who would've thought his actions to disprove her need would only enlighten him to his?

He smoothed back the hair from her forehead. "The reason doesn't matter. I was wrong."

Her face lifted. "What do you mean?"

With all his experience with women, this new vulnerability in his core left him adrift. Flashing a smile, offering a compliment—body language that spoke more than words had been his go-to in difficult situations. Familiar. But stripping it all away until he was laid out bare and naked, his heart exposed—*this* was new and frightening.

He laid his cheek on top of her head. "I wanted to give you your dad so you'd realize you were only filling the void he left when you accepted God as a substitute Father."

"Trent, that's not why—"

"Shh. I know. Believe it or not, I learned a lot from your dad."

Hair scraped his cheek as her head jerked back. "*You* learned something from my *dad?*"

The side of his mouth so eager to grin turned down. "A hard lesson."

Her arms fell from around his waist, and never had he been so keenly aware of the absence of a touch. She searched his eyes. "Someone once told me the harder things are made easier with motion."

Some of the tension eased from his shoulders. "I'm not sure those were my exact words."

"A paraphrase then."

He dipped his head, and they continued their stroll. The bottom edges of the sun disappeared beyond the horizon, causing the tropical sea to turn a dark blue against the fiery-orange sky.

"What hard lesson did you learn from my dad?"

He filled his lungs with the salty air and glanced down at the woman beside him. His vision filled with the top of her head, strands of hair flying on the coastal breeze. The admittance was going to cost him, but he hoped the price wouldn't be too high. "That I'm no different than he is."

He wasn't sure what reaction he expected. Outright denial? Soft assurances? Cutting affirmation? He received none of those. Summer didn't flinch, her step didn't falter, and neither did she look up.

"After meeting Dave, I determined to contact past..." He let her supply the appropriate noun. "Anyway, I wanted to make sure there weren't any kids out there that didn't have a dad on my account."

"And?" She nearly choked on the word, with how strangled it sounded.

"No."

They took a few more steps before she stopped again. Her eyes were hooded, and he couldn't blame her for protecting herself, because even though she said the opposite, he knew his feelings for her were not unrequited. "Anything else?"

How he longed to smooth the crease pleated between her eyes. "Yes."

Tense muscles tightened further, but she lifted her chin as if willing to take the blow head on.

"I found God, Summer. Or, rather, He found me. Or I let Him in." Trent shook his head. "I don't know how to put it." *Make her see.* "You know about my brother Trevor and, even though I rarely admitted it, the hole I've felt all my life." He caught up her hand and placed it over his heart. "It's not here anymore. God filled it when I asked him into my life."

She stared at her hand on his chest. At his hand that covered hers. "The same as He filled mine when I asked."

"Yes." His thumb traced languid circles on the back of her hand. "There is still something missing here though."

Confusion clouded her gaze. "But you said—"

"God filled up that void, but I've recently discovered there's another piece, a very unique and special piece, which I've found and keep trying to place in its proper spot"—he pressed her hand more firmly to his chest—"but for some reason, she doesn't want to fit. Why is that?"

Warm breath fanned his hand in short, rapid bursts. She lifted her eyes to meet his gaze, and they caused a throbbing in his center at the struggle they mirrored.

"Trent, I—"

He brought his forehead to rest on hers. "Why are you afraid to admit your feelings for me?" His voice barely carried above a whisper.

She took a step back and hugged her arms. "I *am* afraid. How do I know you've really changed? That I'm not just some challenge or passing fancy for you? That you won't check me off as another notch on your belt once you've gotten whatever it is you want from me?" She squeezed her eyes shut and let her arms dangle at her sides. When she opened her eyes again, they looked tired and defeated. "I want to believe you. You have no idea how much I want to believe you."

He smiled. Not with elation but a small degree of hope. "I told you before I'd prove you wrong, and I will. One day, Summer Arnet, you *will* believe me when I whisper in your ear"—he leaned down until his face was beside hers—"I love you."

Chapter 33

Bahamas, 1689

Marry him? The two words swirled around in Isabella's mind, refusing to land and stick. She looked at him, took in the grim set of his jaw and squared shoulders. It did not appear the suggestion—nay, command—had appealed to him. But why offer? A sense of duty to his lost friend and first mate?

Isabella swallowed against the churning in her stomach. "I thank you for the offer, but—"

"It was not an offer, as I did not ask."

Insufferable man! Control seeped through her fingers faster than flour through a sifter until her nostrils flared and her hands fisted in the folds of her skirts. "I am not among the numbers of your crew that you may dictate my actions, Captain Montoya."

His gaze swept over her. "That you are not among my *men* I am well aware."

Her chin notched higher. "I will not marry a man who

does not care for me." As surely Hernando had not cared for her mother, the captain did not harbor those feelings that a man and wife should feel toward one another—although that was where the comparison of the two men ended.

He took a step toward her, and she instantly crept back. The intent of the movement thwarted, however, when the captain's strong grip caught her arm and pulled her forward into his space.

"What surety do you have that I do not possess such care for you, Isabella Castellano?"

What say he? Was this an admittance of love from this powerful man's heart? Nay... She shook her head. "You do not love me."

"That word never crossed my lips. But, *sí*, I do care. Though I do not know why nor how nor when, it is there just the same."

Was it enough? Could care grow into love, or would it weaken? She did not wish this man to look upon her through eyes of regret. But what other choice did she have? She could not return to Spain, could not stay in Nassau, and had no other means for travel to a safer location. In truth, she had but one option. And if she had to marry a man who did not love her, she at least had the assurance he was a man who would protect instead of harm. There was also the peculiar warm stirrings in her center whenever he drew near...

Pushing her shoulders back, she met the captain's steady gaze. "I will marry you."

He let out a breath that caused the loose hairs around her face to tickle her cheek. Relief? She had no time to reflect on that, however, as he slid his hand down her arm and captured her fingers. They were lifted, and his lips pressed firmly atop her knuckles, mustache tickling in not an unpleasant way.

"As soon as we dock I will inquire as to a priest so our vows may be spoken."

Her free hand flew to her throat. "So soon?"

"As needs be." He squeezed her fingers in a sign of reassurance.

A knock sounded from the door, which caused Isabella to startle.

"Enter." Captain Montoya's voice sounded strong and sure, which seemed to mock her insecurity.

An elderly man past his sailing prime entered. "*Capítan* Abana wishes to inform you that we have docked, *señor.*"

Captain Montoya inclined his head. "*Gracias.*"

He stepped forward and made to pull her along, as he still had ahold of her hand, but she planted her feet, causing him to halt and look back at her. "You are to be my husband, and yet I do not even know your Christian name."

"Forgive me." He dropped her hand and bowed formally at the waist. "I am José Montoya." Straightening, he hitched a brow. "Anything else you would like to know?"

A thousand things, but the words lodged in her throat.

His large hand held out to her. "Come. There is much to be done."

She eyed his palm and then slipped her hand inside.

———

Nothing could have prepared Isabella for the city which was Nassau. Filth-strewn roads, raucous laughter, crude language that jabbed the air, and scantily-clad women who fairly hung out doorways, not only with suggestive glances but outright spoken entreaties. The smell of ale saturated every breath, made putrid by the stench of many unwashed men.

Eyes followed her every step as she and the captain traversed the part of town said to hold a small chapel. Her shoulders hunched as she tried to hide as much of her body as she could.

The long material of her borrowed gown had since dried, leaving the fabric stiff and coarse. One of the crewmen had offered to ask if the lady he frequented while they were in port had a spare dress, but Captain Montoya had quickly intervened and declined. Isabella would have been thankful for fresh clothing, but not at the expense of her modesty.

"We are here."

She looked at the diminutive building that was hardly more than a few boards nailed together. This was the city's place of worship?

A man stepped through the doorway, and her breath caught. He was the priest? The white clerical collar and long black cassock, sun glinting off thirty-three buttons representing the years of the Lord's earthly life, bespoke his occupation. His face, unmarked by lines of age nor the shadow of whiskers, seemed to argue with his garb. The priest in her town had been closer to the coffin than the cradle. Weren't all holy men of God such that had born years of wisdom?

The man's hands clasped in front of him. "I am Father Rodriguez. How can I help you, my children?"

Captain Montoya—nay, she must start thinking of him as José—stepped forward. "We wish to be married, Padre."

The priest's eyebrows drew together. "Have the banns been read?"

"They have not."

"I see." The young man heaved a great sigh. He alternated his gaze between Isabella and her soon-to-be husband at one side and little Luis at the other. "Have you both come here freely and without reservation to give yourselves to each other in marriage?"

There was no hesitation from the captain. "We have."

Father Rodriguez turned his light-brown eyes on her.

"*Sí*," she croaked.

His lips turned down, but he continued. "Will you honor each other as man and wife for the remainder of your life, and will you willingly accept any children from God and bring them up according to the law of Christ and the Church?"

"We will." Captain Montoya spoke with confidence.

Again the priest's unsettling gaze rested upon her. Throat dry, she nodded her assurance.

"Well then." Father Rodriquez rocked onto the balls of his feet. "It is not keeping with the strict traditions of the church, but rushed weddings are not unheard of."

He stepped aside and ushered them into the small sanctuary. Luis walked in front of them, but turned and took a seat on one of the short pews. Dimly lit by tiny windows and a row of candles near the rear, Isabella stumbled in the aisle. Strong fingers wrapped around her upper arm and steadied her.

Father Rodriguez stopped in front of a wooden crucifix and turned. "I assume it is but vows you wish to speak?"

Captain Montoya looked down at her and searched her eyes. Did he look for an answer among their depths?

"Vows will be sufficient, Father."

"Very well. Your names?"

"José Montoya and Isabella Castellano."

The young priest bowed his head, and out of the corner of her eye, Isabella watched the captain's head lower as well. Following their example, she also cast her gaze to the floor.

Father Rodriguez intoned a prayer in the language of the Church, then crossed himself and kissed his fingertips.

"Now…" The priest's gaze rested upon the captain. "Will you, José Montoya, take this woman as your wedded wife, to live together after God's ordinance in the holy estate of matrimony? Will you love her, comfort her, honor and keep her, in sickness and in health, and forsaking all others, keep only to her so long as you both shall live?"

"I will."

Isabella managed to repeat the captain's words when the same vows were put to her.

"May the Lord in His goodness fill you both with his blessing. *Señor* Montoya, you may now kiss your bride."

José turned to her, one strand of black hair falling across his forehead. For some reason, it softened his usual staunch features and eased Isabella's tense muscles.

He looked into her eyes and then lowered his gaze to her mouth. "May I?"

It took a moment for the question to register, as she'd never have imagined one who commanded others to seek permission for a kiss. She tilted her face up to receive the last symbol that they were truly now husband and wife. The scent of cedar filled her senses as her new husband's head descended. His lips brushed hers for the barest of moments, then lifted and hovered as a bee to an open flower.

Isabella held her breath in that moment of in between. Would his mouth return to hers? Did she want it to?

Before she could find the answer to that question, she was gathered up in José's arms, her body pulled tight to his, and her lips captured.

Not captured. For she found in herself no resistance. Quite

the opposite as her hands slid up and gripped the back of his neck. Her lips giving as much as receiving.

A throat cleared, and Isabella jerked back. Heat rushed to her cheeks, and she lowered her face. To act in such a manner. And in front of a priest! He must think her completely wanton.

Captain Montoya's hold loosened enough for air to pass between their bodies once more. "We thank you, Father."

The young priest raised a hand. "God's blessing on you both."

Slight pressure at the small of her back propelled Isabella forward. Luis stood and followed them out of the small chapel, the press of the captain's hand now directing her to the right and down the dusty road.

Where were they going? What did their future hold—both immediate and otherwise? The *Santa Rosa* lay at the bottom of the ocean, and what was a ship's captain without a vessel to command? Did her new husband plan to return to the sea in some capacity? Would he leave her and Luis in this city of pirates on their own?

A battalion of thoughts warred in her mind, yet her tongue was thicker than *polenta* left too long upon the fire. She searched her being, rooting around for the tight ball of anxiety such uncertainty wound up inside her. It couldn't be found, but how could that be?

She gazed at the captain's profile as he walked beside her. Long, straight nose, the soft pucker of skin above his eye where the fiendish quartermaster had cut him, same hard set to his jaw that had become familiar to her. His focus remained steady. He didn't glance to the right or the left, and his gait bespoke certainty and control. Of their short acquaintance, he had proven himself to be true. She could trust him with her life, her future, and, mayhap, even her heart.

Captain Montoya stopped in front of a corral. Horses grazed within the center of the rough-hewn circular fence. Off to the side, a small lean-to housed an open hearth, where a hot fire blazed. Metal tools hung along the far wall. A large man, his chest and legs covered by a long apron, stepped around an anvil, smiling so wide he showed teeth.

"José Montoya, you are once more returned, and before the promised year, no less." The two men clasped forearms.

Isabella watched the exchange, her curiosity piqued.

The captain once more put a hand to her back, and she took a tiny step forward. "Pedro, I would like for you to meet my wife, Isabella Montoya." He motioned Luis forward with two fingers. "And my new son, Luis."

She startled at the use of her new name and the claiming of Luis as his son, but found the sound of both rather pleasing.

Pedro's eyes rounded larger than his ample belly. "Wife, you say? How did you manage to get such a pretty thing to marry the likes of you?" The man elbowed the captain.

For the second time that day, Isabella felt her cheeks grow warm.

"The Lord blesses, my friend. Now, do you have my horse?"

"Of course. Your stallion gives me nothing but trouble, and I cannot say I am sorry to see him go. My mares however—" The large man looked at her and changed his mind about whatever it was he had planned to say. He continued to regard her, then looked back at the captain. "Will you be needing one of my mares for your wife, José?"

Both pairs of eyes rested on her, but she managed not to squirm under their scrutiny.

"I think not," Captain Montoya said, his gaze still upon her. "We will ride double." He looked to his friend. "Cozy, no?"

Pedro grinned. "Quite cozy."

Not only did her cheeks burn but so did her neck and ears.

"We will need a mount for the boy, however."

She turned to look at the horses grazing upon the tall grass. Which belonged to the captain?

An air of excitement swirled around her, and she looked down. Her new son bounced foot to foot. He glanced up, a grin stretching wide across his dirty face. She bent down to his level and put upon her face a serious look. "Do you think you can handle one of these beasts?"

A shrill whistle pierced the air, and a horse as dark as midnight raised its mammoth head. Hooves pounded the earth as the stallion trotted toward them, his long, flowing mane blowing out with each prance, his tail held high and regal. He stopped just feet from them and lowered his neck across the fence. Captain Montoya stroked the large space between the animal's eyes.

Isabella hadn't been aware of Pedro's absence, but the man had left and returned with two saddles and bridles. The captain accepted the long leather straps and metal bit from his friend. He swung his legs over the top of the fence and landed on the other side. With the horse's head nearly in his chest, he slipped the bit into the stallion's mouth and secured the bridle's straps under the chin. After the saddle was secured, the captain stepped into the stirrup and settled into the saddle. Pedro let down two long boards of the fence, and horse and rider rode through.

Isabella found herself straining her neck as the captain

reined the horse in right beside her. Never had she been on the back of such an animal. Her family hadn't lived far from town, so she'd walked to wherever she needed to go. Hernando had owned a horse, but never had he allowed her a ride.

Large hands encompassed her waist, and she was lifted into the air. A small squeak escaped her lips before the captain reached down and hoisted her the rest of the way until she was settled in front of him. As the saddle was not made for two people, nor her skirts proper to ride as a man did, both her legs draped over one of his. Spine erect, she tried to hold herself as far from his person as possible, as propriety surely warranted. The stallion pranced sideways beneath her.

She sucked in a breath and wrapped her arms tightly around the captain's middle. *Dios*, she was going to tumble to her death at this height.

Laughter rumbled beneath her ear. "If you relax, so will he."

Relax? Not possible. Not when awareness of her new husband so close awakened her every sense. Not when one wrong step of this mighty beast could make him so quickly a widower.

"I will not let anything happen to you."

She let out a deep breath and forced her muscles to relax. In so doing, she leaned into the captain's chest, his arms around her as he gripped the reins in front of her.

Pedro brought around a smaller horse, and Luis mimicked the captain's movements to mount. He urged the mare forward until she was next to the stallion.

The captain raised his hand. "Until next time, my friend."

"Until next time." Pedro nodded his head in her direction. "*Señora*."

She smiled at the man, and the stallion moved beneath her.

By the time they reached the outskirts of town, Isabella had acquainted herself with the rhythm of the horse. Luis seemed to be as natural in the saddle as he had been climbing the ships rigging, so she didn't worry about him as he rode beside them.

"Where is our destination, Captain Montoya?"

A small rabbit bounded out of the brush and across the path. Their mount flung his head in the air. His hooves pounded the ground as he sidestepped. Isabella tensed as the captain wrapped his arm about her waist and pressed her more firmly to his chest. The horse calmed and continued on.

"I think it is time you start calling me José."

They headed away from the shore and the vast ocean. As that had been her constant view for the previous month, so this man had been only Captain Montoya. It would take some time to think of him by another name. "I will try to remember."

"Shall we make a pact? You will call me José, and I will not call you Benito, hmm?"

Snickers sounded from her left, and she found Luis hiding a smile behind a hand. Her own lips bowed. "A fair trade."

"Now, to answer your question, we are headed to my *hacienda*."

That she had not been expecting. "You own property on this island?"

"For some years now. I have crossed the ocean many times carrying treasures out of the New World and bringing them back to Spanish soil. This was to have been my last voyage. And so it is."

"Do you not plan on going back to sea then, Captain Montoya?" Luis asked.

"Plans are a funny thing, Luis. They never seem to go quite how you imagine. Is that not right, Isabella?"

Hers surely had not. She'd plotted a way to be away from Hernando, and while the outcome had proved the same results, the journey getting there had been far different from what she'd thought.

A yawn overcame her, and she covered her mouth.

José pressed her head to his chest. "Rest. We have a long ride ahead of us."

The lids of her eyes grew heavy as the horse rocked her back and forth. Sleep soon crept upon her, and she gave in without a fight.

When she aroused, stars dotted the night sky. The full moon illuminated the path the horse's hooves tread, and crickets called to one another through the thick air. Off in the distance, Isabella could make out the shape of a modest cottage.

"Welcome to your new home, *Señora* Montoya."

Chapter 34

Florida, Present Day

I love you. He'd said the words, but did he mean them? Did he really love her? But then he'd said *one day.* So he didn't love her. He just thought the possibility was there that one day he might love her. Or one day she'd believe him when he said it. So was the *one day* in conjunction with his love or with her belief of his declaration?

Ugh. She'd run the conversation through a thousand times and still couldn't decipher the here and now from the then of the future. What was more, her head hurt from trying to figure it out. Not only the intent behind his words but her own jumbled thoughts and feelings when it came to Trent Carrington. Add to that a heaping dose of impatient anxiety over the editor's decision at *Our World*, and she was a wreck.

"Vanilla latte." The barista placed a tall paper cup on the counter.

Summer walked over and retrieved her coffee. Adele and a

latte couldn't work miracles, but they could help her decompress for a minute.

She sat at a small bistro table and plugged her earbuds into her phone, bringing up her playlist and clicking on "Rolling in the Deep." Her fingernails tapped the beat on her thigh, and she closed her eyes and let out a breath, willing her stress out with it.

The light behind her lids dimmed, and she opened them and looked toward the window, expecting to see a cloud that had momentarily covered the sun. Her vision slammed into a large belt buckle, a tucked-in white shirt framed by a familiar black leather jacket. Her eyes lifted to meet the cocked grin that had become so endearing.

"Fancy meeting you here." Trent dragged out the chair across from her and fell into it.

She pulled the earbuds out of her ears, silencing Adele. "What are you doing in Fort Lauderdale?"

He leaned back and crossed an ankle over the opposite knee. "Wooing you."

An eyebrow rose high on her forehead. "Excuse me?"

"Wooing. You know, to romantically pursue someone." He leaned forward and placed a hand over her forearm. "Or in my case, to prove to you that I am trustworthy of your heart." The tip of his finger drew lazy circles over her skin. "No matter what you may think, this isn't a game to me, Summer."

She tugged her arm out from under his palm and placed it in her lap. "Trent—"

He flashed another smile, this one not quite as bright. "I'm also here doing some research at the university. I've sent the necklace back to the Bahamas with the shipwreck's coordinates. The government is going to take over salvaging the remains. They promised to keep me apprised of their findings."

"You aren't going to be a part of the salvaging process? Even though you're the one who discovered the ship?" She played with the protective cardboard sleeve around her cup. "That doesn't seem fair."

His blue eyes twinkled. "Defending this dastardly pirate now, hmm?"

"Aye, matey." A smile played on her lips. "Do you think they'll find any gold or other treasure?"

"I don't know. It depends a lot on what kind of ship it was and where it had been heading."

"Is that what you've been researching?"

"Some. Mostly I've been digging around trying to see if I can't find any information on the necklace. A piece of jewelry like that must have a history to it. I wouldn't be surprised if a record of it shows up somewhere." He tilted his head. "What about you? Heard from Tabitha Michaels yet?"

A gurgle turned her stomach. It'd only been a couple of days, but the suspense of not knowing was killing her. "Not yet."

"I'm sure you'll hear something soon." He looked at his wristwatch. "Have any plans for the rest of the day?"

Besides driving herself crazy with over analyzation and worrying about the future of her career? "Not really."

Standing, he grabbed her wrist and tugged her up. "Come on. I have something I want to show you."

She barely managed to grab her drink before being pulled through the doors and down the sidewalk to stand in front of his Harley. Trent dropped his hold on her and extended out a helmet. She eyed the thing, then the latte in her hand. A groan rumbled in her throat. No way did hot coffee and motorcycles go together. Even if she managed to keep ahold of the cup, by the time they got to wherever it was they were going, the drink would be cold.

Trent jiggled the helmet, but she held up a finger. "Just a minute." Warm vanilla and ground Columbian beans filled her mouth as she took her first and last sip. Then she tossed it in the trash canister. "That was the most expensive two ounces I've ever consumed."

"I'll buy you another one later, I promise."

"You better." She took the helmet and shoved it on her head. "Where are we going?"

"You'll see."

"Do I get to drive again?" Even if he said yes, she wouldn't dare. The first time had been hard enough, remembering all the steps while his hands were planted on her hips. But it was fun watching him squirm.

"Uh, I think I better drive this time." He jerked up the kickstand and swung his leg over the leather seat.

Here goes nothing. She gripped his shoulders for balance and mounted behind him. The engine roared, vibration moving up her legs. They drove out of the strip mall's parking lot and onto the highway.

Summer let her hands fall to his sides and bunched part of his leather jacket in her grip. She looked straight ahead but couldn't see more than Trent's broad shoulders, bulky helmet, and a sliver of windshield and road. Not exactly a panoramic view, so she looked to the side. Bad idea. All the trees whizzing by made her dizzy. Anchoring her gaze on his back, she let her mind regain its equilibrium. Another bad idea. She went straight from dizzy to hyperfocused.

Was it possible for a back to be hypnotic? That was what it felt like. Like Trent's back was beckoning to her, calling her to wrap her arms all the way around his waist, press her body close, and rest her head right between his shoulder blades.

Should she?

Probably not, but... Her palms slid across firm abdominal muscles, and she scooted even closer until her thighs were an outline of his. Time for the logical side of her brain to rest so she could enjoy this blissful moment. Later she could call herself all kinds of fool.

Trent's hand covered hers for a moment before returning to the handle bars. They slowed, pulled off the road, and stopped.

Grudgingly, Summer disentangled herself and stepped off the motorcycle. She removed the helmet and looked around. Manicured lawn, trails of cement walkways, and a large boxed building right in the center. Even if she hadn't seen the yellow bus off to the side, there was no way she could've missed the school's massive sign. She looked behind her, head tilted. "You brought me to a high school?"

He leaned against the Harley in that carefree way that drove her nuts. "Yep."

"Care to tell me why?"

The smile started in his eyes. "I have an interview here tomorrow."

"Here?" She pointed to the asphalt beneath her feet. "In Fort Lauderdale? At this school?"

The grin reached his lips. "Yep. How else am I going to make you fall in love with me if I can't work on persuading you every day?"

She ignored the last remark. Tried to ignore the flip in her stomach that the words created. "What about *X*-marks-the-spot maps and hidden treasures of history? You're going to give all that up?"

"There's a story in the Bible about a man who searches and searches for pearls. He travels all over looking for that rare thing of beauty." Trent's elbow pushed off the bike, and he sauntered toward her, eyes locked. "And one day he finds it. It's the most extraordinary pearl he has ever seen in his entire life. He doesn't discard it, thinking he can find an even better jewel if he keeps looking. You know why?"

She could hardly breathe from the way his gaze held hers, the tenderness that touched his eyes as he waited for her to respond. Slowly she shook her head.

He reached out and rested his hands on her hips. "Because he knows perfection when he sees it." His thumb lazily grazed the skin on her side where her shirt had ridden up. "So he sells everything he owns and buys that pearl, and he treasures it for the rest of his life."

Summer closed her eyes, the defenses she'd been repeating since meeting Trent crumbling around her like the war-ridden villages she saw on the nightly news. Only one piece of rubble stubbornly remained. "He doesn't end up putting the pearl in a box when he thinks it's become dull and go looking for shiny rubies or diamonds, does he?"

Trent cupped the side of her neck, his thumb stroking her cheek. "He would never do that. He's only ever really wanted a pearl. *That* pearl."

She should take a step back. Allow her mind to think straight with a little bit of space. Remind herself why getting involved with a man like Trent was a bad idea. Instead she leaned into his palm, absorbed the way his touch made her feel. "Is that really in the Bible?"

"Every word."

She scrunched her nose but then smiled. "Somehow I

doubt the pearl represents a woman the man is trying to—how did you put it?—woo?"

He laughed. "You caught me. The parable was told as a likeness to the kingdom of heaven. I took the liberty of giving it a dual meaning."

Her mouth formed an O in a look of mock horror. "Sacrilege."

"Hey, I'm still learning the ropes of this Christian lifestyle." He tweaked her nose. "Give me some credit."

It took effort to peel her gaze away from his, but she swept it back over the looming high school. "You're really going to take a teaching job here? Just to be closer to me?"

He squeezed her shoulder. "Don't forget about the making you fall in love with me part."

She shook her head and forced her lips to turn down to portray a pseudo-seriousness even though she wanted to burst out in giggles. "I could never forget that part. And it seems like you have a game plan already in motion."

"Absolutely." He held up a finger. "Step one, amaze you with my wit and charm."

"How's that going for you?"

"Not as well as I'd hoped, hence the need for step two." He held up another finger. "Get a job nearby so I can wear you down by my persistent presence."

"Do you think that will work?"

"Eventually, even if it takes me the rest of my life."

Summer laughed. "That long, huh?"

"Time well spent, I'd say."

"Sounds like you're determined."

"Nothing could dissuade me."

No, she didn't think anything would. More importantly, she didn't want anything to. Her heart raced. "Might as well start step two now, at least the wearing me down, since you're in town, don't you think?"

His eyebrows shot to his hairline before resettling on his face along with his familiar cocked grin. "Brilliant idea. Summer, will you have dinner with me?"

She clutched her chest. "Wow, this is so sudden. I don't know. I'll have to think about it." Laughter bubbled beneath her palm. "Pick me up at seven."

Chapter 35

The clock on the dashboard read 6:55 as Trent pulled up to the curb outside Summer's studio. Jake, one of his friends from the university, had given him a hard time when he'd asked to borrow his car. In the end Jake had tossed the key across the room with a laugh.

It had been a spontaneous request, one he'd never bothered with before. But even if he'd told Summer he'd spend the rest of his life proving the sincerity of his feelings, if that was what it took, he'd rather make the best impression on this first date—and that excluded subjecting her to helmet hair.

He reached over and grabbed the bouquet of sunflowers, lying on the passenger's seat, before exiting the car and loping to Summer's small porch. The door opened after three knocks, and Trent blinked at the vision before him. Her long hair draped in soft waves, a chunk pulled forward across her shoulder. A navy-blue tunic-type shirt hung past her hips. Long legs peeked from underneath, clad in skinny jeans rolled up at the hem.

He thrust the flowers toward her. "These are for you."

She took them and smiled. "Thank you. They're beautiful." Her back turned as she searched for a vase and filled it with water.

After she set them on the counter, he asked, "Ready to go?"

She grabbed a small handheld purse and preceded him out the door. At the bottom of her stoop, she stopped. "Where's your motorcycle?"

"I borrowed a friend's car for the evening."

Her laugh floated on the breeze. "I should have guessed since you're without faded ripped pants and leather jacket."

He looked down at himself. True, the dark denim jeans and light-blue oxford shirt weren't what he usually wore, but this was a date. "I don't meet with your approval?"

Green eyes sparkled. "I didn't say that."

Warmth surged in his chest and expanded. Something had shifted in Summer. Or rather, in the way she responded to him. In the past she'd reacted in one of two ways. Either distantly argumentative, which was fun and had happened most frequently when they'd first met, or, as occurred more recently, she'd momentarily forget whatever resolution she'd made about him and actually enjoyed their time together, only to later remember and retreat.

He looked down at her as he opened the car door and she slipped in. Tonight she was different. No animosity, no reservation. All twinkles and smiles and laughs and, dare he say it, flirting.

Hope wanted to bubble up like a natural spring of water. He loved this woman with a fierceness he'd never experienced before, and if she was finally admitting to herself her own feelings… Trent tapped a lid on that thought. Running away with dreams of the future would only tempt him to declare things that might scare her and have her retreating like a little rabbit. Besides, there was still a chance her cheery mood had nothing to do with him at all.

He rounded the vehicle and dropped into the driver's seat, cranking the car and pulling out onto the street. "Heard anything from Tabitha Michael's yet?"

Her face dimmed. "Not yet." She twisted her hands in her lap. "I'm trying not to think about it, but that's proving nearly impossible."

If she kept contorting her hands like that, they'd end up in the ER for a broken finger before they made it to the restaurant. He slipped his palm in between hers and laced their fingers together, tugging her closer until both their forearms rested on the center console. His thumb slowly stroked the back of her hand.

He sensed her anxiety seeping out of her. "Better?"

"Much." Her smile was smaller this time, but more peaceful.

Somehow that made his heartbeat quicken even more.

They pulled into the restaurant, and Trent jogged around the car to get to Summer's door before she opened it. He gave an exaggerated bow. "Milady."

She chuckled. "You're a goofball."

One eye closed in a slow wink before he guided her through the restaurant's glass doors.

The hostess looked up. "Table for two?"

"In the courtyard please," Trent said.

She smiled. "No problem." Menus were produced beneath the podium. "If you'll follow me."

They wound around tables and through hushed conversation before being ushered out a back door into a tropical oasis complete with koi pond and a small waterfall at the center and dim twinkling lights roped overhead.

The hostess deposited the menus on top of a small table. "Your server will be right with you."

They sat down, Summer's head swiveling as she took it all in. "This place is enchanting."

Trent smiled. "I'm glad you like it. I've never been here before, but it came highly recommended."

"Let me guess—it's a favorite among the guys at the university to bring dates." The edges around her eyes crinkled.

He dipped his chin. "It might have that reputation."

"I can see why." The exposed bulbs of the hanging lights cast a warm glow over the stone-paved courtyard. Flowering shrubs enclosed the square in privacy and infused the air with a sweet fragrance, and the small waterfall and light instrumental music transported diners into a world of happily ever afters.

A petite woman with a pixie cut and an apron that ended well past her knees approached the table. "Hi, and welcome to The Courtyard. My name is Sylvie, and I'll be your server this evening." She beamed, first at Summer and then Trent, before continuing. "Tonight's special is the blackened mahi mahi with a strawberry mango salsa served on a bed of cilantro lime rice. And might I suggest a Cabernet Franc as a nice pairing."

Summer's eyes rounded. "That sounds delicious, but I'll have a Coke instead of the wine."

"Make that two." Trent closed his menu.

"Very good, sir." The server took the menus and pivoted on her heel.

Leaning her forearms on the table, Summer tilted her head. "So are you really going to give up treasure hunting to be a high school history teacher?"

"Yes and no."

"Yes and no?"

Matching her posture, he leaned forward conspiratorially. "One of the benefits of teaching is summers off."

She laughed. "Do you think you'll enjoy teaching at all, or just bide your time until you can get out there and follow the clues to a new discovery?"

It surprised him how much he looked forward to the school year starting. It had all sounded so dull and monotonous before, a job that lacked adventure, but now he itched to get in the classroom and spark passion for history into the young minds of his students. "You know, your mom said she thought teaching would be fulfilling, and I think she might be right."

Her head jerked back. "You talked to my mom?"

"Yeah. That's how I got the information about Dave Landstrom."

"That's right." She opened her mouth to say more, but the server approached carrying a large circular tray. Two steaming plates were placed before them, the smell of paprika and cayenne from the blackening singed Trent's nose in all the right ways.

"Can I get you folks anything else right now?" the server asked.

Trent shook his head. "No, this looks great, thanks."

Silverware clanked together as cloth napkins were unfolded and placed in laps. The tines of Trent's fork slid through the flaky fish.

"Oh my word, this is good." Summer held a hand up to her mouth as she talked around a bite of food.

If the smell lifting off the steam on his fork was any indication, it was more than good. He popped the first bite in his mouth. Sweet and spicy, it was like melody and harmony playing a hit single on his tongue.

Summer dabbed the napkin at the corner of her mouth. "So there's something that's been on my mind for a couple of days now. Something I can't quite sort out."

"Oh yeah? What's that?" He set his fork down and took a drink of Coke.

The linen tablecloth suddenly absorbed her full attention. She drew lines along it with a fingernail, not once looking up. "The other day when you, you know, said I love you, did you mean—"

Sylvester the cat from Looney Tunes interrupted from her purse on the table. "What's this? A letter. For meee!"

The mindless finger doodling stopped, and Summer stared at her small red leather clutch, breath held and muscles ready to leap as if she were the kitten and that little rectangle accessory were a LED pen light.

Trent watched her for a second. The war between ignoring the new message and pouncing on her bag to see who it was from played across her face. He knew where her mind had gone because his had gone there too. Was this the anticipated e-mail from Tabitha Michaels?

Under the table, he tapped her leg with his foot. "Check it."

Her bottom lip got sucked between her teeth, looking at between him and the bag. "Are you sure? That's really rude, and it's not like the e-mail is going to suddenly vanish and—"

He chuckled. "Check the e-mail, Summer. I'm dying to know just as much as you are."

"Okay." Her smile lit the courtyard more than the dozens of low-wattage lightbulbs. The clasp of her bag unfastened, and she pulled out her cell.

Trent watched her face as she cradled the phone, tapping

and sliding her finger along the screen. Her eyes blinked the rate of hummingbird wings and moved back and forth like a typewriter platen. A spontaneous laugh bubbled past her lips.

She looked up at him wide eyed. "I got it! I got the job."

"That's terrific!" His smile and arm stretched at the same time, and he clasped her hand. "I'm so proud of you."

"She needs me to sign some papers she's attached to the e-mail, and a few other details." Her eyes were radiant with excitement. "I can't believe it. I'm actually going to be an *Our World* photographer."

"I never doubted it for a second."

"Thank you." She squeezed his hand.

The waitress walked by, and Trent held up a finger to call her over. "Can we get the check and some to-go boxes? Thanks."

Divots formed between Summer's eyes as the server returned to the kitchen.

"We're going to the university library. It's open until eleven, closer than your place, and has computers, printers, a scanner, and a fax machine." He answered her unspoken question.

"Are you sure? You don't have to—"

Her words died when he stood abruptly, took one step to her side, and rotated her chair until she faced him. He leaned over her, hands gripped on the chair's armrests, and brought his face down until their noses almost touched. "Stop asking me if I'm sure, Summer. I'm always certain about everything I do." It only took the lifting of his chin to cover her mouth with his in a kiss that would hopefully erase all uncertainty from her mind.

Summer's lips still tingled. A ten-minute drive hadn't reduced the sensation or the realization that, against her best efforts, she had fallen in love with this man.

He parked the borrowed car under a streetlamp, its yellow glow spilling around them. A few other vehicles dotted the parking area, but it didn't seem too many were studying within the university's library. She stepped out of the vehicle, thankful for the drop of temperature from the heat of the day, and walked beside Trent up the library's steps and into the large building.

He led her to a row of computers and logged her in using a guest password. "You should be all set. If you need me, I'll be right over there." He pointed to a shelf of books. "I found an interesting volume earlier that I didn't have time to finish looking through. Hopefully it will hold some answers about our necklace."

Our necklace. The words sent a ripple of pleasure down her spine. Silly, really, because the piece of jewelry was neither hers nor Trent's. And if anyone could claim the discovery of it at least, it was Trent. He'd seen the shadow in her picture. He'd convinced her to take him to that spot. He'd uncovered its three-hundred-year-old hiding place. She hadn't done anything. And yet he'd said *our.* Plural. The two of them. Together. Amazing how one word could snowball her thoughts.

Back to business. She wiggled the mouse to find the curser on the screen, then opened a web browser and brought up her e-mail provider. It took a minute to print out all the pages to Tabitha's attachment. Legal jargon mocked her from the page. Did people without a law degree actually understand this stuff? A jar with pens sat on the table in between the computers. She grabbed one and quickly scribbled her signature at the bottom of the last page.

"Summer, get over here. You have to see this." Trent stood at the front of a row of shelves holding a large book.

The chair scraped the floor as she stood, and a pair of eyes glared at her from behind a computer on the other side of the table.

Sorry, she mouthed and ducked her head, then scampered to where Trent waited. "What did you find?"

"Look." He held the book out to her, his finger pointing to the page.

There it was. The necklace. Not a picture of it, but a sketch. Or rather a picture of a sketch. Every detail had been captured, all the way down to the alternating diamonds, emerald pendant, and teardrop pearl.

Her hand rushed to her chest. "You found it."

"And you'll never guess the story behind it." He led her to a stiff chair. "Go ahead. Read the page before that one."

She sat, her spine rigid as she went back several pages to start at the beginning of the chapter. The author told how he had discovered a journal in a crude metal box among the rubble of what looked to be an old hacienda. What followed were photographs of said journal. The writing was indecipherable to Summer, but thankfully the author of the book had provided a translation.

Word after word she read, fingertips covering her bottom lip and one leg bouncing like a jackhammer. How could one girl in the seventeenth century have gone through so much and come through with such a spirit? Sometimes reality was harder to believe than fiction.

She closed the book, her heart racing like she'd just run a mile. "That's incredible."

"I know. I can't believe we found a firsthand account."

"No, I mean her story, or what was there, at least. I can't believe the journal wasn't found complete. What do you think happened to her and the captain after they were married?"

He took the book from her and placed it on a side table. "I think they lived happily ever after."

She tilted her head and scrunched her lips in the best *yeah, right* face she had.

Laughter filled their section of the quiet library, and someone shushed them from another row of books. "What? A guy can't believe in happily ever afters?"

She shrugged. "I guess. I've just never heard one say it, is all. At least, not without sarcasm."

"Well, I'm serious. It's all written right there." He pointed to the book. "Laced in every word she chooses when talking about the captain."

Summer leaned back and entwined her fingers over her stomach. "I'd like to think so. Everyone deserves to be happy."

Trent nodded absently, a faraway look in his eye, like he wasn't really there anymore. Probably still thinking about Isabella and José Montoya.

Her unfinished question from the restaurant expanded in her chest. She scooted forward on her chair. "Trent."

Focus returned to his eyes. "Yeah?"

"About earlier, before I was interrupted by my phone." She licked her lips.

His head dipped so he could meet her gaze. "Are you ready to hear it?"

Was she? If someone had asked her yesterday, the answer might have been different. Uncertainty had clouded her mind like an afternoon summer storm. But clouds had a way of rolling past and letting the sun shine again, and right then she wanted nothing more than for him to say it.

"Yes."

He reached for her hand and gently pulled until she was on her feet. His legs spread, and he tugged her between them, then drew her down onto his right thigh. "And you'll believe my words are true?" His eyes searched hers, the laughing, teasing, devil-may-care man transformed. He sat unmoving, back straight, the serious air about him unfamiliar.

It was impossible not to get lost in his gaze. The magnetism of it drew her in and stole her breath.

"Yes."

Imperceptibly, he softened. He threaded his fingers through her hair and drew her head down until their foreheads touched.

"I love you, Summer Arnet. You are the treasure of my heart."

He kissed her lips with a tenderness that caused an ache in her chest. As if she were something precious to handle with care, to cherish.

"I love you too." She said the words against his lips.

He stilled. "What did you say?"

"I love you. I've been falling in love with you for a while, but I was too afraid to admit it." She snuggled deeper into his lap and rested her head in the crook of his neck. "While you were uncovering a three-hundred-year-old necklace, I discovered my buried feelings for you. But I don't want to keep them buried anymore, afraid of the future because of the past."

His finger gently drew along her jawbone and lifted her chin until their gazes locked. "I'm sorry I allowed my own pain to hurt others, hurt you. I promise I'm not that man anymore."

"I believe you, and while I still may be prone to err on the side of caution, I'm ready to begin a new adventure. With you."

Eyes smoldering, he lowered his head with a kiss full of promise. Of discoveries, adventures, and a lifetime of love.

About the Author

Sarah Monzon is a Navy chaplain's wife and a stay at home mom to the two cutest littles in the world. Playing pretend all day with them isn't enough, she spends the evening after their heads hit their pillows to create her own imaginary characters. When she isn't in the world of make believe, she can be found in the pine forests of western Washington taking care of her family, fostering friendships, and enjoying all the adventures each day brings.

Her debut novel, The Isaac Project, skyrocketed to Amazon bestseller status while her Sophomore book, Finders Keepers, won the 2017 Selah award for contemporary romance.

Sarah loves connecting with readers at:
www.sarahmonzonwrites.com